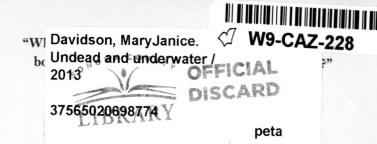

"Wh[...] book [...] [...]"

"Fast-paced and highly entertaining." —*Bitten by Books*

UNDEAD AND UNFINISHED

"[Davidson] proves she can skillfully combine creepy and chilling with numerous laugh-out-loud moments." —*Bitten by Books*

UNDEAD AND UNWELCOME

"Packs a chic coffin." —*The Denver Post*

"Outrageously wacky." —*RT Book Reviews*

UNDEAD AND UNEASY

"Breezy dialogue, kick-ass action, and endearing characters." —*Booklist*

"When it comes to outlandish humor, Davidson reigns supreme!" —*RT Book Reviews*

UNDEAD AND UNPOPULAR

"Think *Sex and the City*—only the city is Minneapolis and it's filled with demons and vampires." —*Publishers Weekly*

continued . . .

UNDEAD AND UNRETURNABLE

"No one does humorous romantic fantasy better than the incomparable MaryJanice Davidson." —*The Best Reviews*

"MS. DAVIDSON HAS HER OWN BRAND OF WIT AND SHOCKING SURPRISES THAT MAKE HER VAMPIRE SERIES ONE OF A KIND." —*Darque Reviews*

UNDEAD AND UNAPPRECIATED

"The best vampire chick lit of the year." —*Detroit Free Press*

UNDEAD AND UNEMPLOYED

"If you're fans of Sookie Stackhouse and Anita Blake, don't miss Betsy Taylor. She rocks." —*The Best Reviews*

UNDEAD AND UNWED

"Sophisticated, sexy, and wonderfully witty book."

—Catherine Spangler

AND PRAISE FOR
THE WYNDHAM WEREWOLF NOVELS

"JUST WHAT YOU WANTED: A WEREWOLF SPIN-OFF TO DAVIDSON'S WACKY VAMPIRE SERIES . . .

. . . That offers serious sexy-heroine competition to Minnesota vamp queen Betsy Taylor." —*Kirkus Reviews*

"Hilarious, fast, excellent read . . . Brilliant . . . [It] has it all!"

—*Fresh Fiction*

"A riotous romp." —*Booklist*

Anthologies

UNDEAD
AND UNDERWATER

MaryJanice Davidson

BERKLEY BOOKS, NEW YORK

THE BERKLEY PUBLISHING GROUP
Published by the Penguin Group
Penguin Group (USA) Inc.
375 Hudson Street, New York, New York 10014, USA

USA / Canada / UK / Ireland / Australia / New Zealand / India / South Africa / China

Penguin Books Ltd., Registered Offices: 80 Strand, London WC2R 0RL, England
For more information about the Penguin Group, visit penguin.com.

This book is an original publication of The Berkley Publishing Group.

BERKLEY® is a registered trademark of Penguin Group (USA) Inc.
The "B" design is a trademark of Penguin Group (USA) Inc.

Berkley trade paperback ISBN: 978-0-425-25332-8

An application to register this book for cataloging has been submitted to the Library of Congress.

PUBLISHING HISTORY
Berkley trade paperback edition / March 2013

PRINTED IN THE UNITED STATES OF AMERICA

10 9 8 7 6 5 4 3 2 1

Cover illustration by Don Sipley.
Cover design by Lesley Worrell.
Interior text design by Kristin del Rosario.

For Turquoise, the best of dogs;
Marble, the new addition;
and Pearl, who's all-around awesome.
And housebroken!

Acknowledgments

Thanks as always to my terrific family. ("As always? Then why keep saying it?" "Hey! Do I muscle onto *your* book's acknowledgments page and make editorial comments?")

To my editor, the always-awesome Cindy Hwang, and her tireless sidekick, Leis. (*Sidekick* . . . yeesh. What was that about? Sorry. I know Leis is a person in her own right. I blame the superhero jargon stuck in my brain like a fish hook, and society.)

Thanks are again due to my tireless agent, Ethan Ellenberg, who can leap tall stacks of contracts in a single bound. No, really! I was in his office a few years ago and a stack of paper started to slide, and he sort of hopped over it. It was so weirdly cool I never forgot it.

Thanks also to my parents, who never mind when I tell sex stories about them to hundreds of people at a time. That's *classy*, man. I'm pretty sure. So far Tennessee, parts of Minnesota, San Diego, and Australia have had to endure me telling sex stories about my folks.

Acknowledgments

Thanks to my brother-in-law, Daniel, who said of my ghostly pale kids, "Your kids are so white, I can see them, and when I close my eyes, I can *still* see them." Yeah, yuk it up, you bastard. Sure it was funny, but look how I ruthlessly stole it the first chance I got. That'll learn you.

Special thanks to my friend Cathleen Carr, who was the inspiration for a sarcastic superheroine who can really pound the brews when she's not pounding villains. The Irish: love them, yet fear them. Ideally, do both.

Author's Note

I make no secret of the fact that I'm insanely fortunate and have landed hip deep in a wonderful life. Case in point: this book. Once upon a time, the book you're holding/downloading was a whim. "Y'know what'd be fun? A novella about a superhero whose most vicious battles against the forces of evil occur within the Human Resources department. Oh, and you know what else would be fun? Having Betsy and Fred team up on . . . I dunno. Something. I'll work that out later. Oooh, and it'd be super fun to do another Wyndham story, this one about Lara (Michael and Jeannie Wyndham's eldest child, and the future Pack leader) set twenty-five years in the future."

"You're right," my editor said. "That would be fun. Here's a contract."

(Really, once you wade through the dozens of e-mails and meetings, and the offers and the counter-offers, at the end of it all, it's my editor saying, "Here's a contract," and me weeping with gratitude on her neck. Say it with me: insanely fortunate. Wonderful life.)

But you guys are a huge reason why I can pitch all sorts of nutty ideas to unsuspecting editors and, like as not, end up getting paid to do something I love. Heck, thanks to you readers, now my family eats Ramen noodles because we want to, not because we have to stretch my last sixty-eight cents and the best way to do that is to invest in a six-pack of Ramen noodles. Thanks to you guys, my kids don't have to buckle down and pull straight As in hopes of a scholarship. They can go to a *party* school!

I could cry, it's so beautiful. So: thank you. Thank you. Thank you.

Yet Another Author's Note

I'm almost done with these. I promise. And normally I wouldn't be wasting your time with this sort of thing; I'd be wasting your time with plot and character development. But this time I accidentally got all deep n'stuff when I wrote these stories (It was an accident! I swear!) and was so surprised I had to share.

Themes (which I normally try to avoid) run rampant through these three stories, in particular women who have heavy responsibilities who (spoiler alert!) run away from them until (spoiler alert!) they realize they have to suck it up and step it up. As Hailey and Fred and Lara come to grips with unpleasantness they had avoided (consciously or unconsciously), I realized *I* had avoided seeing any commonality between them, save for their sarcasm and odd way of looking at the world. Which probably says something about me. Which I probably won't touch with a barge pole.

In addition to being saddled with responsibility they feared as much as they loathed, they also had unlawful authority (Fred the Mermaid even flat-out says to Betsy the Vampire, "We have no lawful authority. Do you know how to make a citizen's arrest? I don't."), annoying sidekicks, severe doubts about their place in the world, and an utter determination to protect their loved ones. Being tremendously flawed myself, I can relate to heroines who have, uh, quirks, so those are the ones who tend to jump out of my brain (*ka-sproing!*) and into my laptop.

My point, at last, is that while writing their stories I discovered that while all the heroines had avoidance issues, as well as the occasional tendency to retreat into but-why-is-it-*my*-responsibility-to-fix-*your*-mess whining, they also had a great capacity to love and to fight for what (and who) they loved, regardless of the potential cost to themselves. So in writing about them, I came to like them an awful lot, not in spite of those flaws but, yep, because of them.

I could never relate to the beautiful, kind, selfless, loving Disney princesses of my childhood. I tended to root for the fembots who were always running around trying to put the beat-down on Jamie in *The Bionic Woman*. Oooh, they were so scary when their girl-masks fell off (often, and inconveniently, during combat) revealing their horrifying fembot innards, but really, all they wanted was to belong.

And let's not forget poor Lisa Galloway, who was so screwed up she not only had surgery to look like the bionic woman, while trying to replace Jamie, she really started to think she *was* Jamie. What a pathetic nut bag! Now there was someone I could relate to! Yay, Lisa, and listen, don't worry about having trouble kicking your smoking habit; everybody smoked in the '70s.

Hailey, Fred, Betsy, and Lara had one other thing in common; they all had Mommy issues, good and bad. Hailey's mom bought her, literally paid money to get her. So while she loves her mom, she also thinks of herself as a baby who didn't have a hospital ID on her ankle, but a price tag.

Fred and her mother, the gracefully aging hippie Moon Bimm, are as different as it's possible for two people to be.

Betsy adores her mother but walks softly around her; the disintegration of her mother's marriage by her father and his second wife had a tremendous impact on how Betsy views marriage—anyone's, including her own.

And Lara and her mother aren't even the same species. No, literally—Jeannie Wyndham is human; Lara is Pack. And destined to boot her mother out of a job, something she yearns for and dreads. I loved that these women could love their moms—fiercely and unapologetically—while at the same time wondering how, *how* did they ever come to be daughters of women so different from themselves?

Anyhoo, here they are: Hailey, Fred, Betsy, and Lara. And they are flawed up the yin-yang. Turned out I was okay with that; here's hoping you will be, too.

Contents

Super, Girl!

For former boss Richard Jansen of Sulzer Spine-Tech,
who once told me (when I was late to work
after being stuck on 494 for three hours
in a snowstorm, and HR suggested I claim those
three hours as vacation time),
"They really know how to take the human out
of Human Resources, don't they?"

And for Janice,
who works for the State of Minnesota, and puts the human back in.

So I was sitting in my cubicle today, and I realized, ever since I started working, every single day of my life has been worse than the day before it. So that means that every single day that you see me, that's on the worst day of my life.

—PETER GIBBONS, *OFFICE SPACE*

Human beings were not meant to sit in little cubicles staring at computer screens all day, filling out useless forms and listening to eight different bosses drone on about mission statements.

—PETER GIBBONS, *OFFICE SPACE*

Asshoooooooooles!

—THE COON'S RALLYING CRY, *SOUTH PARK*

Asshoooooooooles!

—OTTO'S RALLYING CRY, *A FISH CALLED WANDA*

"If we had a billionaire like Lance Hunt as our benefactor . . ."

"That's because Lance Hunt *is* Captain Amazing!"

"Oh, here we go. Don't start that again. Lance Hunt wears glasses. Captain Amazing *doesn't* wear glasses."

"He takes them off when he transforms."

"That doesn't make any sense! He wouldn't be able to see!"

—THE SHOVELLER AND MR. FURIOUS, *MYSTERY MEN*

"Oh, mother. I can't believe you're dying of old age."

"Don't cry for me, Tartine. I've had a full life. Oh, the things I've seen. The first Clinton administration. The Nagano Olympics. Microsoft Windows '95. But I'm forty-one now. Time to die."

—*30 ROCK*, "BLACK LIGHT ATTACK!"

"I'm not going to help you kill her!"

"Kill? I didn't say *kill*! I said *neutralize*! It's a neutral word . . . like Switzerland!"

—PROFESSOR BEDLAM AND MATT SAUNDERS,

MY SUPER EX-GIRLFRIEND

As John Doe dived out of the bullet path—or where a bullet would go if he lingered—he had time to wonder: *When did my life turn into a John Woo movie? Or a Road Runner cartoon? When my burglar parents named me John Doe so I'd have an automatic alias? This is all their fault: yes.*

It really did start out simply. Crime ran in his family, and marijuana is a gateway drug. How else to explain how he'd gone from amiable, sleepy pot user to emaciated, stressed pseudo-ruthless cokehead dealer? It was once again trendy to blame the parents for everything from bleeding ulcers to a life of crime, but he never had a chance.

Dad: "There's no point in trying to have a normal life. Rather than work hard and then throw it all away with reckless behavior, throw it all away while you're still young. It's the American dream!"

Mom: "Also, we don't think you're smart enough for college."

High school guidance counselor: "Smart's not the issue. You seem to have been genetically programmed for a life of crime. I wash my hands of you. And also any prospects I once had of making a name for myself in this field."

Okay, maybe going from occasional pot use to dealing coke was inevitable, but bullets flying past my nose? Sirens shrilling in the background? What is this, the '80s? How am I a cocaine dealer running from the St. Paul police? The only way this could get more terrible is if she *shows up.* He groaned silently, then began to wriggle farther around the corner for more cover. *And me without my pastel blazer and artfully mussed hair. Oh, the humanity!*

He sulked while he wormed his way to safety; as if all this wasn't bad enough, most of the building was under construction, which meant traffic had been a bitch. He'd been told there was only one security guy at that hour, which was true. He was told the guard in question was a retired cop too pudgy and Minnesota-nice to pull his weapon, which was the opposite of true. He'd barely crossed the threshold into the coffee shop when the guy reached.

I just have that kind of face, he acknowledged in despair. His gaze was naturally shifty. He had a tendency to pull in his shoulders when talking, as if awaiting a bullet, which happened a lot. *Everybody* had bullets. He didn't walk, he scuttled. And, completing the genetic treason of his criminally minded family, he had beady eyes: small, dark, squinty. He had looked like he was up to something in the crib, for God's sake.

Still: it took brass ones to turn one's back on generations of family tradition. John Doe's were made of fool's gold, not brass. *Ah, terrible analogy. Fool's gold? Maybe you should stop thinking about your balls and find an exit.*

"Ah, very nice," someone said behind him.

John Doe flopped over on his back like a startled turtle. A turtle in the middle of committing several misdemeanors and at least two felonies. "Where'd you come from?"

"The coffee shop next door." The woman was looking down at him from a great height (at least to his perspective—he was five foot three) with an odd expression. It took him a moment to figure it out, because he was expecting fear or shock to show in her eyes and on her face, and that wasn't happening. There were the crooks and there were the cops and there was everyone else. Everyone else either a) never noticed something was wrong, b) *did* notice and didn't care, or c) noticed and were scared. The ones who noticed and didn't care never engaged.

So he needed a few seconds to name the expression. Annoyed, he decided. Like nearly walking through a cross fire between an angry Minnesota-nice security guard and a convicted felon was going to inconvenience her. *And* let her coffee get cold; he saw she was holding a cardboard drink tray, with two steaming drinks in it. Yep: she didn't want her coffee to get cold.

Well, he was sorry, but he was going to have to inconvenience her. It wasn't his fault. His parents had willfully named him John Doe. *They never even apologized!*

"Listen, I need a—" Meat shield? No; it wouldn't do to freak her out more than she (probably) was. "A hostage. Just to get off the block." And out of the city. And then possibly the country. It was summer in Australia, right? He'd always wanted to see the

Sydney Opera House. "I won't hurt you. Unless the cops make me kill you. Hurt you! If the cops make me hurt you. Is what I meant."

"You are going to make me tardy, which I loathe." She sounded pissy, not afraid. Which was . . . good? Hysterical hostages made everything harder. And noisier. "Inconsiderate thieving asshole," she added.

Asshole?

She was striking—perhaps that was throwing him off. Tall, as he'd noted, with pale skin and small, close-set dark eyes. Not a blemish on her face, because the beauty mark hardly counted as a defect. Her hair was deep brown and a foil for the rest of her, like the color of the rich soil of a flower bed after it rained.

"So, you know." He climbed to his feet, one hand brushing his knees (the John Woo–esque dive through the doorway had shredded his chinos, and why didn't they ever put *that* in the movies?) and the other on the piece-of-shit .38 his gram-gram had given him for his bar mitzvah. *"Oh, I can't believe my wittle baby is all growed up! Give Grammy some yum-yum kisses and then we'll go shoot your gunny-gun!"*

Jeez, Gram, you couldn't give me one of your ex-husband's decent guns? I was thirteen! I deserved a Desert Eagle at the least!

"So, I'm sure you've watched TV so you know the drill."

"Stop now. Surrender. If your inept shenanigans do not make me much later, I'll try to refrain from beating you to death."

"Try?"

"Try," she repeated in a voice so icy he actually shivered despite the rivers of sweat in his armpits. Then she added something that was stranger than this already-strange chat: "You haven't left me a note, have you?"

So sad to run into a drunk, and at this time of the morning. Society is the Titanic *after the iceberg.*

He took a breath. "Listen, you're not in charge here. I'm the one with the gunny-gun." *Ah, hell. Even from the grave you humiliate me, Grammy.* "So you just get over here and then we'll take a quick—What are you doing?"

She had popped the top of the first steaming drink with her thumb, upended the thing, and sucked it down in three monster swallows. He winced and rubbed his throat in unconscious sympathy. Then she did the same with the second drink.

"Hey, take it easy! Look, there's no need to give yourself third-degree throat burns just to avoid me taking . . . you . . . hostage . . . buh . . . nnnnhh?"

Words failed him. Words had failed him because she was now eating the empty coffee cups—yes, she was biting off pieces of cup and chewing and gulping them down, and now she was—was she?—yes! Now she was eating the cardboard drink holder. And washing it down with the handful of nails she must have picked up at the construction site. She was gulping them down—three-inch nails!—like they were gummy worms.

"Oh my God! It's you! You're—"

"Do not," she warned with a mouthful of casing nails.

"—It Girl!"

"Never say I didn't warn you," she said, and launched herself at him.

ONE

Get to It Already.

Hailey Derry seized the small garbage can and spat out a wad of chewed cardboard drink holder. Then she gathered up her work debris, struggled with her seat belt, then lurched out of the car. She scurried past a lawn so perfectly manicured it didn't look real, past the small flock of geese eating and pooping all over the perfectly maintained grass, up the wide sidewalk (so wide employees called it the cement moat), toward the looming HQ of her cross to bear, the bane of her existence, the bet with God she'd lost before birth.

Must have lost. It was the only explanation for her life.

Ramouette, a company famous for 1) producing high-quality target silhouettes, and 2) the utter indifference of its CEO, who came to the office about five times a year, loomed over Savage's southern edge. Savage, Minnesota, was famous for its annual celebration honoring a dead horse, its proximity to RenFest, and the enormous amount of acid most of the population dropped. It was the only explanation, journalists all over the country had agreed, for all the superhero sightings.

That, or there really were superheroes. Not Batman-esque superheroes, whose power was being a wealthy Republican. Heroes with weird powers. And super villains, for where the former led, the latter followed, except when it was the other way around. So, all right, maybe it wasn't rampant drug use. There might be such things as superheroes. But it was Minnesota, for God's sake. Who cared?

Hailey wouldn't think about that right now. She was late (again) and irritated (again) and her cold chocolate was undrinkable (again), and she didn't want to be in this car in this parking lot in this town in this state. Again.

I'm out of the car. Now I need to get into the building. Get to work. You are not a victim. You chose to interfere this morning and you chose to take this job and you chose to be here.

"Fine," she muttered. How did one talk back to inner voices? It seemed counterproductive. Also, her inner voice sounded exactly like her mother, which was so horrifying it didn't bear thinking about.

She would think about her awful job instead. She would ponder that her reactions to the forces in her life tended toward the clichéd: the movie *Office Space* was her *Mein Kampf*, without all the genocide. Or prison POV. Or megalomania. Yes, yes, anyone who had ever been ensconced in a cubicle, while fluorescent lighting beat down on them, thought *Office Space* was the story of their life. But in her case, it was.

Hailey, too, was forced to do meaningless busywork by

someone she didn't respect. She, too, was forced to fill out paperwork that had no purpose other than to make simple tasks harder. She, too, often dreamed of committing arson on such a huge scale Savage would still be smoldering fifty years later. And Hailey, too, had a boss she disliked so much it nearly made her sick to look at the worthless cow.

She was the boss. The head of Human Resources; she only answered to one other person, and Ann Denison hated her job more than she did.

Initially dismissing that as impossible, Hailey gradually came to realize that, yes, indeed, Ann hated running the company more than Hailey hated exit interviews. In her quest to pursue Olympic recognition for her treasured sport, broomball, the CEO had priorities other than overseeing Ramouette's production of iron silhouettes designed for the purpose of people shooting them to knock them over, after which they would be picked up and repositioned and shot at more and more and more.

"You don't find that fulfilling?" she'd asked during her interview.

"Shush," Ann had replied, poring over the broomball world rankings. "I'm in crisis mode here. I've got a serious problem here. Minnesota only made the top seventy-five twenty-two times."

"Upsetting?" she guessed.

"We should be on it seventy-five times!"

"Ah."

"And for sure, first. I mean, come on. That's so obvious it hurts. But not even the top five? Someone's gotten to these guys." She slammed a small fist on her desk, making the broomball trophies tremble. Most people put family photos on their desks, and occasionally computers. Not this one; the space not occupied by trophies was taken up by the broomball rule book and grip tape. "The corruption starts at the bottom and oozes its way through all the layers of the broomball rankings! And they think I'm just gonna sit here? Sit here and let them barf all over all that's good and holy about broomball? My big white Scandinavian butt, I will!"

"I'm sorry." Hailey stood. "I had no idea you were clinically insane. I'll leave you to . . . that."

"No, you can't go!" Ann had said, crumpling the magazine in her agitation. "You have to stay and run HR and, you know, hire people and things so we have people to make stuff and then we have stuff for customers to buy so they give us money and I use that money to get broomball recognized as an Olympic sport, and to practice."

"That was the most succinct mission statement I have ever heard."

"I can't do what I want you to do. I hate that stuff. But my dad's retiring and a bunch of people left with him, so there's all these slots to fill and I just can't, Hailey. Also . . ."

"You have to root out the insidious corruption hidden in the national broomball rankings."

"Yes!" she'd screamed, and then *crawled across her desk* and hugged her. Hailey was so startled and amused she didn't toss her new boss through the window behind them.

So she'd taken the job. To this day, she had no idea why. Well, she knew, way down at the bottom of her brain, where it was dark all the time. But the top of her brain pretended she had no clue.

So here she was, late again. She was supposed to be running a new hire through the worthless maze that was corporate life at Ramouette. One of her minions—their word, not hers, and it had amused her enough that she let it stand, so now there were in-house minion meetings and underling training seminars and Wretch 101—anyway, one of them had interviewed what's-his-name, had been authorized to make an offer of a salary large enough to keep him coming back day after nightmarish day but not enough to pull together savings and eventually depart to a better life. And the poor wretch had accepted.

She raced past reception, hearing the soft drone of Audrey's near-constant, "Thank you for calling Ramouette, how kinnI direct yer call, then?" like some would listen to Zen chants. She'd only lived in Minnesota four years, but she loved the mild local accent. Someone could be in the middle of a murder, but when they piped up with a cheery, "Oooookay, then, I'm gonna shoot this here guy in the face and dismember him and then play with his body in a ritual-type deal, and then I'll just haveta kill you, too, then," it was hard not to smile. (She knew this for a fact. The most depraved serial killer sounded downright adorable when they drew out their *o*s.)

Past reception, she took a left by the restrooms, caught an empty elevator (yes!) to third, another left down a dull windowless hallway carpeted in Corporate Buff, and then was walking through the small HR department toward her office in the back. It had, of course, a real window that opened. A window large enough to accommodate her occasional leaps to the perfect turf below.

"Hi, I'm Hailey Derry, sorry to—"

"Hero. Hero."

"What?" She nearly dropped her laptop. Her eight o'clock had gotten to his feet the moment he saw her. The way he'd greeted her—unless she had misheard, and she must have misheard—was not the only interesting thing about him. He had the oddest coloring she had ever seen. "You—what?"

"Hero. That's you."

She stared, and then, trying a different tack, stared more. He was close to her in height, maybe an inch taller at five-eleven or so, with a rude shock of bright red hair. Not a pretty auburn or a masculine deep mahogany: it was *red* red, Irish red, and he had a face full of light freckles to go with it, and a wide mouth that looked like it was full of smiles and perhaps kisses. A conservative blue shirt and blue- and red-striped tie, khakis, and dark loafers that looked comfortable as well as practical.

For whatever reason, her mind seized on his outfit. *"Every day at Ramouette is casual day!"* one of their more insipid HR slogans trumpeted. *"Except when it comes to customer service, of course!"*

But his eyes. Never mind his clothes, or the freckles, or the mouth she hoped was full of kisses. "Your eyes," she said, and then couldn't believe she'd said it out loud.

"Yeah." He laughed and rubbed the back of his neck. "My mom's Irish. My dad's from Lucknow, in India. So I'm kind of . . ."

Dazzling.

". . . a mix."

His hair and mouth and freckles made him look sweet, like a boyfriend you could snuggle and nag and bang as well as—as—what was the phrase? Pal around with? Yes: he looked like the sort of boyfriend who could also be your friend. But her new coworker's eyes, soulful and large and dark, his eyes made him seem mysterious, like a lover you adored but sometimes wondered about. *When he's touching me in the dark and I'm groaning his name, what is he really thinking?*

Like that.

Exactly like that.

Now he was staring, and she realized she hadn't commented. So she hurried to do so: "Yes. Mix. Yes. You are a mix. That is what you are. You are a mixture of . . . of them. The parents. *Your* parents, is what I mean."

He blinked but, thank all the gods, let it go. "Yeah, so we've established that. Anyway, that's what your name means. Hero. I'm Jamie Linus, by the way, and, yep, I've heard all the jokes."

"What?"

"The jokes. Heard 'em all. That's not a dare to think up different things to say about my dumb name, by the way."

"Your dumb name?"

Hailey, you dim dolt, will you get ahold of yourself right now?

She did. She always obeyed that voice, no matter how much trouble it got her in. Stop that robbery. Fire that idiot. Hire that single mother. Get ahold of yourself right now. It was her mother's voice, but she didn't mind. Since her mother died four years ago, this was as close as she could come to hearing her. *I tuned her out most of my life*, she thought, morbidly aware of the irony, *and only listened after she died.*

"My office, please." She gestured for him to go in, but he courteously stepped back to let her go first. "I must apologize. It was a . . . a chaotic morning."

"Yeah, I heard," he said cheerfully. "It Girl foiled a robbery! Or something. I dunno. But she was right downtown! I only missed her by, what? Ten, fifteen minutes? Argh. *Man*, that must have been awesome."

Ah. That did it. She had no trouble focusing now. Just hearing his pleasant baritone say the hated name was enough to snap her back into her despised job, loveless life, and Pop-Tart-less desk drawer.

Thank goodness. Because really . . . what else was there?

TWO

What Are You Waiting For?

"My dad was a reporter," Linus was saying, *"and my mom* was—*is*—a teacher. Still is, I mean. And what with one thing and another, they got started on this project—finding the roots of names, figuring out what they mean."

"Mmmm. You may have skipped a step in your story." If she wasn't looking at him, things were easier. So she was shuffling the paper on her desk like it was a deck of cards made up of eight-and-a-half-by-eleven-inch printer paper. "Yes. I hear you."

Whatever he said next she missed; she'd found another note. Not hidden or anything. A yellow Post-it, right on top of her closed laptop: *WHAT ARE YOU WAITING FOR?*

Dammit! Had she missed another budget meeting? Or was it about something worse, something secret? These cryptic notes were getting ever more . . . well . . . cryptic. If someone had a problem with her, they should just come right out and say—

"That explains the curse."

"What?"

"Hey, you were listening!" He beamed, so pleased she had to smile. "Lots of people don't. Who can blame them? Roots of names, for God's sake. Pass the snores, right?"

"Ah . . . right." She pulled the note; crumpled it in her fist. Tossed it. Sat behind her desk. "You spoke of a curse?"

"Sure. They were definitely cursed," he went on. "The root of our surname means teacher." He paused. "A kind of teacher, anyway, but that's another whole thing to get into . . . Anyway, my mom loved it and figured they'd live up to it. So they wrote a bunch of those baby name books."

"Oh, yes?" Interesting. She supposed *someone* had to sit down and write those baby name books. It never occurred to her she would know someone who knew someone who did. "Your folks must have given a lot of thought to your name, then."

"Nope. They got so they were sick of digging for hidden meanings in everything. Just . . . so . . . *sick* of it, y'know? Do we want to give him a name that means *hero* or *teacher* or *blessed one* or *pain in the ass* or *weird child with obsessive tendencies* . . . ?"

She burst out laughing, and he laughed with her. "Exactly . . . ugh, right? My folks . . . they just wanted names to be names again. We got a new dog just before I went to college."

"I fear to ask."

"Spot."

"Oh."

"Really jaded."

"I guess so. So if Linus means teacher—"

"It's supposed to mean it, but I think that might be off."

"How come?"

He shifted uncomfortably. "Well, Linus was the guy who taught music to Hercules."

"Oh?"

"Until Hercules killed him with his own lyre."

"Oh."

"Linus equals sucker," he finished.

"What . . . what's your first name again?" she asked, dying and dreading to hear it at the same time.

"Jamie. Which is several pokes in the eye, how's that for annoying?" But he didn't sound annoyed. He sounded almost aggravatingly cheerful. Being around him simultaneously cheered and exhausted her. "It's unisex, so people have to meet me to know if I'm a woman with a weird last name or a man with a weird last name."

"I can see how that would be inconvenient."

"And the root meaning! *Supplanter* . . . what, like Henry VII? Like an invading tyrant? Or a claim jumper out of the *Little House* books? Or a low-level parasite, like dandelions? Yuck. Besides, everybody calls me Linus. People have given me soooo . . . many . . . Linus birthday cards and gift wrap and small Linus statues and blankets. I'm a grown man, for God's sake, and people still give me blue blankies for Christmas."

It's easier if you don't look at him. Because something was wrong with her. She should have found this odd conversation dull, or at least irritating, especially since she was late, would therefore be behind all day, and had to write herself up again for tardiness. Instead, she wanted to keep asking him about names. *Perhaps the flu? It's supposed to be bad this year. Of course, they say that every year. And I can't get sick. Physically, that is.* She could get sick of crime. She could get sick of writing herself up. But she couldn't get the flu, or a cold, or an STD.

"What . . . ah . . ." It was probably on one or more of the pieces of paper in his file, but she couldn't find it. "What do you do here again?"

He arched his eyebrows in surprise and she could almost read his mind: *You're in HR and you don't know that?* "Accounting."

"Oh." Hmm. He didn't seem the type. Far too personable. And gorgeous. And gorgeous. And . . . er . . . what were they talking about again? She should try to hold up her end of the conversation.

"Anyway, you wanted to meet."

"I did?"

He blinked slowly, like an owl. It only emphasized his deep dark eyes. "Sure."

She had no idea why.

"I am a new hire," he said slowly, taking in her confused expression. "You work for Human Resources for the company that has made me a new hire. Ergo, we have some . . . I dunno . . . paperwork at the very least, right?"

"Right!" She had it now. "I *am* in HR! And you *are* a new hire."

"See?" He smiled. It was devastating. There wasn't a sexier grin anywhere. Ever. In the history of grins. In the history of teeth! *Oh, I might be in real trouble here . . .* "We're in agreement already. I love when coworkers get along."

That, she knew, would change. Her rep as resident Hypocritical Bitch would soon reach him. He would dismiss her as napalm in a knockoff suit and avoid her at all costs, which, of course, was all according to plan.

Dammit!

"You have to go away now," she told him. "I have to find the rest of your paperwork."

"Okay." He slouched to his feet. She had no idea how he did that. He was all relaxed and boneless and then he sort of lurched and then he was standing in front of her. He extended a hand and, dazed, she shook it. His hand was warm and dry; his grip was firm. And his eyes . . . "Well, nice to meet you and all. I think I'll go find the bathrooms. And maybe a machine stuffed with greasy food that would kill me if I ate it in huge quantities."

"It's nice," she said soberly, "that you have a to-do list." It was a pale joke, but when he smiled, she felt ridiculously pleased with herself.

Dammit!

CHAPTER
THREE

Linus had been a member of the Ramouette family a week, and liked it.

He liked the commute; since he lived in Burnsville, one town over, it was less than forty minutes. He liked the company property: all that gorgeous green grass, nibbled all day by sleek Canadian geese, and then a vast cement moat swallowed the grass and went right up to the building.

He liked that Valleyfair, the local amusement park, was less than two miles from the office. On his second day, he found a little park—not a real one, a secret park. There was a bench, but it was old and the paint had long faded. There was a duck pond, but the area around it hadn't been landscaped in years, and the ducks weren't fat white domesticated ones, but lean mallards who treated the place strictly as a rest stop. And there were so many weeping willow trees around it, the pond and the bench couldn't be seen from any of the nearby roads. A guy could grab a lunch and walk through the weeping willow branches and plop down on an old bench and enjoy a sandwich. He could watch the ducks and hear the *clack-clack-clack* of climbing cars, followed by shrieks of delight and, if the wind was right, occasional retching.

He liked the company's on-site fitness center, which put the local Bally's to shame: free Muscle Milk! And so many Stairmasters, stationery bikes, and treadmills there was never a line.

He liked the IT department, which was a first. At Ramouette, the IT guys kept to themselves, and their help desk guys were actually helpful. Their boss, Edward something or other, was a weird one, but again: it was IT, and was to be expected, the way you expected dogs to bark and cats to climb trees. When Edward wasn't lurking in the shadows, or holed up with the company server, he didn't bother anyone: yet another plus.

Linus also liked the paid holidays. All twenty-nine of them. When he'd asked why there were so many ("Not that I'm looking a gift Arbor Day in the mouth."), he was told the company's owner hated being there so much, she felt sorry for those who didn't have their own company and so had to come to work, and encouraged Hailey to come up with as many holidays as she could.

Which was why Ramouette observed Christmas Day, Boxing Day, Vernal Equinox Day, New Year's Day, Arbor Day, Easter, Good Friday, Greenery Day, Black Monday, Clean Monday, Maundy Thursday, Valentine's Day, May Day, Independence Day, Pioneer Day, Dan Patch Day, Labor Day, National Freedom Day, Columbus Day, Turkmen Melon Day, Memorial Day, Halloween, Unity Day, Groundhog Day, Lammas Day, Veterans

Day, Presidents Day, Martin Luther King Day, and Thanksgiving.*

All those in addition to three weeks of paid vacation, up to three weeks unpaid (as long as your work was getting done), and thirty days of sick time. All of which could be stockpiled if you didn't use them by year-end. One of the gals in marketing had been on vacation since July 1, 2010.

("Not surprised about all that sick time," Audrey the Receptionist confided while they jogged on side-by-side treadmills at 6:30 A.M. "Nobody was. Hailey's sick a lot. And she makes the rules, so . . .")

He liked the paternity leave . . . thirty days before the baby was born, sixty days after. Paid. The moms got thirty before, ninety after. Also paid. Linus was in his midtwenties and hadn't thought much about having kids. He wasn't old fashioned but wanted, if not a wife first, at least a steady girlfriend . . . no, okay, a wife. A wife to have kids with; he *was* old fashioned.

Anyway, kids were way off in the future, but even to a single guy, Ramouette's parental leave policy was impressive. Might be worth staying here for the next few years. Because if he ever did want kids, Hailey was so smart and so pretty and seemed really, really different and . . . and . . .

Anyway. He liked the pop machines, because Hailey had done something with—or to—the pop vendor, and thus, a big, tall cold fizzy drink cost twenty-five cents. In the twenty-first century!

And speak of the devil—that was the impression he got from others, anyway—he liked Hailey.

---

* These holidays all exist. Look 'em up if you don't believe me!

A lot.

Which was strange, because he'd barely spoken with her once they finished his new-hire paperwork. She was in and out of the office a lot; the owner obviously kept her pretty busy.

Stranger: he seemed to be the only one who *did* like Hailey. Which was a puzzle to him, because she seemed pretty good at her job and cared about getting the best bennies she could for her fellow employees. Exhibit A: a big bottle of Coke for two bits. Exhibit B: you could stockpile a thousand vacation days and take them all at once. Exhibit C: Dan Patch Day.

He was thinking this while he loitered by the watercooler, talking to The Old Coot.

The Old Coot was his boss, the head of the accounting department. Like the accountants at his last job, they were weird. Every accountant he had ever met took pride in the fact that accountants had a rep for being dull, dry, numbers-obsessed dweebs, and then took pride in smashing that rep to shit.

None of that was why he was lingering by the watercooler. He knew the department heads had a meeting in five minutes, an important one about next year's marketing budget, so he knew Hailey would be there. Accounting lost the coin toss and had to host this week's meeting.

"Bruegger's again," The Old Coot was saying. "When HR hosted last month, we got sushi! These guys have no imagination. In the old days . . ."

Stifled groans from the cubicles around them. Linus never lost sight of the fact that though you might think you were in a private conversation with one person, at any given time at least a dozen people you couldn't see could hear it all.

"In the old days," The Old Coot continued, raising his voice to

29

be heard over the groans, "we'd plug in the Crock-Pot in the morning and have hot bubbly chili by lunchtime. Rolls from the bakery, cheese to sprinkle on your chili, all the twenty-five-cent pop you could drink . . . a proper lunch."

"Followed by department heads farting and belching the rest of the day," an unseen voice said from one of the cubicles on the left.

"Disaster," another unseen voice added from the right. "Have you ever tried to proof a P and L statement when all you can smell are chili farts? Hell. Hell on earth."

"I like bagels," Linus said, which was true. Also, The Old Coot seemed to be waiting for him to contribute to the conversation. "And I can't believe there's actually a thing called a watercooler, around which employees can gather and make pop culture references, as we appear to be doing right now."

"Free water," the first unseen voice said.

"Yeah, Hailey put 'em in, so we all just bring our empty water bottles from home and fill 'em here at the cooler."

"Another fabbo perk brought to the good people of Ramouette by HR goddess Hailey Derry." Linus made the comment with total admiration.

"Ha!" Unseen Voice Number Two said. "Goddess, right. Says the newest minion, who hasn't been here long enough to really be terrified of her. Your time's coming, l'il minion."

He thought about letting it go, but couldn't. It seemed at best unfair, and at worst, ungrateful. "You guys, what's the problem? She's pulled all these great bennies for us, she—"

"Can't get her ass to work on time to save her life—"

The disembodied voice from the right broke in. "She can't go more than three weeks without pulling a sick day—come *on*. Anyone who gets sick that often should live in a plastic bubble."

"Paaaaaperwork!" another unseen voice contributed. Linus had the impression of swimming in deep dark water, knowing there were sharks but not knowing how many . . . or how hungry they were. "That girl loves her paperwork."

"She sends out memos reminding all of us to complete our shifts while she gets here late and leaves early . . . adds new codes to time sheets practically every week . . . nauseating."

"In my day," The Old Coot began, and ignored the groans, "memos were on paper. Real paper! From a tree and everything. And we had to fill out real paper timesheets. In ink!"

"Thank God those dark days are behind us," Linus said with a shudder.

"You kids are soft." The Old Coot leaned forward and scooped a paper cup out of the dispenser, then carefully filled it with water and drank it down, his *glug-glug*s not quite as loud as the watercooler's. "You're the soft-boiled eggs of the breakfast world."

"Oh, not this again."

Linus turned, delighted: it was Hailey! He could practically hear mouths snapping shut behind cubicles all over the room. *Wonder if she overheard?* "Hey." *Wow, smooooth. You'll have her swept off her feet in no time.*

She nodded. "Hey. What's wrong, Coot, are you reminiscing about PalmPilots again?"

"Now *those* kept a person on schedule. And speaking of schedules, what the hell are you doing here? Prepared for a budget meeting? And on time—no, *early*."

"Better keep watch for the other horsemen of the Apocalypse," she said dryly.

Linus laughed as Coot rolled his eyes, but was well aware he could be contributing to the conversation, and wasn't. *Say something!*

. . .

(Nope. He had nothin'.)

Say anything!

He gulped a breath and managed, "Apocalypse was actually a girl's name thousands of years ago. It didn't always mean the end of everything. It meant revelation . . . uncovering truth and finding out what's really going on. It was"—he knew they were staring and gamely finished—"it was a good thing. A good name," he finished. "It wasn't weird to have a girl in the family named Apocalypse."

Okay, say something that isn't the thing you just said.

"What's this?" Hailey teased. "Trying to restart a baby name trend?"

He shook his head, relieved she didn't think what he'd said was off-putting. Or if she did, she didn't seem to mind.

"Ohhhh, great," The Old Coot muttered. "New guy's as big a weirdo as Derry."

"What a nasty thing to say," Hailey replied mildly, if absently. She was staring down at a yellow Post-it note. *She must leave herself notes . . . She's always walking around with one of those.*

Her hair was lightening toward strawberry blond, something else that was odd that the people around them didn't notice or, if they did, didn't think was interesting. When they'd met earlier, her hair was dark brown. It set off her pale skin, and made her face seem more striking: wide creamy forehead, straight nose, and lush mouth. No freckles, but a beauty mark riding just above her upper lip; he spent an alarming amount of time thinking about kissing it.

But in a week, her dark locks had lightened to reddish blond. Why anyone would dye their hair a slightly lighter shade every single night was a mystery to him, as beautiful women and their secret tribal rituals always were.

"Jeez, Hailey, you even remembered your laptop. We didn't used to lug entire computers into meetings, y'know. Hell, computers didn't used to be portable! Desktop computers . . . give me a break."

Another chorus of groans by unseen listeners, but The Old Coot was practiced in ignoring them.

"Hey, you know what we had before desktops? Actual desk tops. Tops of desks. And blotters. Blotters will make a comeback. I guarantee it. What's old is new, and all that."

Linus was wondering if he dared ask Hailey out right there, or if it would be better to try to catch her after the meeting, or maybe meet up with her on her way out the—

"Oh my God!" Another hidden voice, this one coming from the kitchen, which was two doors down from the watercooler. Before he could wonder about it, The Old Coot was saying, "It's good you can make this meeting."

"Of course." She shrugged, took one last look at the Post-it, then crumpled it. "I'm right here; let's get started."

"Okay, great. Because with the new rollout next year, marketing's gonna be all over us, and we've got to find a place in the budget—"

"Mighty crap, people! Have you heard?" Audrey the Receptionist bounded out of the break room like a puppy with earbuds. A puppy checking out her iPhone and eating a Hot Pocket. "Some dumbass plowed into a garbage truck, the truck overcorrected and hit a bus, and now the bus is, like, surrounded by toxic waste or something!"

"Jeez," he said, shocked.

"I *know*. It's going to utterly screw my commute." Audrey took another look at the small screen and shook her head, disgusted. "I've gotta take the 494 ramp not even a mile from there. Why can't more parents drive their kids to school? We wouldn't even need buses if they'd step up."

Hailey turned back to The Old Coot. "You tell marketing that I loathe them with everything I have, do not care how many ads they want to run for the rollout, and will not set foot in that meeting until that entire department agrees to stop sucking." Then she whirled and stalked off.

"Whoa," Linus said.

"Yeah, she really hates the marketing guys." Coot shrugged. "I dunno; what's it to her? She's always picking a fight and then doing her ice cube impersonation."

"Knock it off." Linus was startled at how sharply that came out, and consciously softened his tone. "She's got a tough job."

"If she was ever on time, it'd be an easier job."

He opened his mouth to argue, but was still reeling from a) the odd conversation, b) the abruptness of Hailey's mood shift from friendly and pleasant to pissed and abrupt, and c) the fact that The Old Coot didn't look a day over thirty.

("Why is that?" he asked Audrey the Receptionist the night before.

"Because thirty is ancient in twenty-first-century tech years," she explained. "Thirty is the new ninety.")

"What just happened?" he asked aloud, and no one answered.

FOUR

Toldja: If You Don't Act, We Will.

Hailey limped back to the office. Shoving the bus to safety had ruined her clothes: torn pantyhose, scuffed shoes, torn skirt, torn blouse. Grease all over her hands. The heel of her left shoe wobbling at every staggered step. Left bra strap broken and dangling. Hair looking like she'd combed it with a wire whisk. And *unbelievable* dry mouth.

And so, so hungry. Not to mention late for a budget meeting that likely ended over an hour ago. She hadn't even finished writing herself up for being late this morning, and now this.

Audrey the Receptionist greeted her with a, "Whoa! And hey—before I forget, Edward was looking for you. Something about his PO request for more internal fans for the server."

"All right . . . I'll call him."

"Did you pick another fight with the Chipotle guy?"

"No." She limped past.

"The Subway guy?"

"No." Now she was hurrying as fast as she could without breaking into a jog.

"The KFC guy? The bookstore gal? The Caribou Coffee guy? The Dunn Bros gal? The car wash guy? The bakery gal?" Audrey was on her feet, hollering after her. "The gas station guy? Wait, the car wash guy and the gas guy are the same guy . . ."

She was in such a rush she didn't realize she'd knocked Linus over until she . . . well . . . knocked him over.

"Ow!" He was gasping on the carpet, rubbing his nose. "Jeez, you're really bony."

Stupid, stupid, she inwardly raged. *You haven't completely drained the batteries; you could have put him through the wall!* Mortified, she bent to give him a hand up; he was back on his feet in less than a blink, which made him stagger against her. Given the state of her clothes, that should have been embarrassing, but wasn't. More thrilling than embarrassing, truth be told.

"Aagghh! I've never gotten motion sickness that bad before. Or that fast . . ."

"Sorry. I'm so sorry . . . Are you hurt?"

"No. 'Course not."

"Thank God, okay, listen—I'm running late—"

"I know. The meeting's been over for—"

She groaned. "Don't tell me." He was following her to her office, and for once, she didn't mind someone dogging her steps. "Can't believe I missed another one."

"What happened? Did someone—Are you—Did somebody do this to you? Did someone try to . . . ?" He took a breath. "Did you have to fight someone off? Because if you did, we need to call the cops. Right now."

She was surprised to see him go from concerned to horrified anger, and so quickly. Then she realized what he thought might have happened. "No, no. I did it to myself." *At least that doesn't sound exceptionally crazy.* "Flat tire."

"Oh. I've heard you get those a lot."

"It's why I no longer buy American." She got to her office, kicked off her shoes, and sat down at her laptop. At least there wasn't a new note.

And that meant something. That was important. But she was so tired and hungry she couldn't put it together, couldn't put her finger on just why it was important, and resolved to think about it later.

Paperwork. She had to focus on something else. *Had* to. "Linus, I have to write myself up—sorry again about knocking you down."

"Why?"

Hmmm. I assumed he would be quicker. "Because it was a rotten, rude thing to do."

"No, why do you have to write yourself up?"

"I'm in HR," she replied, confused.

"Yeah, but why?"

"To pay my rent?" Was it a riddle? A game? What?

"But why *here*?"

She shook her head, tried to run her fingers through her hair, and gave up after finding a knot of tangles. *Probably oil in it; wonderful. Had to gulp down the spilled oil and eat all the broken glass before I could move the bus. Broken glass tastes almost as bad as Corn Nuts do.* "Linus, I'm not following you."

"You're really interesting, you know that?" He'd taken the chair opposite her desk. She knew she should show him the door but couldn't make herself say the words, much less move. He seemed so . . . so kind and nice and honestly interested. She had liked the way he looked at her during their interview a few days back, and she liked how he was looking at her now, when she was such a walking disaster, when she likely couldn't look worse. It was confusing and wonderful.

"I'm not interesting. I'm very, very dull."

"Dull. Uh-huh. It's the worst-kept secret here that you hate your job. Except you're really good at your job and you go out of your way to get everything you can for us. You put in lots of extra effort for a job you say you hate, to help people you pretend you don't like. And it's possible—don't take this the wrong way—but I think the people here pretend not to like you."

"What?"

"And you hate exercise, but you're always showing up panting and sweaty from jogging or whatever it is you do when you're not *not* going to budget meetings."

"Ouch," she said, hurt.

"I didn't mean it in a nasty way," he quickly assured her. "Just as another point of evidence that puts you in the interesting category. You give off this stiff vibe, but you're sometimes really friendly and nice. And then there's the . . ." Too late, he realized where that last point was going.

Unfortunately, Hailey did, too, and gave him a wry smile. "Yes, continue."

"Uh . . . well, you've got all these minions and underlings and Igors, and they pretend those are mean secret nicknames, but not only do you know about them, the impression I get is that you sort of like them."

I do like them. She did. Nicknames could be wonderful. Like a secret code only a few people knew. A family thing. A friend thing. And since she no longer had a family, and had never had friends, she loved the nicknames, nasty as they were. But she'd done a poor job of hiding it, which made her worry: What else had she made a poor job of hiding?

He's known me a week. I knew he was sharp, but this is . . . this is something more than sharp.

And the notes.

Hmmm.

"Anyway, you're interesting." He leaned back in his chair, started to put his feet up, checked himself, and slumped back in his seat.

She laughed. "Go ahead. I don't have the moral high ground today when it comes to inappropriate employee behavior. Besides, I'm not your boss—just the person who hired you for your boss."

"Right. Thanks." He stretched out long legs and crossed his feet at the ankles, inches away from paperwork. "You're not my boss, but there's something . . . Okay, one thing at a time. So like I said, if you hate it but not really, why are you even writing yourself up? Why do any of this"—he gestured to the room—"if you hate it?"

"I don't know." She didn't. It was one thing to know that she could do a half-assed job, could come into the office no more than eight or ten hours a week, and Ann Denison would never fire her. In fact, Ann lived in fear of Hailey quitting.

Knowing that was one thing; taking rude advantage of it was

something else. If she didn't write herself up for her frequent tardiness, no one would. No one would even say anything . . . not officially, and even if they would, Ann wouldn't care. And that made her think of the notes again. "I guess . . . how can I hold everyone to standards I won't maintain myself? It's not fair, which I agree is a juvenile concept, but I don't have the stomach for it. I guess I'm a terrible rebel."

"Terrible," he murmured, "is not the first word I think of when your name comes up. And it comes up. A lot."

"Yes, I imagine so."

"Can I ask you something?"

"Something else, you mean?" She was pulling paperwork out of desk drawers and hunting pens. She could at least sign off on payroll today, even if nothing else got done.

"Yeah. Uh . . . we're close to the same age, right?"

She blinked even as she found a hidden Snickers and wolfed it down in three unlovely bites. "Mmm gsss sssoo." She was twenty-six. He was twenty-four.

"It's just, you seem older."

"Ffffnnnkks fffrrr nnnthnng."

"In a good way, in a good way! You just . . . you know how they say some people are old souls? I never met one before. You're one of those; you have an old soul tucked behind a young face."

You would, too, if you spent your days shoving school buses and foiling robberies and getting stabbed trying to break up a rape and then having to eat the damned knife to have the strength to pummel the rapists.

"Which is also interesting," he finished.

She swallowed the rest of the candy and held on to the wrapper. She would eat it as soon as he was gone. Also the four empty file folders she'd found. And possibly the pencil shavings out of the electric sharpener. A pity there had been no time to replenish her work stash. But her work stash might be what led to those unlovely notes.

The whole thing made her tired. And, to be honest, a little angry. She'd stopped asking herself *why me, why me, why am I the one stuck with this, woe, woe* years ago, but sometimes it snuck back into her brain. "Well, thank you, I suppose. And now I have to kick you out. Work, work, work. But I'll see you tomorrow."

"Prob'ly not; tomorrow's a holiday, remember?"

"It is?" Her heart sank. Literally: it actually felt like it swelled from adrenaline and then dropped down to her belly button. "I won't?"

"Greenery Day."

"How could I have forgotten?"

"Can you believe it's that time of year again?" he asked with exaggerated surprise. "Japanese nature holidays just sneak right up, don't they? To think I've left my Greenery Day shopping 'til the last minute."

She cracked up; she couldn't help it. Which got him started, so in seconds they were both yowling like hyenas behind her closed office door.

"Well," he said at last, wiping his eyes, "happy Greenery Day Eve." Ignoring her snort, he added, "Uh, maybe you'd want to get together tomorrow for a—"

"Of course!"

"—movie or someth—What? Oh. Great." He smiled again, that wonderful smile. His obvious pleasure in her acceptance almost negated her embarrassment that she'd hurried to say yes before he had a chance to finish the question.

Which was insane. Knowing what she knew and, worse, what she didn't know.

I don't know him: bad. He's a nice boy, but exactly that: a boy. Worse. Or not. And that's the worst of all.

They worked out the details—lunch, tomorrow, Big Bowl in the Galleria, 11:30, maybe a movie after. Then he bid her a courteous good-bye and shut the door behind him with a firm click.

She instantly stuffed the wrapper in her mouth, followed by several pens she kept for emergencies, the ones out of ink.

Funny, she mused, chewing. *I feel loads better, though nothing has changed. I'm still a mess. I still work here. Evil has still not been vanquished. I'm still getting those annoying notes.*

And I can't wait for 11:30 tomorrow.

FIVE

Seriously: Did You Think This Was a Joke?

Linus found Big Bowl with no problems but hadn't known he would. So because he left himself plenty of time to arrive, he was forty-five minutes early. And delighted to find Hailey already waiting. Part of him had spent the night worrying she'd forget about their date, or would change her mind before they even sat down, or would rush off before the pot stickers came because she'd double booked herself.

So he spoke without thinking when he saw her: "Hey, you're here! Great!" And was mortified by his big mouth, and relieved by her smile.

"Oh, I wouldn't miss it." Then she frowned, as if she might have said too much. He was pleasantly startled to see her hair was lighter today; the red was fading to pure blond.

They sat, chatted with the friendly waitress, ordered dumplings and soup and pot stickers and peanut noodles. And talked, of course: about people they knew, about their homes, about (of course) their jobs, and other shared interests.

"I was really hoping for an It Girl sighting."

Hailey instantly frosted: "Why? She's not real. And if she was, well . . . that would make her a glory-seeking moron."

Which was how he found out Hailey Derry had no love for heroes.

"Oh, come on," he coaxed, stupidly ignoring the warning signs. "I've lived here half my life. I know—"

"Half?"

"Maybe a third. We moved here when I was little, then headed up to Duluth until I finished my UMD degree. Anyway, I know people who've seen her . . . She's real."

"A real idiot." The waitress plunked down two plates of dumplings, and Hailey speared one with a single chopstick and tossed it into her mouth. "Who does things like that? Who could, and who would? She's a YouTube myth. They talk about her because they can't get *her* to talk. They can't prove her and it just makes them want her more. My mother—" She cut herself off and sucked down another vegetable dumpling.

Whoa. Deep water. "Yeah? Your mom? She says she saw her?"

"Ah . . . no."

"Was she from around here?"

"Briefly. Like you." Hailey smiled a little, more a quirk of her lips than a warm expression. "I was born here and then . . . we left."

"Okay." Linus felt like he was in a minefield. A minefield of pot stickers. He tried to sound noncommittal, like he didn't much care what she was saying, or wasn't listening very hard. It was strange, but sometimes that was the best way to keep someone talking. "Born, then left."

"Yes. She had to—she was infertile, see? And unmarried. And rich. Don't forget that last part; it's important later." Another small, bitter smile. "She went to a clinic. Several times, in fact. Got pregnant, stayed here through her pregnancy, my birth, all that. Then left. Promised never to return. And never did."

"Okay." He sucked down half his ginger ale. He couldn't recall being on a more stressful first date.

"The point is, she had to spend a lot of money to get me. And my mother always valued the things that were the most expensive, the things she actually had to work for. Coach bags. Louis Vuitton suitcases. Clé de Peau Beauté cream. A last-minute lunch rez at Menton. Dinner at Addison's. And me."

"Okay." *Weirder and weirder. It's wrong that her intensity is turning me on, right?*

"Anyway." Hailey had trailed off and was staring over his shoulder, then seemed to regain her train of thought. "She died a couple of years ago. And I didn't have anything to hold me to New York. So I came back here. Where I began. Where she first started to value me, before she ever saw me. Long, *long* before she knew me. Which brings me back to my point—the only reason people have any interest or liking in that person—"

"It Girl."

"Awful, awful name—yes. My point: they can't *know*. So because it's not quantifiable but is *assumed* to be extraordinary, she's valued. If you found out she was your next-door neighbor, you wouldn't be interested anymore."

"You mean *you* wouldn't. Because if It Girl was my neighbor,

I'd only have about a zillion questions. Savage and It Girl: a killer combo!"

"That's the other thing."

"Yeah?" The waitress had returned with more plates brimming with noodles and dumplings, which she was wolfing down in a way that both alarmed and intrigued him. *The weirdest things this woman does that get me hot. Swear to God!*

"You might not yet realize this, since you haven't spent a lot of time here in the last two decades, but this town is strange. The company you work for is strange. This entire area is very, very odd."

"Yeah, but in a good way, right? Ha!" His chopsticks had blocked hers just in time. "You can have the last vegetable pot sticker. I get the last chicken one." He whacked her chopstick again, eliciting a giggle. "Begone!"

"Fine, take it." She leaned back, smiling, but the smile disappeared when she again looked over his shoulder. "I don't have a problem with the notes, I don't think. But there are more direct ways to get your message across."

"Okay. I'm just gonna pretend that the thing you just said had something—anything—to do with the other things you said. Because otherwise you'll know you've lost me."

She leaned forward. He was a good boy and did not scope her cleavage, which he absolutely could have, since she was wearing a forest green tank top under a black linen jacket. Linen pants, too, and little green shoes; his ex from college had been into pretty shoes, so now he noticed women's shoes, and knew Manolos were *so* 2005. He didn't necessarily want to notice them, or know Manolos were so 2005, but it was just how things were now. Breakups change people.

"Linus, listen. We work in a town called Savage, which once upon a time had the slightly less awful name of Hamilton until a rich guy named Marion Savage bought a horse called Dan Patch and, when that horse won a few races, they changed the name of the city."

"Wait." He paused, slurped the forkful of peanut noodles, swallowed. "So Savage is named after a horse?"

"If only. Savage is named after the guy who *bought* the horse."

"Marion was a guy?"*

"Like that makes any of this better? Oh, and at least a third of us graduated from Cretin High School—yes, that's *Cretin High School*, and we work for a company that makes big metal animals that people can shoot at, and our mutual boss hardly ever comes in because she's determined to turn broomball into an Olympic sport. Let's see, did I miss anything?"

"I don't see why you're down on the horse. He was a terrific horse. Audrey the Receptionist told me Dan Patch broke world records for speed."

"As a *harness* horse," she replied, scorn heavy on *harness*. "My point is, get out. Get out while you still can, I pray you."

"This explains Dan Patch Drive."

"Yes."

"And Dan Patch Lane."

"Yes. Don't forget Dan Patch Day. It's horses or Cretins around here."

"And superheroes."

"Myth," she said. She wiped her mouth, stood, grabbed her

---

*This is all true!

purse, and said, "I have to go the bathroom. It was lovely talking to you."

He figured she wasn't coming back from the bathroom and . . . nope. She was not. When he asked the waitress for the check, she replied that his date had paid the entire bill and left. ("She was in a hurry to get somewhere, huh?")

Date? Is that what that was?

He hadn't walked five feet into the parking lot when he saw the small crowd gathered around a thirtyish, tearful redhead cradling a squalling (also redhead) infant. "I locked my keys in—stupid, stupid! And shut the door, and then Renee was locked in! And I didn't know what to do and I forgot my phone and then that lady fixed it! There, baby, it's okay. Mom's here."

"I don't think it was locked, ma'am," a teenage girl said doubtfully, looking at the rear passenger door. "Your door's busted, though. Good thing you didn't really lock her in. Guess you just didn't yank good enough."

Curious, Linus peeked around the teenager.

The handle of the door had been twisted, as if it were made of steel-colored bread dough instead of steel-colored steel.

(Much later, he realized: eagerness to see him might not have explained her showing so early. She'd picked a booth near the windows and took the side with her back to the wall. She had an excellent view of not only the entire restaurant but the parking lot outside.

And what was that about notes?)

CHAPTER SIX

Why Aren't You Doing More?

A couple of her fellow employees—and someone she didn't know—were amiably grumbling about being back at work so soon after Greenery Day. Hailey got there for the last of the conversation (shockingly early for her, which was to say, only twenty minutes late).

"Can't believe it's gonna be another whole year." The Old Coot sighed, comfortably sprawled in one of the plush chairs in the reception area. He looked up and waved. "Hey."

"It goes by so quickly," Audrey the Receptionist agreed. "But Arbor Day will be here in no time." She turned to face the new hire and held out her hand. "Hi. I'm Audrey the Receptionist. You must be Jennifer." And then, when she spotted Hailey, "Whoa."

"Now, don't make a big deal out of this," Hailey warned, digging in her purse for the last of the M&M's.

"You're shockingly early. Which is to say—"

"I know."

"—only twenty minutes late," Audrey finished.

"I *know*."

"Jennifer, this is Hailey, the head of HR. Don't do *anything* she does."

"That's sound advice," Hailey said to Jennifer, who was another petite, pale blue-eyed Nordic blonde from the wilds of southern Minnesota. "Welcome aboard. One of my minions passed on your new-hire packet to me, so we'll get you through this paperwork and get you set up inside." She scooped the last of the candy into her mouth, chewed, realized she was also chewing a couple of pennies and a paper clip, and in the future resolved to look before she chomped. Or at least keep the candy separate from the non-candy.

"She has tons of minions," Audrey the Receptionist said helpfully. "Someday you, too, might be one."

"Dare to dream." The Old Coot poked at his iPad. "This thing needs charging *again*? It's only been twenty hours! In my day—"

"Shut up," Hailey and Audrey said. Hailey glanced at Jennifer. "Uh, I don't normally condone telling colleagues to shut up."

"Like I said: don't do anything she does."

"In fairness, she only tells me to shut up. Everyone else she tells to hush. But Aud's right: not doing anything Hailey does is a surefire way to go right to the top," The Old Coot said. "Or get saved by It Girl."

"That makes *no* sense," Audrey pointed out. "One thing's got nothing to do with the other, you twenty-nine-year-old senile freak. And there's no such thing as It Girl."

The Old Coot ignored her. "But no fair 'accidentally' parking your car on the railroad tracks in the hopes that she'll save you and you'll get something new for YouTube. Not to mention a new in-my-day-superhero-vigilantes-actually-tried-to-cover-their-faces-and-*not*-get-on-the-news story."

"Oh, I'd never," Jennifer said, looking from The Old Coot to Audrey the Receptionist to Hailey, her glances so quick they could almost hear her eyeballs clicking: back and forth, back and forth, *click-click-click*. "I don't . . . There's no such thing, anyway, right? Like Audrey said?"

"My *name* is Audrey the Receptionist."

"You really should try to get our names right," The Old Coot said kindly. "It's the least you can do."

"The least she can do is nothing," Hailey pointed out. *The least you can do* followed by someone doing something besides nothing was a pet peeve of hers, along with people who thought switching sides meant *doing a three-sixty*.*

Jennifer tried again but was still giving off trapped-like-a-rat-in-a-room-with-crazy-people vibes. "It Girl—I figured she was one of those, whatchamacallits . . . a meme. Or an urban legend. Something."

"That's the spirit!" Hailey cried. *Meme! Oh, that's wonderful! Planking, Faith Hilling, It Girling! Either way, a silly fad no one actually takes seriously.*

"Not this again," The Old Coot groaned. "Of course she's real. People have seen her."

"Do you hear yourself?" Audrey the Receptionist cried.

_____

*Author: I hate that.

"Life is not a Marvel comic book. There are no superheroes. I feel dumb just telling you that. What, did you also see a blurry picture of a Sasquatch and decide Bigfoot's real, too?"

"It would be terrific," Hailey said, "if you didn't compare It Girl to Bigfoot."

"New kid rules the tie . . . so, Jennifer, is It Girl real? And if she is, is she real-real, or if-it's-on-the-Internet-it-must-be-true real? Or a hoax or a hallucination or a sinister government cover-up?"

"I'm—I'm not sure."

"Well, guess. Or narrow the question down further: which one of your new colleagues is batshit crazy for believing everything she sees, and which is the logical fountain of organized thought through which wisdom flows?"

"I'll just go find my desk and stuff now," Jennifer said, slowly backing away. She bumped into Hailey and didn't notice, just backed away more quickly.

They listened to the receding *clack-clack-clack* of Jennifer's heels hitting tile, then the *thud-thud-thud* of them hitting carpet.

"That poor kid." Hailey sighed.

"She's not going to make it," Audrey the Receptionist said. "Not if one harmless conversation about which of us needs psychotropic meds freaks her out. This is no place for the timid. Just the weird. And you."

"Me, what?" Hailey was fumbling for her phone . . . Linus was texting her again. A good trick, since she hadn't given him her cell number. "What?"

"Come on. You know what. I know you have hair ADD, but you've gone eight shades darker in three days."

That was only the truth; Hailey's mop of unruly strands had

been medium brown when she woke up two hours ago. She did not want to think about what that meant, and so did not.

"I just think you could try a shade slightly longer than, oh, eleven hours? Maybe? Sometimes you have. Sometimes an entire week goes by and your hair remains the same color. It's eerie, but also nice."

"Hush," she told her absently. Again, Audrey was correct, and again, Hailey didn't want to think about what that meant.

Besides, she was quite fond of Audrey the Receptionist. It was hard not to like someone who found the whole your-job-is-your-identity thing so silly she referred to herself, constantly, by her first name and job title. All the time. Everywhere: at work, at home, at the grocery story, at family reunions. "My hair is my hair, and it's silly that we're talking about it at all."

"You just do not even care that you're so utterly, utterly weird, do you?"

"Not for a while now," she admitted, and hurried back to her office.

"Twenty-four hours!" Audrey the Receptionist called after her. "Maybe even thirty-six! Hey, how about forty-eight whole hours with the same hair color? Just think it over! That's all I'm asking." She plunked back down in her chair. "It's *not* that much to ask," she said to no one, and turned back to her computer.

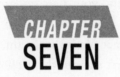

CHAPTER
SEVEN

"Ah," Hailey said upon entering her office. Linus was instantly on his feet when he saw her. "There you are. I got your texts." Another unpleasant fact she did not wish to dwell on, but had to. Best apologize first, and then get to it. "I know you must be angry about our lunch, and I'm sorry I had to mmmmm uumm mmm."

She'd mumbled the last because he'd grasped her by the shoulders, and kissed her on the mouth. She was so startled she dropped her briefcase, mentally groaning at the thought of the folders spilling everywhere (stupid broken zipper!). No, wait—that was verbal groaning, specifically, *her* verbal groans. Possibly because Linus was an amazing kisser. A wonderful kisser. An astounding kisser. What briefcase?

"Astounding!" she said, pulling back with real regret. "You

are wonderful! Which is bad. Why did you do that? It was . . .
ah . . . astounding. Yes. The perfect word."

"Yeah, thanks, I had to," he replied, which made no sense.
Worse, she didn't much care. "I mean, you're a department head
and I'm just an accounting cog. Probably you'd get in trouble if
you nailed my lips at the office. Not that I'd mind," he assured
her. "I wouldn't! And I wouldn't sue for sexual harassment or
anything. Unless that's what you're into. So I figured we'd talk
and I'd ask you and then I sort of forgot about that and kissed
you."

"I never understand half of what comes out of your mouth,"
she complained, but she was glowing. She knew it; she could
actually feel herself all warm and flushed and happy and ready
for more kisses.

Which was all just awful, really. Under the circumstances.

"You don't understand half of what comes out of *my* mouth?"
His eyebrows arched; his sweet mouth curled into a darling
grin. "Have you heard *yourself* ever?"

She sighed. By not smacking him, or suing him, she'd made
the situation worse. And now there was nothing for it but to
plunge. *Glowing feeling fading . . . fading . . . gone.* "Look, you don't
have to do that."

"What?"

"Pretend to like me to cover up the notes."

"*What?*"

"I just want to know what your purpose is. To out me? To
complain about my work habits? To put more pressure on me as
an individual or us as a society? What?"

"Are you talking about those Post-its you walk around with
all the time?"

"It's not all the time," she said, trying to keep her anger in check. "It's only since you got here, which you must very well know. What I want to know is why—"

"Hailey: I've never left you a single Post-it." He rolled his (big, dark, beautiful) eyes and shook his head. She had the impression he wanted to shake *her* but had decided against it, at least for the time being. "Why would I ever be okay with words on a tiny yellow piece of paper when I could see you in person and hear your voice and look at your eyes and your weird, always-changing hair and your four-seasons-ago Coach Lena flats?"

She stared down at her feet. "Four seasons—okay, this proves you're spying on me. How else would you know how long I've had these—"

"I am not spying on you! I'm not leaving Post-its and I have no idea where you live, although I'd love to be invited over for dinner and you could run off and leave anytime you wanted though I'd hope you'd stay at least through the first course, and I'll cook if you don't want to because—"

He was like a human blender of words. "Again: I never understand half of what you say, and I also never gave you my cell phone number." She truly hoped he wasn't going to morph into a full-blown crook weirdo stalker she would then have to pummel after eating the contents of her In bin. "But you've texted me multiple times, the notes started showing the same week you did—" Had he only been there a week? Had all this madness been happening for a mere seven days? She felt like she'd been listening to yet not understanding him for much longer. She felt like they'd known each other and amused the hell out of each other for much, much longer.

She also wished he'd kissed her for much longer.

Stupid thinking, especially if he turns out to be dangerously deranged instead of merely deranged.

"Sure, I've got your number—you gave it to me." His hand plunged into his front left pocket (khakis, she noted approvingly, which was fine for business-casual Friday) and he pulled out a tiny yellow stamp.

No: it was a Post-it note. She saw he had very carefully folded it with crisp corners, and folded it again, and again, so it was teeny and yellow and a bare half-inch across. "I have little pockets," he mumbled, his pale freckled skin blushing, "and didn't want to lose it, so I was careful when I stuck it in there."

"That is so adorable I might pass out." It was. *I must stop saying these things out loud to him.* She carefully unfolded it, observed her cell number written in handwriting not her own, then carefully refolded it (teeny origami!) and gave it back, feeling loads better. "I didn't write that." In fact, she had a solid idea who did. The relief that Linus seemed to like her for herself was enough to make her knees weak. Or was a residual symptom of his kiss. "I didn't leave that for you. Isn't that great?"

"Oh." His blush deepened. "I guess you didn't mean for me to have it, then. Here." He tried to hand back the teeny origami but she wouldn't take it.

"That's not what I meant! I'm sorry, I didn't mean—it's fine that you have my number. It's not a state secret or anything." She felt awful, knowing he thought *she* thought he'd been a creep and, worse, a creep she did not want to give her digits to. His dear face was rapidly nearing the color of a ripe beefsteak tomato. It was strange, but his mortification touched her almost as much as his kiss had. His sweet kiss and his dear face and now he couldn't look at her; he was in an agony of embarrassment and she had never felt more tender and protective of anyone, ever, in her life. "See? I can prove it. Like this."

Then she seized his shoulders, yanked him forward, and kissed him back.

CHAPTER
EIGHT

Sometime later (seconds, hours, a month?) they both came up for air. They'd staggered around her office like two people trapped in a sack together, their arms around each other, kissing with the fury of two people who had remembered that often the best part of a relationship was the part they were embarked on right that moment, in her office, on her Corporate Yawn–colored carpet.

Linus hadn't even remembered when they'd left their feet. He was having trouble remembering any specifics at all. He had been so glad to see her and so happy to kiss her and so angry to realize she thought he was *pretending* to like her and then— pretending? What the *hell*? Who would? And why?

He had no idea how someone could fake being enchanted by a beautiful smart wonderful woman like Hailey Derry (hero,

hero). He hadn't been able to think straight for days; who could *fake* that? The thought upset him all over again and he instinctively put a hand to her. She took it, turned it over, and planted a soft kiss on his palm that he instantly felt . . . somewhere else.

"I never thought the name Linus was especially erotic." She shook her head and let him take his hand back (not that he was in any rush to do so). "How little I know."

"That's right. More fool you!"

"It's the name. Do it to me, Linus. Fill me up, Linus. Ooooh, give it to me haaaard, Linus!" She raised her voice to be heard over his helpless laughter. "If you kissed me as some sort of negative reinforcement because I ducked out on lunch, it was an utter failure."

They were both sitting on the carpet, thoroughly rumpled. They'd both called a halt right around the time they both went for the other's shirt buttons. ("Uh . . . probably not the best idea." "Right." "In my office, I mean." "Right." "To be continued." "*Damn* right.")

He shook his head. "It wasn't negative reinforcement. I was just so damned glad to see you. You came rushing in like you do, in a hurry, and I've sort of been worried about you, but when you rushed in, you looked so gorgeous the reason I was waiting went right out of my head." He sobered, hopped to his feet, then helped her to hers. "Hailey, I've got to talk to you. And you have to stay in this room with me until you've answered my questions. I'm not trying to come on like some Rambo jerkweed chauvinist, but come on. Something's up."

"Rambo jerkweed chauvinist?"

He didn't smile back. "You disappear all the time, you come back looking like somebody's beat you up, your mind's on something else—a lot." He took a breath, then let it out. "I'm the new guy and even *I* know something's wrong. I talked to Audrey the Receptionist while we were waiting for her girlfriend to pick her up the other night, and she said you were totally fine, and that you're kind of a nut about your privacy, which I totally respect—"

"He said, butting into her privacy." But she was smiling, so he plunged ahead.

He tried again. "I know we haven't known each other very long—"

"Only a week! Isn't that amazing?" She looked so happy when she said that, every thought went out of his head except for, *Must kiss pretty girl more now, yes, yes.* "It feels like longer."

"Huh?" *Must kiss pretty . . .* Linus shook himself. "Right. But you're in trouble, Hailey. Aren't you? Tell me. Let me help." He took a breath. Waited. Thought, *Yep, I'm really gonna ask her this.* Said: "Don't get mad, but you're It Girl, aren't you?"

"Yes."

CHAPTER
NINE

"Okay. I know it sounded crazy, but I just had to—wait. You said yes. You admitted it."

"Yes. Also, I hate that name. Rhymes with Zit Girl and Pit Girl and Hit Girl—people all over the Web think I'm plagiarizing Mark Millar." She'd finished adjusting her clothing and now stood on one foot, rested her hand lightly on his shoulder, then slipped her other shoe back on. "Now then. Since you didn't hack my digits, that means—"

"Hailey, come on. If you don't want to tell me what's wrong, you've at least got to agree to call a cop!"

"I'm It Girl." She actually shuddered as she said it. "That's what's going on. My God, I actually said it out loud and everything . . ."

"No, come on. Okay, I admit, it was a silly idea, okay?"

"Why?" She'd slipped her other shoe on, and was now unbuttoning his shirt (hooray!) and then rebuttoning it (boo!), this time with the appropriate buttons going into the appropriate holes. His head was still so full of her scent and her smile he was amazed he'd gotten any buttons into any holes. "What's so silly? Other than the absurdity of a grown woman finding out she's living the life of an escapee from a graphic novel."

He'd been almost sure, but her quick response threw him. "Look, I know you're in trouble. Please, *please* let me help. Okay, so you're not It Girl . . . It was a dumb idea. I mean, you work hard for us—when you're here—but you're kind of, um, disorganized . . ." He gestured; files were everywhere. "And you're always late or leaving early; and even when you're not at work, you're always rushing off somewhere. You're never around when . . . um . . . when . . ." Just like that, he'd talked himself back into the silly idea that Hailey Derry was It Girl.

"All those things you said, they're true."

This was not how it went in the movies. The cornered superhero would have all sorts of reasons why they weren't Superman or Vomit Girl or Hernia Boy or whomever, and they'd be able to back it up with airtight alibis by faithful butlers, statements that were typed and notarized. They didn't say, "Yep, you got me. You have found out my deep, dark secret. Woe, now the truth is out! Anyway, try not to blab it all over town."

"Look, I'll prove it."

They didn't say *that*, either.

Then Hailey rummaged through a desk drawer, pulled out a jumbo box of staples, and gulped down not only all the staples, but the box they were in, and then the stapler they'd been intended for.

Which, once he got over his shock, was the coolest—

"Linus?"

—thing—

"Are you all right?"

—ever.

"I've got you."

CHAPTER
TEN

"Thank God." Hailey sighed when Linus opened his eyes.

"That was awesome," he said weakly. He moved his head enough to realize it was pillowed on her lap, that they were still in her office (thank goodness for doors that closed, and employees who, unlike Hailey, went to meetings in other parts of the building), then started to sit up. "And I didn't faint."

"No, no."

"I blacked out."

"Of course."

"Because I was a little shocked."

"Yes."

"And also extremely turned on. That was awesome! I never knew a woman could look so damn hot while chomping down staples. So all the blood left my head and rushed . . . uh . . . somewhere else . . . and . . ." She was laughing so hard she almost dropped him. "Okay, but we agree I didn't faint like a girlie girl, right?"

"Oh, yes. Absolutely. Your rep as a stellar stud who never faints when confronted by a freak who—"

"*Don't say that.*" Surprised, she drew back a little. "Sorry. But don't, Hailey. You're not a freak. You're terrific. You are the polar opposite of a freak, okay? Run yourself down like that again and I'll kiss the shit out of you."

"That will certainly teach me, all right."

"And you suck at keeping your secret identity a secret."

"What secret identity? Do I have a costume? Do I rush around the country shoring up falling buildings or catching planes before they crash only to dash off and go back to my job as a mild-mannered HR director, always on the alert for evil and help desk seminars? No. If I'm in a situation where I can help, I do. I'm no different from an off-duty EMT. They'll help if they can, even if they're on their own time. That's just how things are for them. And me, too, I guess."

"Then why not tell the world?"

She snorted, which on any other woman would have been unlovely, but on her, was hot. "To what end? To draw tons of attention to myself? To hold press conferences, maybe write a blog? And I couldn't just say it, could I? I'd have to prove it. Over and over, and eventually on live TV, and again, to what end?"

"Doesn't it bug you, knowing people are arguing that you either exist or you don't? Sometimes right where you can hear them?"

"Well, I'd rather they didn't compare me to Bigfoot, but

beyond that . . ." She shrugged. "It's no more inane than most workplace chitchat."

"But why'd you tell me?"

"Nobody ever asked me before."

"You're kidding. Nobody? Come on. Nobody? Ever? *Really*?"

"Really."

"Hailey, come on. I've been here a *week* and I figured it out. Other people know, I promise."

She shrugged again. "If they do, they've never said. And what am I going to do, run around asking people if they think I'm It Girl? Linus, I promise you: the world is full of people who are mildly interested but, in the end, don't give much of a shit either way. Their own lives and their own problems are much, much more interesting than 'It Girl vs. Sasquatch: Live on pay-per-view!' Trust me."

"Jeez."

"I know."

"This is one of those times you sound a lot older than me."

"Sorry."

"It sounds so bleak and horrible when you put it like that."

"No." She shook her head. "It just sounds true."

"Does this—" He broke off and thought about it a little more while Hailey prowled the room, putting her office to rights. "Hailey, does this—these things you can do—do they have anything to do with your mom having trouble getting pregnant?"

"My God." She was staring at him and he realized (when had *that* happened? While he'd been passed out on her lap?) her hair had dramatically lightened in less than five minutes. "You are *quick*, Linus. To put it together so—I mean, I had to think about it for years. So apparently I'm older, but you're smarter. And, yes. I think so. My mom needed the clinic to get her pregnant. She donated eggs and they had to do things to the eggs, and once I was born, she got the hell out of Savage and never came back. She died a couple of years ago . . ."

"I'm so sorry."

"Thank you . . . and I kind of drifted back here on my own. One of these days I'll get really brave and go see those doctors." She shoved her (now blond) hair back from her face. "But not today. Today I must fight evil, and make out with an accountant some more. My kingdom for a ponytail holder."

"Is that because you ate the stapler?" he asked excitedly, jabbing his finger at her hair. "And it'll fade as you, um, digest the stapler? And the staples? And the box?"

"Yes."

"But right now you're super strong and fast and everything?" She was smiling again. "Yes."

"You're thinking about how you rushed across the room in half a blink and handily caught me as I swooned, aren't you?"

"Noooooo."

"Liar."

Her beautiful smile lit up her face. "Yes."

"What?" He was dazzled; it was hard to look away from her. Good thing he didn't want to. "Why are you looking at me like that?"

"It's just . . . it's so nice, Linus. Telling you these things and you not treating me like a fr—like I'm different." She paused and her wistful expression actually hurt his heart like a cramp. "I didn't know it could be nice."

"Nice is an understatement. And different is awesome." He

went to her and smoothed the light strands back from her eyes. "Different kicks ass. Different is the sexiest thing ever."

Then he kissed her for a lovely long time, and breathed in her sweet smoky scent, and felt her small, warm, strong hands on him, and forgot about It Girl and lost himself in Hailey.

Too, too soon Hailey had to call a halt. "Not that I don't think we need to go somewhere private and finish this," she said, letting go of him so quickly he staggered. "Oh! Sorry! There, let the blood rush back into your head. The bigger one," she added with a wicked smile. He groaned but kept his hands off her. "But if you're not leaving nasty little notes for me, someone is."

"And they wanted me to have your cell phone number."

"Oh, sure they did." *What else to eat? What else? Need to be on the safe side. Who knows what depth of evil they've gotten up to in their nasty little dungeon?* "They probably waited to start this until there was a new hire. You're their red herring, Linus."

"Oh. Very nice." He sounded pissed on her behalf as well as his own, which she could not help but adore him for. "You sound like you know who it is."

"It's not much of a mystery. Just like me being able to do the things I do isn't much of one."

"What? Come on, Hailey! You're the *only* one who can . . ." He trailed off and she knew why. He was thinking about all the odd things on YouTube, the videos that had been proven fakes and the ones that hadn't. The Web, curling and coiling around the planet with strands of information reaching everywhere, always. As technology made the planet smaller, it also demonstrated to people just how little they really knew about the places they lived and the people they knew. "You don't think you're the only one, do you?"

"No, Linus, I am not unique in my freakery." She said it without a trace of self-scorn so he wouldn't get upset on her behalf again. "There's just no way." She almost told him her number-one suspicion, but held back. She knew about Linus and he knew about her, and not just what they could do to each other. They knew the other would be in their life for . . . well . . . ever. Time enough to explain that her mother donated over two dozen eggs to the clinic. Time enough to point out the strong likelihood of super-powered half siblings running around. "But Savage *is*. Especially once you consider the stupid horse. But aside from that, there are all sorts of military bases around, and private companies with military contracts. Camp Savage, for instance, was a military intelligence school. Cargill made ships for the U.S. Navy. The Pine Bend Refinery—one of the largest oil refineries in the country—is just a few miles from here. A couple of decades ago there was a military gunpowder plant not twenty miles from here. I'm telling you, this whole sleepy midwestern town thing, it's true on the surface, sure. But scratch a little and there are all kinds of secrets. The newsies have been asking, 'How can there be superheroes here?' Ye gods, Linus, how are there not *more*?"

He shook his head. "This is a lot to take in. And I'm still really horny. But . . . the notes?"

"It's not just the notes. It's the stuff they preceded. Before you came—this is another reason you're the red herring, by the way—before you came it was actually pretty quiet around here, and had been for a long time."

It was strange, and she could never explain it. Some weeks she was constantly leaping the two stories from her office window to rush into town and foil crime, and also pick up a Subway foot-long (roasted chicken breast, Dijon, tomatoes, cukes, black olives, green peppers, salt and pepper, vinegar and oil). Some weeks her "bitch sense" never so much as twitched. It was the heat. Except, because it was Minnesota, it wasn't. It was society. Okay, but society was everywhere. It was a social protest. Except it wasn't. It was a day that ended with a *y*.

Well. Yes. That was as good an explanation as any. Except all the days ended with *y*.

She explained this to Linus, who listened carefully and then shrugged. "I don't think someone orchestrated that. Sometimes people wanna do bad, a lot. And sometimes, not so much."

"Overly simplistic," she scoffed.

"And big-time realistic," he countered, softening the words with a small smile. "Hon, if you try to find the logic, you'll give yourself a migraine."

"'Hon'?"

"Yes. As in, *Attila the*."

"Oooh, later for you, you liar." She ignored the shredder and went for the potted plant in the corner, a sad little geranium she frequently forgot to water. "Sorry, little buddy." She wolfed it down, grimaced at the dirt, and ate that, too.

"Whoa," Linus said, even more big-eyed than usual. "That's awesome."

"Nuh-*uh*," she said, lightly spraying him with dirt. "I can eat anything and convert it to energy. That's it. Doesn't mean I like it. Any of it. Dirt tastes like dirt. Dead flowers taste like dead flowers. Staplers taste—"

"Right. Got it."

"Plus I'm a stress eater."

He didn't want to laugh, she could see, but couldn't help it. She frowned at him, broke the pot, then started eating the shards. "I see the funny side of it. Occasionally. So that's all right."

He was grinning, and reached out with his thumb to brush dirt off the corner of her mouth. "We're gonna have a good time, aren't we?"

"Oh, yes," she promised, and gulped down the last chunk of the broken flowerpot. "Starting right now."

CHAPTER
TWELVE

"When you agreed we'd have fun," Linus was saying as he hurried down the hall to keep pace with her, *"I sort of thought you meant we'd both call in sick for the rest of the day and spend the afternoon naked."*

"Well, that, too. But I've had enough of the notes, and I do not like, *at all*, that they had no problem manipulating me into doubting your motives."

"Okay, when you said *at all* like that, it made me incredibly nervous. So, just for the record, I'm going to try hard to not do anything that would make you talk about me like that. Ever, ever, ever."

"'Get to it already.'" They were through HR, past reception.

"What?"

" 'What are you waiting for?' " She was nearly stomping down the hall. Past R & D. Past Marketing.

"Hailey?"

"The notes. 'Get to it already, what are you waiting for? If you don't act, we will. Did you think this was a joke? Why aren't you doing more?' "

Linus was gaping at her, appalled. "That's what they wrote you?"

"Yes, it's just nag-nag-nag with those people."

"Those people?"

"At first, I assumed it was about work. I have, as you've noticed, a terrible attendance record. But why be sneaky about it? This is the easiest company to work for in the history of business. No one needs to be sneaky about anything, and we all know it. And then you showed up. And then accidents started happening that required immediate action. *My* immediate action."

"The school bus," Linus remembered.

"Children. They endangered *children*. Because they didn't think I was performing up to par."

"Who?"

"Oh, who else? Who would be passive as well as aggressive? Who would hide behind documents, behind words, while challenging people to act, even as they *don't* act? Come on, Linus. It's obvious."

"No way."

"Yes." Past the break rooms, the conference rooms.

"Even for them . . . I mean, I know they're awful, every company in the world knows they're awful, that they're a necessary evil, but this is *evil* evil."

"Yes!" She stopped. They were there. "The ones whose job it is to spy on their colleagues and then inform on them. The Brownshirts of every company in the world. Who have most of the power while we pretend they don't, and they pretend they're not dangerous." She glared up at the sign. "The IT department."

Linus looked up. "Abandon All Hope and Get Pwned" was over the bloodred double doors in dark cursive font a foot high. "If I hadn't abandoned hope already, I would now."

"Maybe you should—"

"No way."

"As you like." Hailey kicked the sinister red doors open and marched into the Information Technology department, their dire motto directly over her head for a second.

CHAPTER
THIRTEEN

The room, kept cool and gloomy, seemed to swallow them. But when Hailey came through the doors, she brought enough light in to scatter at least three IT drones, who scurried out of sight, squeaking and squealing.

"So at last, you've come." Edward Smegger turned slowly in his large black office chair, the back so flared it looked like a throne on wheels.

He was dressed in an alarming uniform of red jeans, white lab coat, and loafers in traffic-cone orange, but no shirt or socks. His shoulder-length gray hair (premature . . . Edward was thirty-one) looked more scraggly and mad scientist-ish than usual. He was so thin the bones of his wrists looked like they could be used as bladed weapons. "I wondered when you'd be here, you pathetic drone."

"She's not pathetic," Linus warned.

"Thank you, Linus," she replied. "Now then: we've had this talk before, Edward. This is not appropriate workplace attire. And you're supposed to display your employee badge above the waist at all times."

"The clip hurts my nipple," he complained.

"At least this isn't jarring or weird," Linus muttered.

"And out there? In your world you think is so safe and so sane?" He stroked the small white object in his arms. "Your apathy, your refusal of your gifts . . . is that appropriate for the workplace?"

Distracted by what the man was holding, Linus raised his hand, as if waiting to be called on, and when Edward nodded, asked, "Are you petting a fake cat?"

"I'm allergic," he explained primly, stroking the glassy-eyed stuffed animal. "But l'il Éowyn of Rohan understands me. She's the one who told me what to do. She is my constant companion, my one and only true friend. And she is here with me now . . . at the scene of my ultimate triumph."

As God is my witness, Linus thought, entranced, *I can't think of a thing to say.*

"Moo-ha-ha-ha!" The laughter, which startled the hell out of them, got deeper and villainy-er. "Moo-ha-haaaaa! I—ack! Graaa-uk! Uk! Uk-uk!" Edward coughed, then rubbed l'il Éowyn on his throat like a poultice. "Sorry. I've been holding that in—"

"Your entire life, I think," Linus finished, triply freaked out.

"Yes, possibly," he admitted. "No need to hold anything in any longer. Not now. Now that we've succeeded. Now that we've moved you to act. L'il Éowyn counseled patience, and in the end, it was rewarded. All this . . ." He gestured to the gloom-shrouded computers, the chilly atmosphere, the minions lurking out of sight, watching and waiting to see who won. "She told me how to fool you."

"Fool her?" Linus yelped. "It took Hailey about ten seconds to figure out you were the bad guy. After she realized *I* wasn't the bad guy. And also after . . ." *Making out for a while*, he'd been about to add, then decided against it. "And Hailey was right . . . it's obvious. Of course the bad guy's in the IT department! You spy on what we're doing on our computers—"

"You're not supposed to surf Rotten Tomatoes or ESPN or update your Facebook on company time," Edward whined.

"—so you can rat us out like, I dunno, Nazi Germany or whatever—"

"The Nazis were into animal conservation, and they were anti-tobacco. And they came up with the Volkswagen."

Momentarily thrown (*Really? The Volkswagen?*), Linus plunged ahead. "And when you're not spying, you're sneaking around and sitting in judgment because we keep crashing the network but we don't know why, and no matter what sort of help we need, you pretty much stamp *No* on everything, and of course you see everything, you know everything. You control the information!"

Hailey was staring at him.

"Wow," he said, surprised. "I guess I've got some repressed anger at the IT guys."

"Think so?"

"Edward, I'm sorry, you didn't deserve all that vitriol. Probably. God, the stress of—"

"God is dead! Only the IT department can help you now."

"It's just that sort of attitude that gets you in trouble with HR," she warned. "As I said during your last disciplinary action, telling employees God is dead and that your department is all the God they need in their cringing pathetic lives is not appropriate workplace behavior. We've got a really easygoing CEO, but even she thinks telling people you're the only God they need is uncool."

"You are living a lie!" L'il Éowyn went flying as Edward abruptly stood. "Hiding behind your paper identity, when you owe the world your gifts!"

"The only thing I owe the world are taxes and, possibly, children. And then, of course, more taxes." She turned to Linus. "My mother always said we should replace ourselves, kid-wise, and move on. So I think we—"

"Okay, whatever you want, *please* don't take your eyes off the villain," Linus begged. "He is *freaking* me *out*." Linus had never before sensed such overwhelming evil from a single person. Sure, everybody knew the IT guys were creepy, asocial weirdos who spent far too much time staring into screens of any sort. And, yeah, you didn't ever want to meet one in a dark alley. Or cross one. Or engage with one in any social setting, ever. But Edward's sheer malevolence was more than unsettling. He was a generally scary—

"I have made you great, It Girl!"

—nut job.

"And in return I and all my brethren are treated with thinly veiled contempt!"

"Then I apologize," Hailey said in a tone that was frightening in its pleasantness. "I had no intention of veiling my contempt at all."

"You shut us off from society, cast us off from the world! We're cut off from the rest of the world not just physically but psychologically! We have nothing to do but fester and—"

"Go insane?" Linus guessed.

"Well, yes. Like mushrooms," he admitted. "Evil mushrooms who can run a network from anywhere on the planet."

"Oh, please. You guys get off on being different. You take pride in it. We don't cut you off; you guys do it all on your own. You isolate yourselves; it's your nature. And don't get me started on your idiotic Help Desk Muppets!"

Edward gasped so hard Linus wondered if the man was having a heart attack. He shook a trembling finger in Hailey's direction. "Judas!"

"Actually, Judas means *praised* and *admired*. So, yeah. Hailey's definitely a Judas."

Hailey was rubbing her forehead. "Please stop sticking up for me now. Edward, you and any other hacktivists you've hidden back there will cease and desist looking for bad situations and making them worse so I, or the National Guard, eventually have to intervene. Then—"

"What's a hacktivist?" Linus asked.

"A trendy term for cowardly sneaky trespasser."

Edward was rubbing his forehead in a gesture identical to Hailey's. "Yes, that's . . . that's one I can't defend. There can be no denying it's sneaky of us," he admitted.

"Edward, here's how it is. I'm going to continue living my life, and if I'm running around doing the job of a cop or a firefighter or just working on annual reviews, it's my own business and none of yours. And you? You're going to jail.

"I don't know what you did to the school bus, and how many

other 'accidents' you've been responsible for to encourage me to step up, but you can be sure you won't be doing anything like that *ever again*. You will turn yourself in. You will confess. You will *not* take a plea bargain. You will go to jail for quite some time. You will behave; you will forget you ever dreamed the dreams of super villains."

"Why?" he asked, and Linus was afraid: it was a reasonable question. There was no proof. There were only Hailey's hunches. Edward didn't have to admit anything to anyone. He needn't have confessed what he did to Hailey and Linus. He'd *wanted* to, which wasn't the same thing. Linus doubted Edward would just stop. Why would he, when it was getting him what he wanted?

Even worse, would this lead to a smackdown between the superhero and the villain, an ultimate battle the likes of which the world had never seen and, also, wouldn't have much interest in? Did he want such a tired cliché to happen right in the middle of Ramouette's IT department?

What would the consequences be, especially with the company picnic coming up in less than two weeks? Would factions be further splintered? Would Hailey get fired for employing a super villain? Would the super villain bring a wrongful termination suit against Ramouette? Would the state of Minnesota's department of dislocated workers get involved, guaranteeing hundreds of lost man hours? He foresaw entire square miles of paperwork ahead, and was afraid.

"Why?" Edward asked again. "Why stop now when you're so close to accepting what you are? When you're almost ready to understand that—"

"Don't," Linus warned.

"—with great—"

"If you say *with great power comes great responsibility*, I will do something terrible," Hailey warned. "More terrible than I already had in mind, I mean. And if you don't turn yourself in now, today, you will never recover from what I'll do to you."

"Why?" Edward asked, sounding curious.

"Because I'll do things to you I won't be able to take back. For starters, I'll dissemble and eat your entire server, right now. The whole thing. Every bite. I'll get it *all* down, Edward. You won't be able to stop me; I could break your arm with one hand while smashing up the hard drive with the other. I've never actually eaten a fan before, and the server's got a good one. You need them to keep the tech cool.

"The more I'll eat, the stronger I'll get. The stronger I'll get, the more I'll pull a *Hailey smash* all over this department, your car, your home. Even if you've backed it all up somewhere else, this is your baby. We all know it. It's actual, physical tech you will never get back. Tech I'll convert to energy and use to, I don't know, have sex for a week without stopping, with Linus here. That's what will happen to your Precious. I'll use it to have sex. And you won't have it anymore."

"*Tons* of sex!" Linus added.

"And that," she added, watching all the color fall out of Edward's face, "that's just the first thing to pop into my head. I'll spend days thinking about how to fuck you up. Weeks. *Years.*"

It broke him. Linus saw it at once. It wasn't the threat. Not even the threat of more threats. It was her face and her tone. She had looked sorry; she had also sounded genuinely sad when she spoke of doing things she couldn't take back. Like she knew what it was like. Like she had experience with being fucked with, and was sad because she knew the march of events was inevitable.

It broke him, and he agreed to everything.

CHAPTER
FOURTEEN

"Toldja," **The Old Coot said, watching as the Savage police** hauled a cuffed and raving Edward to a jail cell far, far away.

"Inevitable," Audrey the Receptionist agreed. "The second time he told me the only god I should pray to was the server god, I figured he was bound for, I dunno, prison, or the bottom of the Mississippi, or one of Hailey's sensitivity training seminars. Some wretched fate that would make him pray for death. He must have done something more evil than usual to get you up in his face like that," Audrey noted. "What, did he call you out about being It Girl?"

For a second Hailey couldn't breathe. She actually doubted her ears: Had Aud the Rec really said what she thought she had? She stole a glance at Linus, who looked remarkably serene.

"That's it, isn't it?" The Old Coot asked, observing Hailey's frozen expression. "What'd you do, threaten to eat his tech? If I was It Girl, that's what I would have done. Actually, I would have trussed him with barbed wire until he looked like an insane hedgehog, then made him watch while I ate allllll his back-ups."

"How—How—I—How?"

"Are you kidding?" The Old Coot looked at Audrey, who was slowly shaking her head. "Is she kidding?"

"'Fraid not. That's the extent of the cloud this woman walks around in."

Hailey knew she sounded idiotic but was unable to stop. "There's not—I don't understand—You couldn't—"

"Seriously with this?" Audrey the Receptionist asked, incredulous. "For God's sake, you leap out two-story windows and are constantly seen eating things that would kill anybody else. There's a bus crash or whatever, and suddenly you remember you have to race home and feed your nonexistent cat, and then while you're feeding the cat we all know you don't have, someone mysteriously saves the lives of a dozen first graders. Then you come back looking like you've been—I dunno—shoving buses off railroad tracks? Of course you're It Girl! Or a super villain. But we thought you were in on it."

"In on what?" Linus asked. He figured he could get away with it, being new. And Hailey looked so shocked, he was worried she might pull a Linus and faint. Black out, rather. Fainting was for sissies. He took her hand and she clutched at him with panicky fingers.

"Well. We don't talk about it so much, but we all know you're It Girl. We try to look out for you. And in return we figured you've been looking out for us, getting us all those awesome paid holidays, keeping the boss happy so she's not here trying to get people to practice broomball with . . ." The Old Coot turned to Linus. "Basically Hailey here keeps the *human* in *human resources*. We thought you thought we knew that."

Astonished silence from Hailey. The Old Coot and Audrey the Receptionist traded glances, then shrugged. "Either way," Audrey said, "we've been watching out for you. We know you don't have a life except for"—she waved a hand, vaguely encompassing Ramouette's offices—"this. And now, maybe"—waving a hand at Linus—"that. So the least we can do is cover for you."

"Why?" Hailey burst out. Linus was startled—and moved—to see her eyes were brimming with tears. "I'm never—You guys always—And it's not like I—"

"Hailey, jeez." Audrey sighed, giving her a quick, one-armed hug. "We *live* here. Our families *live* here. And you're here, too—you could live anywhere in the world. You could be driving anybody else crazy. But you're here. Driving *us* crazy."

The Old Coot nodded. "That means a lot."

"You spend your days in Savage looking out for our families and friends while also pretending you hate looking out for our families and friends. Which is weird, by the way. But that doesn't mean we don't know what it costs. You have *no* life. So we back you up whenever we can. You didn't—Come on. You knew we knew, right?"

"Toldja," Linus coughed into his fist.

"Oh, sure. Yes. Of course. I—" She was smiling and dashing tears away with the back of her hand. "But I have to go home now and cry for a while. And then have sex with Linus."

"Weird," Audrey the Receptionist commented.

"And inappropriate. In my day, HR heads did not run around foiling evil and banging new accountants."

"Shut up, Coot," Hailey said, and kissed him on the cheek, and hugged Audrey so hard she groaned and clutched her ribs, and seized Linus's hand and dragged him out.

"Tell you what, Aud, they didn't do that, either," he mused, rubbing his cheek. "Hmm. Maybe we should get her something extra-nice for Dan Patch Day."

"Pass. I'm gonna take my seventy-four days of accumulated sick time and grow back my ribs. Workers' comp might hear about this!" Audrey the Receptionist shouted after the departed It Girl. "But probably not! Let that be a lesson to you! Ow, my ribs . . . How many shopping days is it until Lammas Day?"

CHAPTER
FIFTEEN

They had every intention of making it to his apartment. No, her apartment . . . it was a shorter drive. No, the Red Roof Inn was shorter still. No, the secret park.

"Secret park?" Hailey managed between kisses. They'd gotten into her car and kissed. She'd stopped at the stop sign and they kissed. She stopped at the yield sign and they kissed. She didn't stop and they kissed. "Where do I live again?"

"No, here . . . take a left. Over here." He pointed and she drove and then she'd stopped the car and he'd gotten out so quickly the seat belt hung on and almost yanked him back inside the car. He wrestled free of it while she leaned against the hood so as to not fall down laughing, and they ran toward a bunch of trees to the left of the small road leading away from Ramouette.

She gasped in wonder at the small secret park, not perfectly trimmed and manicured like non-secret parks, but overgrown and just wild enough to be interesting but not ugly. The pond, about fifteen feet wide, looked so tranquil as to not seem quite real, reflecting the willow trees, which waved gently in the breeze.

His fingers were on her blouse and she tried to help him, then realized she didn't give a good damn about the buttons and yanked.

"Ow!" He clapped a hand to one eye.

"Oh my God!" Stupid It Girl strength; it hadn't worn off yet. "I'm so sorry, let me see."

She bent forward, intent on his face, and he snatched her to him for a sound, searching kiss. Then he pulled back with a breathless, "Psych! Just kidding. Can you fly like Superman? Can I be Lois Lane, except without that weird chiffon dress she wore in the first movie? She looked like she was wearing my mom's bathroom curtains."

"Please shut up now." She'd shrugged out of her blouse, her bra. "You've never seen anyone here?"

"Not once. Uh, take off more clothes, please." He reached out and cupped her breasts in both hands, then leaned down and breathed on her nipples, and then kissed them. She nearly lost her footing; it felt like he was kissing her somewhere else entirely. She (gently) grabbed his ears and pulled him to her mouth and kissed him with the intensity she'd felt, but tried to control, since he said, "Hero, hero." He didn't know her, then, and he said that. He knew the truth now, and he was still here.

She had no idea that simple acceptance could make her so wet.

She wouldn't break the kiss, so they managed to undress and help each other without once coming up for air, and then she was carefully pushing him onto the soft grass and climbing on top of him. She'd pushed him down on the bank and his head was actually pointing down toward the pond, but she didn't care if he didn't, and he didn't seem like he did. It was possible he'd forgotten the park entirely.

Her knees were on either side of his hips and, while she steadied herself with one palm on his chest, she reached back and found his hot hard length. She squeezed gently and smiled at his groan, then lifted up just a bit and slooooowly lowered herself onto him, closing her eyes at the pure sweetness of it.

"Oh, Christ."

Yes, those were her exact sentiments.

She began to ride, getting used to him, letting him get used to her, easing up and down, surprised and thrilled at how slippery she was, how slippery he was making her.

"Don't stop. Anything you want. If you don't stop. Money, fur, jewels. Farmland, puppies, caterpillars. Orange juice. A Starbucks franchise. A gift card for Red Lobster. Don't stop."

She leaned down and kissed him. "I have no need for caterpillars and I hate lobster," she whispered into his mouth, and she felt him reach around and grip her ass. "Ummm . . . that's nice. Do that harder. I'm charged up enough . . . you can do that a *lot* harder."

So he clutched and kneaded her pale flesh until his knuckles whitened and the veins stood out on his neck, touching her with force that would have badly bruised anyone else, force that made her want only more of it, more of him. Watching him lose himself in her tipped her over and she fell into her orgasm; it hit her with such rapidity that she was surprised.

Still shuddering, she felt his warmth burst inside her and was surprised once again.

"Hailey," he managed after several minutes. "I'm officially ruined for other women, forever."

"I should hope so." She licked the sweat from his collarbone.

"Also, I fell in love with you after you abandoned me at Big Bowl to help that mom free her kid."

"Well, good."

"And my head's gonna pop off."

She pulled back and looked; he *was* quite red-faced. "Oh, Linus! Your head was pointing down but I didn't think you cared at the time."

"I *still* don't care. I was just letting you know the situation. My head can keep filling with blood until I burst something; I don't give a shit. Won't even feel it. Won't notice . . . aaahhhhh." She'd pulled him to a sitting position. "So, this is what it's like to not pass out."

She hugged him to her and heard an, "Oof!" and then got a hug back. He grinned at her. "We're gonna have fun, aren't we?"

"For the rest of our lives," she promised, and carried him to the car.

"Hi. I'm Audrey the Receptionist."

He smiled. First days were always the worst, but everyone had been pleasant so far. With the economy only starting to recover, he was grateful for a good job with a good company.

And Ramouette had of late been making quite a name for itself; it had always pulled a profit, which was a good trick given Minnesota's economic woes. But now it was making waves with its innovative benefits options, big number one being, "As long as your work is getting done, take all the vacation time you want."* No one in the business world was quite sure what had changed in the last several months, and as someone

---

*Netflix actually does this!

whose first love was marketing, he'd been anxious to join the team.

"This is Gerry, our new marketing director." The HR rep—who insisted on referring to herself as one of Hailey's twisted minions and had never actually given him a name except Minion Number Four—had been taking him around. He took that with an internal shrug: there was one in every company.

"It's nice to meet you," Gerry said, shaking her hand.

"Same. Hailey's on her way," Audrey the Receptionist told the minion. Audrey was short, with ebony skin and a square-shaped face she emphasized with square glasses set in purple lenses. Her handshake was quick and firm. "She says she'll finish the new-hire stuff when she gets here. Hailey's our head of HR . . . She's running a little late."

Gerry said graciously, "That's how it goes sometimes. And Four-ninety-four was awful."

"Yeah, that's how it goes with Hailey sometimes, and by sometimes I mean always, and every day is Monday and Four-ninety-four is continually awful. Hey, Coot, what are you getting them for the engagement party?"

"Them?"

"She and Linus are getting married next spring," the young man—who was surely not a day over thirty—explained.

Did she call this boy Coot? All right: there were *two* in every company.

"Did you say Linus?"

"Yeah, Jamie Linus," Audrey the Receptionist replied. "Don't call him Jamie because nobody will know who you're talking about, including him. He started here a few months ago . . . He's an accounting stud with the eyes of Marlon

Brando and the freckles of Howdy Doody. Somehow he makes it work."

"Marlon Brando, now there's a true Hollywood god. In my day—"

"Shut up, Coot. Gerry, don't pay any attention to his feeble mutterings."

"All right," he replied cautiously. A transplant from New York, he'd assumed midwesterners would be a little more bland.

Just then the front door opened and two more young people came in. The man had the most startling large brown eyes Gerry had ever seen, eyes that went oddly with (the receptionist had nailed it) the Howdy Doody freckles.

But it was the woman who caught most of his attention, and not just because she was a striking, slender brunette with a pretty mouth and lovely pale skin. She looked as though she'd been in an accident—torn panty hose, smudged skirt and blouse, hair straggling out of its ponytail.

"Hey," the coot and the receptionist said in perfect, unsurprised unison.

The woman greeted them with, "Sorry. Nasty one on the way in—the cops were waiting for the firemen to grab the jaws of life. But it wasn't as bad as they thought. They were able to get the door off after all, jaw-less. You must be Gerry." She held out a small, dirty hand for him to shake.

"Yes, my God, are you all right?"

"Hailey likes to work out in garages, not gyms," Audrey the Receptionist explained as if that made sense to a normal person. "She feels that if you don't leave with oil in your hair and a torn shirt, you didn't do it right."

"I've got to stop commuting with you," the freckled man

groaned. "You've made me late three times this week. And it's Tuesday."

"Gerry, I'll just clean up and we can get to it," Hailey said, unperturbed by the comments. She was a lovely woman, glowing and proud even in her dishevelment. "You're going to like it here."

"I'm sure I will." *All right, there are three in every company . . . no, four . . . Still, they seem like fun. Not much point going in to work if you don't like the people you work with. Nice kids, for sure.*

"We all love it," she explained. "A lot of companies say they are, but they aren't, not really. But Ramouette is." The woman seemed to almost glow with contentment and joy. "We're a family."

Undead and Underwater

Hey, Davidson! What's your deal with vampires and mermaids, anyway? Are you unable to write stories about regular people with regular problems?

Apparently, yes. So I figured I'd better cough up some background. Although the next story can be read as a stand-alone (my editor and I work hard to make sure any of my books can be read on their own, and by *my editor and I* I mean *my editor*), it's got characters from my *Undead* series as well as my Fred the Mermaid series. Betsy Taylor is a young vampire (age thirty when she died, and less than five years dead) as well as the (reluctant, annoyed, and annoying) queen of the undead. She's trying to run things without running things, as she finds it absurd that she's the boss of thousands of vampires, most of whom are older and (supposedly) wiser. At the least, she figures they shouldn't need a scolding mommy type looking over their lives. But whether the vampire in question is *in* trouble or *causing* trouble, Betsy and/or her husband, Eric Sinclair, have to look into it. The first book in the series is *Undead and Unwed* but, as above, any of the books can be read out of sequence.

The Laurel to Betsy's Hardy is Dr. Fredrika Bimm, a half human, half mermaid marine biologist with the social warmth of Lisbeth Salander, and none of the hacking skills. Her mother (Moon Bimm) is a hippie; her father was a traitor to his people, the Undersea Folk. The Fred trilogy covers her childhood, education, love life, struggles as the world's only known human/Undersea Folk hybrid, and her eventual outing of the Undersea Folk to the rest of the world. Once engaged to Prince Artur of the Folk, Fred fell in love with a colleague, Dr. Thomas Pearson, and they're now engaged to be married. Fred is on excellent terms with the Undersea's royal family, but some of her father's people don't like her and/or don't trust her. Fortunately Fred, unlike Betsy, is not a recovering Miss Congeniality, and has never given much of a hoo-ha about being disliked.

Seen by both humans and the Undersea Folk as a sort of goodwill (ha!) ambassadress, Fred does have one thing in common with Betsy: they think the vast majority of their "people" can and should take care of themselves.

Post-outing, although most people on the planet are embracing the idea of real mermaids, many also think that the whole Undersea Folk reveal is a hoax.

Fred's stories can be found in *Sleeping with the Fishes*, *Fish Out of Water*, and *Swimming Without a Net*. The events of the next story take place after *Undead and Unstable*.

Author's Note

I was scared when it was time to move to Boston. Although I'd lived all over as an Air Force brat, most of my time had been spent in the Midwest, and all I knew about Boston was what I'd seen in my future in-laws. Naturally, I was terrified. ("If we don't yell," my mother-in-law explained, "they don't listen. It's the natural order of things. I said, *it's the natural order of things*!")

I hadn't expected to love it, but I did. A landlocked landlubber most of my life, living in a beautiful historic harbor city was a revelation. So was the seafood . . . They had *fast food* seafood! And of course fresh lobsters. And amazing chowder.

The very best chowder can be found in any of the Legal Sea Foods restaurant chain. When we visit my in-laws, we try to eat there at least once: chowder, bucket of steamers, arctic char. Bliss. It's no coincidence that the only thing Fred has planned about her wedding is where the bride and groom will eat on their wedding night: Legal's.

Author's Note

Also, there isn't a bridal salon on either side of the John Fluevog store on Newbury Street in Boston's Back Bay. But, as Betsy Taylor would point out, there ought to be.

Also, velvet clogs seem to be finally, mercifully disappearing from boutiques the world over. Proof! Proof Betsy may not have utterly trashed the timeline beyond repair.

"Now, get this! We ain't partners. We ain't brothers. And we ain't friends. I'm puttin' you down and keepin' you down until Ganz is locked up or dead. And if Ganz gets away, you're gonna be sorry *you* ever met *me*!"

"I'm already sorry."

—JACK AND REGGIE, *48 HRS.*

I've done far worse than kill you, Admiral. I've hurt you. And I wish to go on hurting you. I shall leave you as you left me . . . as you left her . . . marooned for all eternity in the center of a dead planet. Buried alive. Buried alive.

—KHAN NOONIEN SINGH, *STAR TREK II: THE WRATH OF KHAN*

I don't want to speak too disparagingly about my generation (actually I do, we had a chance to change the world and opted for the Home Shopping Network instead).

—STEPHEN KING, *ON WRITING*

She clawed for her cell phone, fumbled, dropped it, caught it with the tips of her fingers and then dropped it again. She fell to her knees on the concrete and scrabbled for it as scalding tears burned her cheeks. Thank God it hadn't been in her purse. Thank God she'd kept it in her jacket pocket because her clutch was too small, thank God, thank God.

After a thousand years of groping for it in the far-from-perfect glow of street lights, she had it, and thumbed familiar buttons.

"Mama?" she asked as the voice she loved answered her call, as she always, always did. And part of her was comforted, and part of her was rueful: *I'm in my early twenties, for God's sake, and, like, crying for my mommy? Laaaaame.* "Mama, I'm in such bad trouble. They're tried to kill me and they couldn't; they're gonna kill her and get back to me. And it's exactly what I deserve. She'll be dead because of me. And then I'll be dead because of me. I don't think you can fix it."

Her mother wasted no time. She soothed, she directed, she promised to fix it. All her daughter had to do was sit tight.

Soothed, Madison was surprised to see she was still on the concrete, her stockings in shreds around her knees and the darkened New England Aquarium looming behind her. Boston wasn't ever especially quiet, but at two A.M. on a Monday it was close.

She climbed to her feet, still looking at the building. *Looming. Why did I think that? I work there, I always wanted to work there. Better, she used to work there, and prob'ly will again. It was my favorite place in the world when I was ten and it is today and it's not looming, it's . . . it's just there.*

The building hadn't changed. She had changed. Always wanting more and never satisfied, the Fehr family motto. She promised herself, as she had many times, that This Time It Would Be Different.

(It was always the same.)

Forget the building: Mama was on the case. She knew people all over the world, important and scary people, and had buckets of money to boot. Mama would come up with something.

Or someone.

Madison Fehr limped toward the Marriott. She couldn't go home; they had her clutch, which meant they had her driver's license. They were welcome to the cash, and her credit cards would be cancelled within the next half hour. Mama was even now calling to book her a hotel room where she could—

(cower)

—lay low and—

(creep away and cower)

—stay off the radar for the next few hours.

Whatever Mama did or whoever she sent, Madison would (finally) be her mother's daughter and have the courage to face it/them. *Be brave and hang tough and probably things aren't that bad. Be brave and hang tough and probably things aren't that bad.*

It didn't work. It hadn't for two days.

CHAPTER ONE

Fredrika Bimm, grumpy mermaid and former future queen of the Undersea Folk, stalked across the cobblestones past the Marriott Long Wharf, zeroing in on the pit of all evil and despair, the loathsome housing for malice that was the New England Aquarium. The sky was overcast, gray, and threatening to spit chilly rain. Her mood had never been so foul on a day she didn't have to go to a bridal/baby/housewarming/new pet shower. And that was foul indeed.

What has Fehr done? And why call me? If her former boss, Dr. Barb, hadn't been so insistent . . . but she had been, which sucked Jonas in, and then *he* got insistent . . . which meant she was in Boston, the very last place she wanted to be.

It was all that wedding stuff. Correction: weddings stuff. Plural. Bad enough she was Jonas's Bitch of Honor. But the other wedding was worse: her own. She was the bridezilla. ("A bridezilla," Jonas had said, his voice faux trembling, "to fear above all other bridezillas, a bridezilla the likes of which the world has never seen and pray God will never see again!" It hadn't helped one bit that he'd been right.)

Ugh.

Tedious shopping trips spent tediously trying on tedious wedding finery. Tedious visits to florists and their tedious inventory. Bakeries: major, *major* tedium, not to mention sugar highs followed by sugar lows. Places that rented tedious tables and tedious tablecloths and tedious tuxes.

All that. Times two.

She was gnashing her teeth so hard she wondered if she'd crack a molar. But that might not be a bad thing. An emergency trip to the dentist would get her out of all sorts of tediousness. Yes, an after-hours dental visit would solve so many problems. Fred cursed her never-so-much-as-a-cavity teeth. Why couldn't she have inherited her traitorous (dead) father's fangs? But noooo, she got her mom's flat grinders instead. Her father had been a predator in every sense of the word and, as with all his kind, went around with a mouth full of sewing needles; her mother was a gentle hippie whose idea of a naughty meal was putting store-bought ranch dressing on her (organic) salads. Fred got the hippie's teeth.

Fred sighed. Ah, it was all a simple daydream, but no matter how much she fantasized, a dentist in shining armor wasn't going to rescue her. And if one had, she'd be so thrilled to have wiggled out of her responsibilities (if that's what they even were), she wouldn't have needed the nitrous oxide. She'd giggle like a hyena while the dentist advanced on her with pliers or, worse, refused to validate her parking.

Gnashing her hippie grinders, Fred momentarily regretted she hadn't been lurking on the bottom of the Caspian Sea when Madison Fehr got up to her shenanigans du jour.

Whatever you've done, Madison Fehr, whoever you're afraid of, you are absolutely afraid of The Wrong Person.

CHAPTER
TWO

*It was strange that Fred noticed them at all. But she was a nat-*ural procrastinator, and often when she was trying to avoid a problem, she'd let her attention get caught by just about anything.

It was a slow evening at the NEA; Tuesdays often were. School had let out, and it was the dinner hour, so all the buses full of children were long gone, as were the people who wanted to swing over to Faneuil Hall to suck down a lobster roll and/or cup of chowder and/or a brownie and/or fried rice for the trip home.

And because there weren't a hundred people milling about the entrance, her attention was caught by a tall dark-haired man who was standing perfectly still. That was unusual; Boston was lousy with people hurrying, always hurrying to get from Point A to Point Q (the roads did not go in straight lines, ever).

If I had access to a time machine, she mentally grouched for the hundredth time, *I'd go back and tell the FFs, "Great job finding the place, O mightily clever Founding Fathers, and, yes, I understand why you feel finders keepers is a legitimate reason for genocide and territorial conquest. I won't judge: it was a different time.*

"And thank you also for the Constitution: great job! Quite enlightened. And don't feel too bad about the parts you missed; later generations did eventually get around to acknowledging that freedom only for white men isn't exactly freedom. In fact, by definition, it's the opposite. Again: different time. Not judging.

"But perhaps deciding to pave the cow paths—that is, paths trampled by bovines whose only concern was finding the tenderest of grass and alfalfa as opposed to the most efficient way to go from A to B—was utterly, utterly stupid."

". . . stupid."

She glanced over and saw him, a man who would have been striking under any circumstances. His sheer height, breadth of shoulders, and impeccably tailored navy suit demanded respectful attention. But what was odd was how he stood in the middle of the cement apron, arms stretched out and face tilted toward the (cloudy, sullen, threatening-to-rain) sky, smiling. Almost like he was . . . all right, it was silly, but she *was* a marine biologist, so she knew what a stranded mammal caught under open sky looked like. She was looking at a male Homo sapien, basking like a leopard seal, one decked out in a terrific suit about to snack on a dozen penguins.

(Later, when she knew what he was, she thought it was

interesting that she would have instantly compared him to a pred-atory species; he and the woman were, in fact, apex predators.)

All that, still, might have escaped her notice—or at least only captured her attention for a second—but then the shrill woman said it again, echoing her thoughts: "Stupid!"

"Sticks and stones, my love," the man replied in a cheerful baritone. He was turning in a slow circle while still staring at the sky, so blissed out she wondered if he was high on some-thing. (She found out later he had been: high on the great out-doors, high on the color of the sky, high on how the air smelled before a spring rain, high on being in the company of his queen. Thus: no accounting for taste.)

"Sinclair!" she cried in the tone of a woman annoyed beyond her capacity to bear such things, but the fond smile made her tone a lie. "Will you please get a grip? Stop staring up and spin-ning around like friggin' Mary Tyler Moore on Nicollet Mall, okay?"

"Shush," he said, still basking, eyes still closed, arms still stretched out, still blissed out despite (because of? No . . . impossible) the shrill blonde. "Do you know how long it has been since I was outside—"

"Twenty minutes."

"—in a coastal city—"

"Year and a half ago, on the Cape with Marky Mark and the Fuzzy Bunch."

"—during daylight? And you must promise never to call Michael that to his face."

"I'm not promising anything, and okay, that thing about daylight, that's a fair point. Also: Who can turn the world on with his big weird smiiiiile? Who can take a sucky day, and suddenly make it all seem super lame?" she sang, horribly off-key while (worse!) butchering the lyrics to the Mary Tyler Moore jingle. "Well, it's you, Sink Lair, and you should know it! Each day you really, really blow it! Schmucks are all around and you're driving me crazy, stop spinning around like you're in a daze-ey . . ."

"We're gonna stake it after all," was his (tuneful!) response, at which point the blonde shuddered and said the most puzzling thing yet: "No matter what I do to make things right, this time-line gets worse and worse."

Tourists, thought Fred, annoyed they'd caught her interest for even a few seconds. *Proof I'd rather think about anything else except whatever mess Fehr's in. What's the* actual *line from the jingle? Ah: How will you make it on your own?*

The man put his arms down and snapped his long fingers: *crack!* "The phone! I need to call them."

"Again?"

"What, again?" he replied easily, reaching into his suit jacket pocket to pull out an iPhone, sliding his fingers across it, then holding it to his ear. "It's been hours, long lonely hours, and I— hello? Yes, may I speak with them? Yes, again."

"You're gonna drive the poor guy to suicide! *Also* again."

"It's me!" the tall, handsome, dignified man said, in a tone that was not at all dignified. "Who else would it be? I must speak to the babies. Put them on at once, Marc."

"Aw, God." The blonde sighed, shaking her head and staring at her shoes. Which were striking, Fred noticed. She herself had been known to wear flip-flops to a fund-raiser, but recognized

beautiful foot gear when she saw it. These were high heels—
spike heels?—with a black base, and beautiful bright flowers had
been painted over them in vivid reds, greens, yellows.*

As the blonde began to pace, Fred saw she had no trouble
walking in the teetery heels. They could have been last year's
ratty tennis shoes, they seemed to fit her so well.

". . . yes, well, Elizabeth is on her way to meet the young lady
in question, and I have more shopping to do for the babies. So
would you please put Fur on for Daddy. And then Burr. And
then both!"

"Cannot believe, cannot *believe* you're turning into one of
those guys, Sinclair. I might not ever save you again if you keep
this up."

". . . that's all right; I shall wait . . . Hello? Marc?" He glanced
at his companion, who was rubbing her temples. "Are you having trouble hearing me . . . ? Perhaps this is a poor area for . . .
Hello? Marc?" He began shouting into the phone. Perhaps
Marc was trapped in a blizzard with a dying cell. "Tell my babies
Daddy is calling and I have bought them all kinds of snacks and
shall buy still more! Fish snacks! From Boston!"

Argh, enough. She could stare at the tourists all day; it wouldn't
make Fehr go away, it would only make everything take longer.

Her phone buzzed and she pulled it, glanced at it, then
texted Jonas back: CAN'T SEE YOU NOW BUSY MAYBE
LATER. Sure, like *that* would have any effect.

She pulled her badge and her key card, and headed to one of
the side entrances for employees. Not that she was one. But

---

*Alice + Olivia Devon painted floral patent leather pumps.

being a mermaid who used to work for the NEA had its advantages: pretty much every aquarium in the world wanted her to have drop-in privileges. Her old boss, Dr. Barb, had given her an ID and the keys to the castle more or less in perpetuity.

Fred didn't give the tourists another thought until she found herself trying to push the blonde's nose out through the back of her head.

Tuesdays! Sheesh.

CHAPTER THREE

Betsy Taylor, vampire queen and exasperated wife, noticed the lanky, frowning redhead at once. There weren't many people around, for one thing, and her husband, Eric Sinclair, had gone insane; that was the other thing. Betsy was, therefore, interested in anything that did not involve acknowledging her husband's recent insanity. Thus, the redhead, who seemed in a hurry yet was dithering outside the Big Boston Aquarium or whatever the heck it was called, caught her eye.

Leaving her insane husband to go about his insane business, Betsy followed the redhead, who looked to be in her midtwenties and was dressed in a torn T-shirt (not artfully torn, *torn* torn, as in, it was old and ratty and the fabric had given way due to wear and tear, as opposed to tear and tear), a pair of paint-spattered jeans (also *torn* torn), and (shudder!) pastel blue flip-flops. None of which Betsy much cared about; besides, you couldn't make people care about their shoes. The accessories she appreciated were the employee ID around the redhead's neck and, presumably, the key card to go with it. She was too old to be an intern, and wasn't dressed like someone in corporate, but the fact that she was here after hours with ID was promising.

You picked a bad day to linger, Red. And a . . . yeesh! A bad day to skip a shower. Do all the employees smell like that?

As the redhead started to let herself into a side entrance, Betsy walked straight up to her, tapped her on the shoulder (literally speaking), and then seized her brain (figuratively speaking). "Take me inside, please. Right now, no questions." *Please* had been unnecessary; the redhead had no choice. Still, Betsy hadn't been raised by wolves. At least, not entirely. Though she'd been known to hang out with them now and again.

And in they went.

The first thing that struck her was the immense size of the place; the outside building had been whopping but still hadn't come close to showcasing how the aquarium was essentially a gigantic warehouse on the bay filled with all things fishy.

The second thing that struck her was fishy: the odor. It wasn't awful, but it was pretty constant . . . it was how the woman smelled, but concentrated. She knew her brain would adjust and eventually tell her nose it didn't smell like much at all in there. *Get to work, brain, start lying through my teeth! Or whatever you need to do in there to fool my nose.*

The third was the sense of desertion. The place was a tomb—literally; there were fish skeletons all over, and the size of the place emphasized how empty it was. Betsy stifled the urge to shout, "Helloooooooo" for the childish pleasure of hearing the echo.

All in all: excellent! Maybe this little cross-country errand wouldn't take long. Maybe she and her insane husband could be back on the plane tomorrow morning, where he could cheerfully continue his insanity at thirty thousand feet. When his insanity ran its course, as she prayed it must, she, too, would be insane, and all their friends. But they'd be insane together! One great big happy family of utter nut balls.

She fished out her cell and double-checked the info. Madison Fehr, former intern at the aquarium. In some kind of trouble, the kind where a coroner had to be called and police reports filed. Madison's mother had pulled a Princess Leia: *Help me, Obi-Betsy. You're my only hope.* And so here she was.

"Do you know Madison Fehr?" she asked the redhead, who was staring ahead like one of those creepy stuffed animals that could walk or bark or turn a somersault, but did nothing but stand and stare after the batteries ran down. "Is she here?"

The redhead grimaced . . . a good trick, since most people she mojo'd behaved like robots she alone could command. No expression, no input of their own. Just blind, unquestioning obedience. "Yes," she replied, the *ugh* plain to hear in her voice. "And, yes."

"Okay, take me to wherever she'd be in this cement cavern. Can you do that?"

"Yes. And, yes."

"Then giddyap, Red."

The redhead actually *turned around* and met Betsy's gaze, which no one mojo'd had ever done. She gave Betsy a look that clearly conveyed what she thought of the instructions, then slooooowly obeyed.

I must be losing my touch! Or she's a special case. People either instantly submitted to her hostile takeover of their brain, or fought like pissed cats. Or it didn't work with them at all. Not this . . . this eventual, sullen obedience. Betsy was less than five years dead; she had no idea what to do but plow ahead. *Some people have a higher tolerance for booze, some for drugs, some for ye olde look-into-my-eyes vampire mojo. Live and learn! Or if you can't do both, try for just one. And I know which one I'd try for . . .*

She followed the redhead through the semi-gloom, trying not to be distracted by the exhibits of shiny fish, lobsters, and jellyfish. She was surprised to discover that parts of the Aquarium were more like classrooms and research labs—she'd figured the whole fishy warehouse to be one big tourist trap. See the penguins, learn about them, then buy a stuffed one for the low, low price of $49.99.

But, no, people apparently did serious work here as well as hosing down seals, cleaning up the IMAX theater, and selling things no one needed at outrageous markups. Did you have to get a master's degree in marine biology or fish zoology or whatever before you could say, "Ticket, please"?

One of the labs opened into a sort of kitchen area/staff break room, and it was down there that she got a look at Madison Fehr for the first time. She hadn't been able to smell her; all she could smell were smelt. Or whatever they fed the seals and sharks and rays and clownfish.

Well, she'll be relieved to see I'm here, was Betsy's last thought before Madison started screaming and the redhead punched her so hard she flew out of her shoes.

Her shoes!

CHAPTER
FOUR

The girl's shrieks jolted Fred out of her stupor, and she'd never been so glad in her life that Madison had a low stress threshold. Even as Fred let herself be taken by the adrenaline rush, she could feel that other woman's hold on her thoughts slacken dramatically and, the more she moved and thought on her own, disappear entirely. Even her physical touch had been startling and unreal: the woman felt uncommonly cool, like she had Freon instead of blood running through her veins. It was a relief to be away from her in every way.

Hitting someone had never felt so satisfying. Not even when she had killed her father. "Don't you ever," she told her as the blonde sailed over the small break room table, "don't you ever"—and crashed into the wall just behind it—"don't you *ever*, *ever* do that to me again!"

Although the woman landed in a heap, that did not allay Fred's rage and fear. So she rushed over, picked her up with both hands by her (rapidly ripping) collar, and slammed her back down on her brain-hijacking blond butt.

"If you ever—" Slam! "If you *ever*!" Wham! "*I will kill you. Not you-borrowed-my-shirt-without-asking-I'm-gonna-kill-you kill you. The-minute-you've-finished-throwing-up-you've-gotta-call-the-cops-or-we'll-never-get-those-dogs-away-from-the-corpse kill you.*"

She took a breath and kept on: "The police. The police will make slideshows out of what I do to you." She seized the treacherous twat to go for one more wall toss, only to have the blonde catch her by the wrists and gently but firmly thrust her back, a good trick from her position flat on the floor: no leverage. Fred flailed a little but didn't fall. She was again aware of the coolness of the woman's hands. *They're cold enough to be a doctor's.*

"All right, those I deserved, but now you're getting a little foamy at the mouth, and getting beaten to death is gonna wreck my week, so just . . . settle. Okay?"

Anyone else would be out. Anyone else would have an urgent date with an ER attending. She took it and then she stopped it, and neither act appeared to take much toll. I am in real trouble here.

"Dr. Bimm . . . ohmiGod . . . And you . . . You're here, too . . . Aw, jeez . . ."

Fred had forgotten about Madison, the screaming witness to the beat down. *Gad, the poor thing must be scared out of her tiny mind.*

Fred took a breath and puffed a lock of hair out of her eyes. She'd torn her shirt again. A pity it hadn't been the woman's face. "Okay, Madison, it's all right. You were right to call me." Never would she admit how that confession stung like acid. "She's down, okay? Madison, look." Fred actually grasped her (heaving) shoulders and turned her twenty-five degrees to the left, the better to see the mysterious blonde who was, incredibly, trying to stand. "I got her."

Or not. But she must know—her ass is still on the floor, she'd bet-ter know—I'll put her through the wall, not just into the wall, if she tries even one more thing.

Though having her brain kidnapped had been horrifying, Fred wasn't going to deny being surprised and happy. Sur-prised because she'd gained new respect for Madison . . . If this woman was after her, her former intern had a serious problem indeed.

Even better, Madison's problem wasn't going to take weeks of her time, or even days. Hell, twelve hours from now she could be snuggling into bed with her fiancé, Thomas. Twelve? Non-sense . . . the Marriott Long Wharf was all of five hundred yards away. Room service sundaes while she and Thomas did their best to make sure they'd get hot fudge stuck in wonderful places . . . a date to remember. She hadn't seen him in weeks, and they'd barely had time to get their shirts off before Madison had called in tears . . .

But that was then and, as Fred had just realized, Madison had done the right thing. Fred would never admit it aloud, but she was ashamed of (some of) the unkind things she'd thought and said about Madison. *If I hadn't been here—if that rotten bitch hadn't kidnapped my brain and used me to get into the building—Madison could be dead.*

"It's okay," Fred assured Madison again, and the blonde on the floor said the same thing at nearly the same time.

And, "I got your message; I came to help." They both said that, too, and then broke off and glared at each other.

Finally: "I'm here now, everything's all right."

"Will you *please* stop reading my lines?" The other woman had gotten to her feet, something Fred found amazing and ominous, and was gingerly feeling her face and neck and head. "Okay, so . . . okay, that's still there . . . and there's no hole *there* . . . so my skull only *feels* like a ceramic pot you chucked out a window. And ow. And ow. Ow-ow-ow."

"Who *are* you?"

"Again, Red, you're reading my lines, not yours."

"Like hell," Fred snapped back. "You should know, with every word that drops from your insipid mouth, I get more and more pissed."

"You'd think that would shut me up. And yet here I am. Still talking."

Yes, that *was* annoying. "Whoever you are, you picked the wrong dolphin-loving ex-intern to mess with."

"I'm guessing you're not talking about yourself." She pointed to a wide-eyed Madison. "And I'm *not* messing with her. You are."

Fred shook her head so hard she almost knocked herself over. Listening to the nonsense made her feel like she was on shaky ground, like her brain was vulnerable and *this close* to being hijacked again. Being under the blonde's control had been like trying to think through a brain drowning in quicksand. Just remembering how it felt to have a voice that was not her own controlling her nervous system made Fred want to vomit up her lungs.

"This," the blonde was saying, limping to one of her pretty shoes and stuffing it back on her foot, "this is what I get for answering the phone. And listening to what the person on the other end says. And then agreeing to act. And then acting by coming to Boston with my insane—never mind. The point is, I've brought it on myself. Ow. Anybody ever tell you, you hit like someone wearing brass knuckles over their brass knuckles?"

"No." Oddly, that pleased her. "How are you even conscious?"

"It's a secret. So I'll just tell you: I've got a hard head. Like, concrete hard. Cement hard. Trying-to-get-Sarah-McLachlan-to-stop-making-those-sad-animal-abuse-commercials hard. Also you smell weird, does that have anything to do with it?"

Fred wondered if a side effect of being possessed was to feel like nothing anyone said made sense for at least ten minutes afterward. "Does that have anything to do with what?"

"The badass beat down you just gave me. And I couldn't mojo you." The woman was looking at her thoughtfully and, though she wasn't behaving in a threatening manner, Fred sensed she was more dangerous now than she'd been before. "Not all the way, anyway. You shrugged it off after a while. That's never . . . huh. Why do you smell like fish?"

Fred blinked. *This was . . . yes. This was happening.* "You're in an aquarium, you idiot."

"Touch-*ee*. Betsy Taylor, by the way." She stuck out her hand.

Fred looked down at it, then back up into Betsy's blue green

MaryJanice Davidson

eyes. Then remembered *mojo* and jerked her gaze elsewhere. "I'm not shaking your hand."

"Ouch again. It's okay; they warned me about people from Boston."

"I'm not—" Fred shut her mouth. *Why am I having a conversation with this creature? My kingdom for a spear gun.*

Undeterred, the woman continued, "I'm Betsy Taylor. You must be Madison Fehr. We got here as soon as we could. Sorry if I scared you."

"That's okay." Madison was hiccupping, from fear or adrenaline or both, but got hold of herself enough to shake Betsy's hand. "I didn't handle that very well. I haven't handled any of this very well. I'm rilly, rilly sorry."

"Yeah, I was hoping we could talk about that. And about you, of course. I take it that whatever jam you're in, she's not part of it?" Jerking a thumb in Fred's direction.

Madison, still hiccupping, shook her head. "No. Not yet, but she probably will be, and it's my fault." For the first time, Fred saw how wretched Madison looked and sounded. The girl was barely out of college, had the money to buy anything she liked, and usually looked carefully put together.

Madison tended to dress like she still went to an exclusive East Coast private school: pleated khaki skorts, crisp white blouses, navy cardigans, and her I'm-only-an-intern-but-they-gave-me-this-cool-lab-coat lab coat. Hair pulled back into a curly platinum ponytail. Minimum-to-no makeup . . . the *only* thing she and Fred had in common. Madison didn't need it, and Fred had always found stuffing her pores with foundation, tugging on the delicate skin around her eyes with pencils and

128

makeup brushes, and plastering her lips with wax preservatives to be exquisitely stupid.

That other one was wearing makeup: bronzer and blush. She didn't need it, either, which pissed Fred off. Irrational and irrelevant, but tonight she was a slave to her baser emotions.

"I don't suppose either of you are in a smoothie mood, huh?" Betsy asked.

CHAPTER
FIVE

"If neither of us is the problem, what's the problem?"

Madison was having trouble meeting either woman's gaze. "Um, I'm the problem. Me and the bad guys. Okay, these guys I met? They think I'm Fred? And they wanna kill lots of Undersea Folk?"

As Fred stared, Betsy—sounding truly unpleasant for the first time—said, "I hate when women make everything a question? I don't understand how you can't hear how annoying that sounds? Like you can't get your thumb out of your butt and be assertive?"

Fred snorted; her sentiments exactly. She hadn't anticipated having even one thing in common with Betsy Taylor.

"What do you mean, the bad guys think you're me?"

"And who are you?" Betsy asked.

"Don't do that." The only thing that made Fred more uncomfortable than the people who recognized her were the ones who pretended they didn't recognize her. "If you've ever watched TV or been on the Web, you know who I am."

"Wow, the ego on *you*. And if I'm calling you on having a big ego, it's time to reexamine your life. Let's try one more time: Who are you?"

"This is my work friend," Madison lied. Fred did *not* consider the platinum-haired dimwit a friend. But *this is my pain in the ass* sounded unkind, even to her ears. "Betsy, this is Dr. Fredrika Bimm. She's one of those mermaid people."

"By *mermaid* people do you mean *heavily medicated* people?"

Fred slapped the counter in her annoyance. "Oh, come on! It's been all over the news for months. Mermaids are real, they're called Undersea Folk, and we're all going try to live in peace. Hum your favorite parts from 'Come Together' and it'll all fall into place."

"I've been busy with my own stuff—does this sound familiar since I just said it? So how about you get to the actual reason we're all in a big fish warehouse on a Tuesday night after the place is closed when I could be around the corner enjoying an oyster milkshake at the—the"—Betsy held up one finger in the universal hold-on-a-second gesture, fumbled through her dark green tote bag, then whipped out *Boston For Dummies*—"Union Oyster House. Says here it's the oldest tavern in America."

"You called a tourist for help?" Fred asked Madison, who had the decency to blush at the shame of it. "And you! Step *away* from the guidebook. First, you should have gone with Rough Guides. They're not as bossy. Second, mermaids exist, I'm one of them, and that's probably why Madison's in trouble. I have to speculate, though, since Madison hasn't coughed up the reason she's in trouble. As for you . . ." Fred seized Betsy by the arm and hauled her up the stairs . . . and up, and up. Madison tripped along behind them, wringing her hands. Fred was unaware women did that outside of gothic novels. "I can see we're gonna be stuck in neutral unless I can get you past this one thing."

"You mean about you being clinically insane? It's okay, though," she added hastily as they came to the top level, and the top of the tank. "My husband is, too, so I'm not judging. What does any of what you're doing have to do with—Hey, a turtle!" She peered into the enormous tank, home to several dozen species of fish and reptiles. "And sharks!" Then: "Whoa."

She had whoa'd because Fred had kicked off her flip-flops and stripped down to her . . . nothing. Yep, she was down to her nothing. Then she stomped over to the stairs beside the side of the tank, ascended them, and—

"I'm pretty sure you'll need a note from a parent or a doctor before you do that. Seriously. Will you get down? Hey—don't!"

—dropped in.

The NEA's Giant Ocean Tank* *was a four-story live exhibit at the* heart of the aquarium. More than twenty feet deep and over thirty feet wide, the thing held two hundred thousand gallons of salt water as well as turtles, stingrays, eels, reef fish, sharks, assorted excrement from same, discarded food from same, coral reefs—lots o' stuff, in other words. The water itself was bathtub warm.

---

*that's what it's really called! You can actually hear the capital letters.

From inside, Fred could see wavy, indistinct versions of Betsy and Madison looking down at her. She was a little nervous. Not out of fear of the tank's inhabitants. Like all Undersea Folk, Fred shared a low, telepathy-based form of communication with the fish here, and they were (for the most part) on friendly terms. Yes, they'd gone on a hunger strike a couple of years ago when Fred refused to pipe in more Pet Shop Boys (coral reef fish adored '80s glam rock for reasons unknown to Fred, who loathed it). Yes, there were occasional power struggles. But in general they got along.

No, she was afraid of how the other two would react. Though she had outed herself as a mermaid-human hybrid to the world, she was still overcoming decades of conditioning to keep her deep dark secret a deep dark secret.

Speaking of which, time for the show, especially since she couldn't swim without her tail, which made snorkeling a challenge: she stretched, wiggled in place, and felt her legs recede and her tail come forth. Not that her legs went anywhere, or her tail came from anywhere. It was difficult to describe the process, which she'd found personally frustrating as someone with a background in biology. It was like her legs were ... subsumed, she supposed. Like getting a tan: the tanned person looked different, but they were still the same person. Even when she couldn't see her legs, she knew they were there, knew they were a part of her.

She swam back and forth for a minute, letting Betsy get a good look and glad for a chance to work out some muscle tension. Then with a powerful flick, she zoomed up to the top, her head popping out with a satisfying splash.

Betsy was clutching the top of the tank, white-faced. "Oh my God."

"I see you've grasped the situation."

"Oh my God!"

"This is what I was talking about." Fred made sure she was within reach of the ladder before shifting back to her legs and climbing out. "Somehow you've missed the fact that an entirely new sentient species has existed with yours for millennia and picked the last six months to expose themselves."

"I'll say," she muttered, eyeing Fred as she gathered up her clothes. "Nice rack, by the way. Unreal! Not your rack. The situation."

"Only to some." But she smiled to soften her comment, then wondered why she wanted to soften anything for the tote-bag-toting, nonsense-spouting, thought-hijacking bitch.

"I can't believe it!"

Betsy seemed so astonished, and so sympathetic (though that was a little weird—why would she have sympathy?), Fred found herself warming up to her.

"You sometimes have a *tail*? You're a half mermaid thingy or whatever so sometimes your feet just *disappear*?" Betsy sounded more distressed now than when Fred was tossing her into break room walls. "So half the time you can't wear shoes! Half the time *you can't wear shoes*! Even—"

"What?"

"—if when, even if when you have feet and buy the cutest pair ever, sometimes your feet just *vanish*!" She staggered and, startled, Fred put out a hand to steady the tall blonde. "I'm so, so sorry!"

"It's not that bad." *Was she serious?*

"No, just—I don't mean to—you're very brave. I could never be as brave as you with this; I'd take it much harder. I don't know what to say. I'm so sorry."

She was! Why am I surprised Madison asked an idiot for help? Fred went to the secret towel cache she tucked beside the exit, briskly dried herself, then started putting her clothes back on. "Anyway. Per Madison, here, somebody tried to kill her because they thought she was me. Is that right?"

"That's the condensed version, yeah." Again, Madison stared at the floor. Fred didn't know if she was glad the girl had no comment about what she'd just seen, or miffed. You'd think someone who *rilly, rilly* loved dolphins would be just a teeny bit blown away by seeing a real mermaid in the flesh, so to speak. "The long version makes me out to be pretty stupid."

I'm sure. "So now that—"

"I have to tell my husband about this!"

"As you like, but right now we have to deal with—"

"Whoa, okay? Whoa, *whoa.* I'm gonna need more than thirty seconds to process what you just did."

"You've had months, like everyone else," Fred forced out through gritted teeth. "Unless you've been off the planet, there's no excuse for—"

"I *wish* it was as simple as being off planet. You know? I absolutely wish I'd been *only* off planet, fighting space lizards or feeling Khan's wrath or whatever, so instead of someone yowling, 'Khaaaaaan! Khaaaaan!' they'd be all, 'Betseeeeey! Betseeeey!' But I was time traveling and in hell and getting my friend Jessica pregnant and things just sort of stacked up on me. And big damn deal! I don't have to justify my to-do list to you. Great, you're a fish."

"*Part* fish. No, dammit, no fish, I'm a mammal!"

"Yeah, a mammal with fish scales. Is that why you were able to shrug off my mojo, and smell weird?"

Remembering her desperate battle to think her own thoughts, Fred muttered, "Shrug off isn't how I'd have described that. And I do not *smell*."

"I don't think you smell, either, Dr. Bimm."

"No, no," Betsy soothed. "Don't take it wrong. It's not a bad smell. It's just different. It's not your fault—I've got a super sensitive nose. And I'm still learning, so at first I thought it was just me, but now I know it's just you."

"What?" Nothing. Nothing this woman babbled made sense, ever.

"Okay, this is a terrible example, but I'm hoping it'll help so that you'll be able to overlook the terribleness of it: You know how when you walk into a good sushi restaurant, you smell fish? And it's not a bad smell, but it's a smell? You're the sushi restaurant of my . . . er . . ."

"Olfactory canyon?"

"Yes! That! But again, not in a gross or smelly way."

"I dislike you intensely," Fred said. She'd had enough of the blonde, enough of the other blonde, enough of the tank, and enough of the entire mess, which *still* had not been explained to her satisfaction. "Did you mean it about wanting a smoothie?"

"Really?" Betsy's face lit up and Fred was startled at how quickly she could go from pretty to gorgeous. "You're not teasing, right? Because if you are, that's just not funny. So are you? No? We can? Smoothies? Now?" She threw her arms around her, which Fred found alarming and touching. *A little touching. Barely touching. Not really touching at all.*

She figured the woman had a lot of friends. Probably she

made positive first impressions on others, ones who didn't mind her penchant for thought rape. She could see how Betsy could grow on her. Like a fungus. Like . . . blonde athlete's foot.

So I'd better work doubly hard not to let her in me or let her win me over.

Thus resolved, Fred explained how easy it would be to score smoothies in Boston on a Tuesday night.

CHAPTER SIX

"Whoa."

She must say that a lot, Fred concluded, though she was pleased to see Betsy enjoying the marketplace. The scents, sights, and lights were dazzling to Fred, and she'd lived in the area most of her life. What must it be like for . . . er . . . for someone who was from . . . uh . . .

Fred realized that she still knew nothing about Betsy except she could hijack brains and didn't need to wear makeup. So that would have to be rectified while they ate.

"It used to be a meeting hall in the seventeen hundreds," Fred explained, finding herself in tour-guide mode but not minding. She loved Boston. It was a city that looked old but felt young. "No taxation without representation was debated right here. Samuel Adams and George Washington were both here to pitch their cases. Ted Kennedy and Bill Clinton have been here."

"Great, but it's weird you're counting those last two as a mark in this place's favor. Whoever's been here, it's great. Look at all the food to choose from!"

"And all thanks to the cradle of liberty. You're welcome, the rest of America."

"I had no idea the Founding Fathers invented smoothies."

"Of course they di—" She glanced at the blonde, who grinned back. "Ah. Very funny."

"Yeah, well. Couldn't resist messing with you."

"Try harder."

"This . . . is . . . so . . . cool!" During their conversation Betsy took in everything she could. She was walking while staring, looking all around and even up at times; it was amazing that she hadn't stepped on someone or knocked them over. "What are you guys gonna get? Can we eat inside? It's cold out. Where should we sit?"

Not that cold. Most people are so happy when spring shows up, they'll sit outside in a thirty-degree drizzle. Hmm.

Fred, obeying the demands of her shellfish allergy, opted for a salad. Madison had a daiquiri; Betsy opted for a strawberry smoothie. "It's so fresh," she moaned around the straw. "Tastes like they picked 'em this morning. I live near farms—I married a former farmer—and this is still the best one I've ever had."

"Yes, fascinating. Glad you like it, now let's get to it." *I don't know why I'm here, but it's not to be her tour guide.* They had picked a (relatively) private table on the second floor, in the far corner (if a round room could be said to have corners). As it was past the dinner hour, they had most of the tables to themselves. "You said you live near farms? Where are you from?"

"St. Paul. Which, you're gonna point out, is a big city and farm-free, and it is, but it's not farmer's *market* free, and that's where we get a lot of our fruit."

Fred looked at Madison. "You dragged whoever she is out here from Minnesota?"

Madison looked uncomfortable but, to her credit, managed a truthful answer. "I didn't drag anybody anywhere. I was hoping for help, though. I don't want to lie about that."

Fred turned back to Betsy. "How do you even know Madison?"

"I don't. I don't know her mom, either, but her mom knows me, so here I am."

Her hip buzzed; Fred ignored it. "Let's try this again. From the beginning. What's going on?"

"Madison's mom called me," Betsy said between slurps. "Said her kid was in trouble and would I please go see what I could do, and my husband is going insane so I figured a change of scenery might help, and here I am drinking the best smoothie of my life after meeting a grouchy mermaid."

Fred took that in, then turned to Madison. "You ready to jump in?"

"Careful," Betsy cautioned. "She might mean that literally."

"I called you and then my mom, and she called Betsy, and here I am and here you guys are." Madison lowered her voice, though no one seemed to be paying attention to them. "I didn't think Betsy would get here so fast."

"That's what I do. Get places fast. D'you think they'd make

me a custom smoothie if I said *pretty please*? I'm thinking peach and raspberry . . ."

"Are you two being obtuse on purpose?" Fred demanded.

"Mmmm . . ." She appeared to think about it as she licked her straw. "No?"

"I don't think so . . ." Madison said doubtfully.

"Are you trying to goad me into beating you to death? Because you should know it's not difficult to goad me into beating you to death."

Madison sighed. "I met this great guy—I thought he was great—and a couple of his friends at the NEA, and they thought I was you and that was okay when they were just being touristy, but they want to kill you, Fred, and when they found out I wasn't you, they tried to kill me. I got away and called Fred and my mom."

"And you called your mom because . . ."

"She can always fix things."

"And your mom called Betsy because . . ."

"Betsy's the queen of the vampires." Madison waited, as if that was a normal thing for a normal person to say. Then she stirred, as if remembering something: "Oh! My mom's a vampire, too. Did I forget that part?"

CHAPTER
SEVEN

Fred took a breath. Held it for a count of ten. Gave up at five, whooshed, then said, "Let's take it from the top."

"Again, she might mean that literally. She gets off on stripping naked and then jumping into things. So just, you know, be aware."

"Your mom is a vampire."

"Yes."

"And Betsy is also a vampire; she's the queen of them."

"Yes."

"All right. I can see why you wouldn't want that to be gossip fodder. What I don't understand is—"

"Wait, wait." Betsy had put her straw aside, upended her near-empty glass over her open mouth, and was now thumping the bottom of the glass to get the last precious drops of the smoothie. "That's it? You're taking that in stride? You don't want to take five and have a minor freak-out?"

"No. I believe you both."

"Because, there being mermaids? Doesn't prove that there are vampires."

"It doesn't disprove it, either." The strength. The way she took a beating that might have killed a regular person. The thirst. The . . . What did she call it? The mojo? Those also helped prove her point. "Okay. So your mother, who is a vampire, called the qu—the quee—" The vampire part was believable . . . or at least, not unbelievable. The queen part was harder. This woman was a leader? People looked to her for guidance? *The horror.* So she veered off topic for a few seconds. "How is it that your mom's a vampire? You're adopted, right?"

Madison nodded and stirred her daiquiri, which she had barely touched. "Yeah. Mom's raised lots of kids. She left England a while back to get away from the douche boat she married. She—"

Fred knew she shouldn't, but did anyway: "Douche boat?"

"Cross between a douche bag and a dreamboat. Like Bradley Cooper in the *Wedding Crashers.* I think I read that in *EW.*"

"Right." Madison nodded. "Mom wanted kids, but not his kids. And once she came to America and settled in and got established and died and came back, she started taking in orphans."

"Define *a while back.*" Old money, that's what Dr. Barb had told Fred several months ago. Interns were sometimes a burden, sometimes a blessing; the coin flipped and you got what you got. Madison wasn't the first intern Fred had to put up with because

Someone Important got her the slot. Fred had been expected to play nice with the Fehr-haired girl because her mother was rich and a generous sponsor of the NEA. So *old money* could mean—

"You know how people say so-and-so's been here so long, their family came over on the *Mayflower*?"

"Yeah," Betsy answered. "Except in Minnesota, we say they're so old they were the original Ole and Lena."

"Okay. My mother really *did* come over on the *Mayflower*."

Fred just stared.

"Uh-huh, rilly, I'm serious! A long time ago, hundreds of years, a small group of disgruntled English citizens decided to head forth to a new land in the hopes of—"

"I understand *that*." *The last thing I need is a history lesson from Madison Fehr.* "That must be—Your mom must have some good stories."

Madison sighed. "You'd think. But, no. At least none she'll share. I get a lot of *you've got no idea how good you've got it*, but all moms do that. It's, like, a mom rule. So my mom knew about Betsy." To Betsy: "She gets the newsletter, so she had all your contact info."

"What?"

Madison ignored Fred's squawk. "And I told her I was in a jam, and she sent Betsy here to help me."

Betsy smiled. "Not quite right, since there's not a vampire on the planet who can send me anywhere." She said so in a perfectly pleasant tone. *So why*, Fred wondered, staring at her, *did all the saliva in my mouth just dry up?*

Madison had caught it, too; the whites of her eyes were showing all the way around, like a horse about to rear. Between one second and the next, the room seemed darker and colder; between one breath and the next, the world was scarier. Because Betsy had spoken one sentence. And smiled as she did it. Fred had felt that sort of indifferent menace before: from hammerhead sharks.

"I mean—I mean, then you agreed. When you heard my mom needed you. That I needed you. When she told you—when she *asked* you and you agreed to come. But you didn't have to. Because no vampires can send you. You came because you wanted to. Out here."

"Well, it's not like I can't watch my TV shows online," Betsy replied, instantly back to herself. Or was she? *Maybe the giddy twit is the mask, and her true self is the vampire no one can send anywhere.* "Take a breath; you look like you're gonna faint."

While Madison managed a sickly smile, Fred leaned back in her chair and studied Betsy. She was glad she'd chosen the venue she had. Yes, on the one hand they were discussing matters that were complex and dangerous and, most of all, private. Things you didn't necessarily want to discuss in public. Things that, if overheard, at best would bring eye rolls and titters, and worst, wooden stakes.

On the other hand, the chances were good that Betsy and/or the bad guys wouldn't try anything in such a public place. The more she learned about Betsy, the happier she was that they weren't in a big empty aquarium at night with lots of natural soundproofing.

"Okay, I get why you're here, Betsy, but why not contact Madison directly? Go right to her for the scoop? Why skulk around—"

"I never skulk."

"—and hijack my brain?"

"Barely. More like temporarily borrowed. You got it back, didn't you?" Betsy shrugged. "I wanted to see things for myself straight out. As much as I could, I wanted to get a fix on the bad guy, right? Which worked out exactly as I planned, except for the part about how you weren't the bad guy."

Her cell buzzed. "Dammit, Jonas! Enough! Take a hint." She glared at it, irritated, then did what she should have half an hour ago and clicked it off. Her best friend had been bugging her for hours to have dinner with him, and, yes, she'd been out of town for weeks and wanted to hear his news, and she had missed him, too, but the last thing she needed was to have Jonas—

"There you are, you uncommunicative tart!"

—dragged into this.

CHAPTER
EIGHT

Jonas Carrey, her best friend since the second grade, bounded up to their corner table and greeted her with, "Forgot to shut down your cell tag, dummy." To Madison and Betsy: "You guys know she's a scientist, right? Unreal." To Fred: "So I was able to Sherlock my way right to your doorstep, not that this is it, exactly. And—hello!" He'd hello'd! because he'd gotten a look at Betsy. Who was, Fred had to admit, very pretty if you liked vulgar blondes with nice racks and long legs and big clear greenish blue eyes and wiseass grins.

"Go away, Jonas."

He ignored her, which he'd also been doing since second grade. "If you're waiting for Fred to remember her manners and introduce us," he said to Betsy, shaking her hand, "I hope you packed a snack."

Betsy laughed. "I don't need to, here. And be nice to poor Fred. I kind of dropped in on her tonight."

Kind of?

Fred gritted her teeth. Years of experience had proven Jonas would remain as long as he liked; nothing short of knocking him unconscious would prevent his presence. Since he was already here, and presumably protected under the earlier probably-won't-make-a-scene-in-a-public-place logic, she reserved knocking him unconscious as Plan B. "Betsy Taylor, this is my friend, Jonas Carrey. Jonas, this is Betsy. She's in town visiting Madison for a few hours." *Please let it only be a few hours.* "I think you met Madison last year."

"Meetcha." He stepped to the empty table beside them, snagged a chair, and settled in. "So what'd I miss? What's going on? And hey—great shoes."

The vampire looked absurdly flattered. "Thanks. I know they don't look it, but they're pretty comfortable."

"Alice and Olivia, right?"

"Yeah." At once Betsy was a great deal more animated. "Yeah, they just screamed, 'Spring!' at me and it was a cloudy chilly day and I'm one of those people who's always cold so I couldn't resist."

He nodded. "I know how it goes. The heart wants what the heart wants, and so do the feet."

"Jonas, please stop talking about shoes or get out of here, but you've gotta pick at least one."

Jonas held up his hands. "Oh, simmer, I'm just making conversation with your new friend—"

"Not. My. Friend."

"So just put *down* the glass of haterade."

"That's wonderful," Betsy said, smiling. "I'm stealing it."

"That's okay," Jonas said, "I did, too. Amazon forums, would you believe it? But seriously, you guys—why are the three of you sitting up here almost by yourselves in a giant food court when none of you are eating much of anything, when *you've* barely been back in town ten hours"—nodding at Fred—"because of something *you've* done." Nodding at Madison. "Is it super-secret mermaid stuff?"

No one seemed to know how to answer him until Betsy spoke up. "No. Super-secret vampire stuff."

Fred was astonished, and then frightened, and then admiring. *That fanged cow wants Jonas to be curious. She had a very specific reason to tell him what she did and she did it in a very specific way. She wants people I care about in this. She wants them nearby. Because that will make me be careful. Maybe I'll be so worried about keeping Madison and Jonas out of trouble, I won't have time to kick her undead ass all over the NEA break room. Nice one, blondie. Maybe you only look like a vapid dumbass.*

The irrepressible Jonas took it well, considering. "You guys are vampires now?" he gasped.

"Not her." Betsy, jerking her head at Fred. Then she nodded at Madison. "Her mom. And me."

"Is that why you're chilly to the touch?" Fred asked. She'd been wondering about it before, but in the ensuing excitement had forgotten. But now she was thinking about Betsy grabbing her wrists in the break room, how cold her grasp was. "You can't keep a ninety-eight point six body temp anymore?"

"No," she said with a sad sigh. "I'm always cold. Even in summertime. It's a terrible burden."

"Try swimming the Arctic Ocean in January sometime," Fred snapped back, unmoved.

"Ooooh," Jonas said, leaning back in his chair. "Is there gonna be a mermaid-vampire smackdown?"

"There already was," Madison said, picking up her drink, looking at it, and putting it down once more. Fred estimated she'd drank about twenty milliliters at most. A waste of a daiquiri. "It was rilly horrible."

"Whaaaaaaat?" Jonas's chair came forward with a *thunk*. "And I missed it? Dammit! I knew I should have tracked you down the first time you blew off my text. The event of the century and I was stuck on the Red Line! So who won?"

"I think it was a tie. Then Fred stripped naked and swam in the Giant Ocean Tank and proved she was a mermaid because Betsy never watches TV."

"And *where* was I? Son of a bitch!" Jonas smacked himself on the forehead, like a man vigorously checking himself for fever. "Okay, from the top. Seriously, guys. Start over. I wanna hear everything. We're wasting valuable time, time that could be spent making me feel like I was there and didn't miss the awesomest evening out ever."

And because Fred and Betsy had the same thought, though they didn't know it (*I still have questions and Madison still hasn't told us everything*), the mermaid and the vampire thought that was a fine plan.

"Does he do this a lot?" the vampire asked. Fred noticed that, as she'd sucked all the liquid from her smoothie, she'd begun eyeing Madison's all-but-untouched drink. *Hmmm. Unnatural thirst? How often does she have to suck down blood? And when did she last do so? Hmmm.* "Just plop himself in the middle of something and assume he belongs?"

"Since we were seven." Fred sighed.

Betsy's smile widened. "Yeah. I've got one of those, too." She didn't elaborate, but unless the vampire was an Oscar-caliber actress, she was looking at Jonas with genuine fondness, and for that, Fred could almost forgive the mind snatch.

CHAPTER NINE

"So I came to town for the Tall Ships thing—"

Fred winced. *Don't do it. Don't. Don't. She might finally be ready to tell the whole thing. At last you'll have answers. So keep your piehole shut tight.*

"—but, like, they were late or whatever, or I was early, because—"

Jonas frowned at her. "Don't, Fred."

"—the ships weren't there."

"Of course not!" Fred had held herself in as long as humanly (or Undersea Folk-ey) possible. "That's in the summer, as anyone within five hundred miles of Boston knows, it's *always* in the summer. Who comes for Tall Ships in the spring?"

"Okay, I can see how that would annoy a local," Betsy conceded, "but come on, are you gonna interrupt after every sentence? How many hours have you allotted to story time? I could be hanging out with my insane husband right this minute."

Which was worse, being reprimanded by a thieving vampire, being confronted with Madison's essential stupidity, realizing that Jonas would rip into her snobbery when he could get her alone, or knowing the vampire was correct? "Nnngghh. Go on. Sorry."

"And also, I thought maybe mermaids would be interested in tall ships, and maybe I could meet a couple more. You, um, you said you'd introduce me to some, but you've been super busy."

I will not feel guilty. I will not feel guilty. I will not feel guilty for politely blowing her off.

"And also, I was hoping to meet some people that I'd met online, doing the PR stuff for the NEA and for you."

"For me?"

"Fred doesn't even do her own PR stuff; she wouldn't stick you with it," Jonas agreed.

"Except I did," Fred said slowly, remembering.

Jonas threw up his hands. "Well, *great.*"

"Madison offered to catch the e-mails for NEA's 'Ask a Mermaid' page." Just saying the name of the thing out loud made her want to break things. "The volume. You wouldn't believe the volume of stupid, stupid, stupid questions. There were almost as many of those as there were sex questions. You wouldn't believe what some people wanted me to do with my tail."

Betsy made a strange sound and clapped her hands over her mouth; Fred realized she'd barked laughter without meaning to. She took her hands away and said, "It's awful you had to be exposed to those and then exposed Madison to those."

"Well." Fred coughed. "Madison was there and she offered and she's good at it." Fred saw the young woman blush with pleasure, the first time that evening she hadn't looked like she was coming down with a violent stomach virus. "And she offered to do the press releases, too, and I said sure."

Jonas was nodding. "Okay, yeah, I get it." To Betsy: "Fred hates that shit. If she had her way, she'd dig a hole in a Cape Cod sand dune and live in it and hardly ever leave it except to bitch at tourists for building sand castles in her yard and maybe bathe."

Fred kept her mouth shut. *It's not like he's lying. Ahhhh . . . my own sand dune . . . my own hole in the beach . . .* The thought was so haunting and beautiful she wanted to cry.

"Okay, so I was rilly, rilly flattered that Fred trusted me with it."

More like couldn't be bothered with it and didn't care who did it as long as I didn't have to, but okay. Sure. Please go on.

"I figured if I did a good job, maybe I could meet some more of your Undersea friends."

"Awww, Madison." Jonas patted her hand. "That's where you went wrong. Fred doesn't *have* any friends, Undersea or other- wise, except me, and that's just because I lost the coin toss with God."

Betsy had now snaked Madison's drink for herself and was sucking it down. "So you dumped your job on Madison, who did her best to make you proud . . ."

"Hey!" Fred said sharply. "It was never my job. Dr. Barb set the whole page up after the Folk outed themselves on CNN. There are pages on the website for the penguins and the sea turtles, and those aren't my job, either."

"Yep, that's true. Fred's former boss is my current sexy squeeze . . . She told me you weren't keen on the idea, which is Freddish for *get away from me with that thing before I vomit and embark on a killing, puking rampage.*"

"What did she expect? I had next to no privacy after all that. People would come up to me and do the weirdest things. Mermaids don't grant wishes, that's myth number one I'd like addressed and then smothered. Thank God I was the unofficial bridge between the races, because after a while the royal family appointed actual capable ambassadors, which we all should have realized they should have done in the first place. I'll be the first to admit: even though I signed on for it, I sucked at that job."

"We can't all be recovering Miss Congenialities," Betsy said cheerfully.

"Okay, whatever. After a few months it got so bad I got the hell out of Dodge. I've been tagging along with my fiancé while he makes the fellowship rounds." Fred pointed to her head. "This weird red is not my natural hair color."

"It's nice, though," Betsy commented after eyeing the fake hue. "Auburn, with deeper auburn lowlights."

"Thank you," Jonas said, bowing from the waist. He managed to do it from a chair without looking ridiculous. "Fred kicked up such a fuss you'd think I'd shaved it instead of dying it Awesome Awesome. (And if that's not a real name for a hair color, it should be.)"

"I didn't ask you to do that," she snapped. "I had a box of Yuck-O Brown Number Twenty-one all ready to go." Even now, the memory of Jonas's horrified screams made her shudder. He'd actually knocked her to the ground to wrench Yuck-O Brown Number Twenty-one out of her hand, then dragged her to a salon and personally supervised the cut and coloring. "That was three hours of my life, gone forever."

"Oooh, I wish my friend could do that!" Betsy said, looking at Fred's hair with renewed interest. "She just laughs at my home-dye errors. What color is it under all that?"

"Green," Fred answered curtly. She did not want the discussion veering further toward her hair.

"Sorry, what? Green? Your natural hair color is—oh, right. Mermaid thing."

"Ooooh, but all those who truly lurrrrrrv her see it as blue," Jonas said, fluttering his eyelashes.

Fred longed to punch him. "Some people see it as blue," she admitted. "I hate the ambiguity . . . Blue, green, who gives a shit? It just perpetuates the stereotype that the Folk are magical. We're not."

They looked at her.

"We're not!" She shook off their stares. "Anyway, thanks to Jonas, I'm harder to recognize now. Case in point, Betsy: you had no idea who I was."

"You should set the bar higher," the vampire advised. "I've been dealing with a bunch of my own shit lately. Me not knowing who you were isn't the same as the average gal on the street not knowing."

The thought that Betsy would willfully ignore spectacular current events further irked Fred, who wasn't blind to the irony. She hated the fuss and she got annoyed when someone didn't know about the fuss. *Jonas is right; he really is one of my few friends*, *and for years he was my* only *friend. This sort of thing is the reason why.* Still . . . "This was an unprecedented event in history!"

"Hey, my shoe closet wasn't gonna organize itself, okay? And that's only one of the things I got stuck dealing with. I've got more on my plate than whatever the latest fad is."

"Fad?"

"Anyway," Jonas broke in, "Madison was nice enough to help you out with work you had no intention of doing. And then . . ."

"Then I met these guys—they sent lots of stuff to Fred's page—"

Not my page! Fred closed her eyes but said nothing.

"And they seemed rilly nice and they, like, had all these great ideas to help the Folk—cool stuff like how to use legal precedent to show the world that anything abandoned in the ocean, y'know like ship wrecks and pirate booty and all that, they had a way to prove how it all legally belongs to the Undersea Folk."

Ah. This was sensible. Though most of the planet (the ones who didn't think the mermaid thing was a hoax) outwardly embraced the Undersea Folk, some countries had gotten touchy about the Folk's vast treasure. A few of the dignitaries realized the Folk had in their possession, among other goodies: caches of Confederate gold, Blackbeard's treasure (scooped from caves of the Cayman Islands), Incan gold from lakes in the Colombian Andes, King John's crown jewels, fist-sized diamonds from the wreck of the *Flor de la Mar*, and other priceless artifacts (including the *Kusanagi-no-Tsurugi* sword, the *Aphrodite of Cnidus*, Michelangelo's *Sleeping Cupid*, and the Lighthouse of Alexandria) and began legal proceedings to get "their" property back.

The Folk's response to this was simplicity itself: finders

keepers. As King Mekkam said, "How can treasures that rested on the bottom of the seas for centuries, treasures gone so long no one living even remembers them much less requires them, how can such things belong to any lander now living?" The king had been too polite to point out that the Undersea Folk were well within lander laws regarding salvage: they took the risk, they got to keep the goodies. It was a growing problem; Fred acknowledged to herself that she would have looked into the strangers' ideas just as Madison had.

"Anyway, they had other ideas, too, and so we agreed to meet and they thought I was you and then they tried to kill me."

Betsy, who'd had a look of polite interest on her face, sat up straight, the better to look straight at Madison. "You're kidding."

Fred, who could feel her eyebrows arching (they were also red, thanks to Jonas's tireless efforts to drive her mad with minutia), asked what, to her, was the obvious question: "How could they think you were me?"

Madison sucked in breath, then let it out. "CauseItoldthem-Iwas."

Jonas cringed, waiting for the inevitable shit storm from Hurricane Fred. When no one said anything, Madison continued in a small voice: "I told them. I said I was you."

It took Fred a moment to find her voice. "Why?"

"Yeah," Betsy said, also puzzled. "Why would you ever say that? Of all the un-fun weirdos you could be, why would you ever—"

"I'm handling this, Betsy."

"—ever—"

"Do you mind?"

"—*ever* want to be her?"

"Because that's all I've ever wanted to be!" Madison flashed, anger chasing shame in her shout. "Why d'you think out of all the aquariums in the country—"

"How many can there be?" the vampire from Minnesota asked. "Six? Seven?"

"Sixty-three," Fred and Madison said in unison. Madison continued alone. "Why d'you think I ended up here? I've been following your career since your research project at Woods Hole. People don't really like you—"

"You are wise to see the truth," Jonas noted.

"—but they fall all over themselves offering you fellowships and grant money. Then, boom! You're a mermaid."

"Boom?"

"And not just any mermaid—"

"A seriously grumpy one. With blue hair except when people think it's green."

"Betsy, *shut up*."

"Okay, but you know I'm right."

"I know what you think of me—another spoiled brat intern playing at marine bio on her mama's money—"

"I didn't think you were a *brat*, per se," Fred mumbled. She could feel herself blushing but, unlike Madison's rosy cheeks, it wasn't from pleasure. *Everything she's said is right. So who's the real dumbass, Fredrika Bimm?*

"But that was fine! I figured if I was useful, you'd like me and we'd hang. You didn't care that I was rich and you didn't care who my mom was. I—I loved that. D'you know how many people I've met who don't care about Mama's money and connections? I could count them on one hand—I could count them on three fingers. You just weren't interested and I thought—I thought if I really put myself out there . . ." She trailed off, shook her head at her own silliness, and continued. "So I started answering the really important e-mails as you. I figured I'd set up all this research funding and legal strategies to help your friend the prince, and when it's all said and done, they're pissed I lied, they're pissed I'm not you. And like a pathetic fool I go along with it! And now we're all in this mess."

"It's like an episode of *Three's Company*, with the goofy mis-understandings. Plus attempted murder and the pretty high chance at least one of you will end up shot in the face." Betsy grimaced and shook her head. "*Hate* getting shot. Stings like crazy."

"Oh, wow, now I've got questions for you, Betsy." Jonas turned his chair with a loud scrape, the better to face her. "When you say *stings like crazy* do you mean *stupid mosquitoes* or *ouchie, that's gonna need stitches*?"

"How did you get away?" Betsy asked, ignoring Jonas.

"Well, they grabbed me and got my clutch, and then I played dumb long enough for them to let their guard down, and then I ran like hell, and I think, I think instead of coming after me they took off, because I never saw them outside the building. Mama got me a room at the Marriott. I was afraid to go home."

Jonas's eyes narrowed at Fred; she could pretty much read his thoughts: *Let the playing-dumb thing go.* It was good advice; she heeded it.

"Good for you," Betsy said, nodding in approval. "That's my rule of thumb, too: when in doubt, play dumb and then run like hell. But they're still after you, right? They didn't try to kill you because you weren't Fred."

Madison was reluctant to contradict the vampire, who'd been

so nice to her, but had to correct the misunderstanding. "Well, sure they did. They were *so* mad."

"Yes, because they were really there to kill me." Fred kept her tone low and gentle. "When they found out you weren't me, they knew they had to kill you, or you'd warn me. Which you're doing."

"Ohhhhh."

"So Madison's mom called Betsy, and Madison called Fred. And you all met inside the NEA. Fred let you in?" Jonas asked, turning to Madison.

She blinked, surprised. "No, I got there first. We agreed to meet but I only had to come a few hundred feet."

"How'd you get in after hours?" Fred asked.

"Oh! They tossed my clutch and someone found it right outside the hotel and brought it inside and the manager recognized my name and brought it right up. No credit cards," she added with a resigned shrug, "or money, which I figured, but they left my library card and my frequent flier—"

"Okay, okay. So who wants Fred dead?"

"Aw, man." Jonas rubbed his eyes. "If we're gonna make a list of Fred's enemies, I'm gonna need a drink."

Fred smiled sourly. Annoying and unpleasant as it was, Jonas was right: it would be a long, long list, and making said list wasn't even half of it.

"We'll all need drinks." She sighed, and they got to it.

CHAPTER
TEN

Jonas's help compiling the list of Fred Haters was invaluable, as Betsy and Madison pointed out. Fred, meanwhile, had a headache that got worse with each name.

"Boo-hoo," Jonas replied. "You're just tired. You'd be the first to admit you're not the victim here."

"Not the victim," she agreed, "but it's still not much fun listening to you rattle off the names of those who loathe me."

"You should see my enemies list," Betsy said, as if Fred would find that comforting. (She was annoyed and grateful that the vampire's comment did, in fact, make her feel a little better.) "It was bad even before I died."

"About that . . ." Fred had been so caught up in Madison's mess that she'd had no time to indulge her curiosity, which was considerable. When she'd woken that morning, she had no idea more people she'd never met wanted to kill her, or that there were vampires outside of fiction. "You say you literally died? And came back? Because Madison said the same thing about her mom." *And was disturbingly matter of fact about it. Guess it's true: if the weirdness is in your own family, if weirdness is all you know for the first few years of your life, it's hard to see it.* "So you truly do die?"

"Oh, sure," the vampire said cheerfully. "*Truly*'s not the word for it; I was deader than the color-blocking fad. Of course, I would have returned from the dead no matter what, since it was a huuuuge matter of personal vengeance."

"Against whoever murdered you?" Fred asked, sympathetic. *What must that be like, to experience your own murder . . . and then get better? Did her killer steal her brain first, like she tried to steal mine? Did she know what was happening at the end? I cannot think how awful that must have been, and what am I saying? I don't like her and I'm not going to like her, so who cares, who cares, who cares?*

"Worse. Against my stepmother, who, when I wasn't even in the ground yet, stole all my designer shoes."

Jonas, still scribbling names, gasped.

"And she's not even my shoe size! Pure spite, that's all it was. My Manolos, my Beverly Feldmans, my Zanottis, my YSLs, my Jimmy Choos—"

"Please stop, I can't bear it," Jonas begged.

Me, neither.

"—my black satin rose Roger Vivier pumps."

Jonas shrieked like his armpit hair had caught fire.

"And left me to be buried in her crappy knockoffs that didn't even fit."

Jonas dropped the pen. "Tell me, *tell me* how many ways you killed her."

"Didn't. My dad would have freaked; plus it would have ruined Christmas."

"More than your dying?" Fred asked dryly.

"I did put her tacky jewelry through her own blender," the vampire admitted. "I won't deny it was super satisfying."

That had been the high point (egad!) of the last hour. When the list had reached seventy-nine—

". . . and don't forget your old college roommate. And your mom's next-door neighbors. And my next-door neighbors. And our seventh grade English teacher. And your ninth grade English teacher. And the swimming instructor at the Y. And the yoga instructor at the Y."

—Fred begged for a break. "Besides, they'll be kicking us out soon; it's getting late."

"Oooh, let me order another smoothie before they close," Betsy said, rising at once.

"Make it a double," Jonas said. "C'mon, I know where the best ones are."

Fred's hand closed around Madison's bicep. "Not you. I wanted to ask you something."

"Sounds ominous," Jonas said. Fred momentarily wondered if letting her friend go on a smoothie run with a vampire was smart, but her options were limited. And as before, she figured the chances of undead shenanigans were low. If push came to bite, Jonas was capable of handling himself. Insecure homophobes often took his extreme metrosexuality for homosexuality. This sometimes led to shoving matches escalating into punching matches, at which point Jonas would draw on his black belt(s) and make them his metrosexual bitches.

Once they were down the stairs and deep in conversation

about shoes, have mercy, Fred turned her full attention to Madison.

"Oboy." Madison wouldn't meet her gaze. "Here you go with the yelling, I bet."

"Not too much," Fred lied. "Look, I get that you were in a huge jam and I know you were scared, but would you please explain what possessed you to bring vampires into this? The queen of them, no less! I understand your mom wanting to help you, but sending us a vampire was not the way." Wait. Sending *a* vampire? Fred flashed back to Betsy and the gorgeous imposing guy outside the NEA. He'd been trying to make a call and Betsy had been trying not to punch him. When she didn't know them, she compared them to apex predators. *Mrs. Fehr sent us vampires, plural. That was her solution. Christ.* Followed by, *One of the vampires she sent keeps remarking on the other vampire's lack of sanity. Christ twice.* "You mom couldn't control the situation from New York. They could have turned on us. In fact, Betsy *did* turn on me."

"She didn't; she didn't know you were my fr—you were someone I knew. It's not turning on them if they don't know you're one of the good guys."

"Big risk," she warned. "Especially with lives not your own. Right? And if your mom's on the coast and Betsy's in Minnesota, how did you—or your mom—even know her? Just because I'm half UF doesn't mean I automatically know the life story of every other UF on the planet. So how could your mom know about Betsy's history? Or even that she died and came back?"

"History?"

"Yes, Madison, history: events that happened before." *If you don't kick-start your neurons and start thinking, this is gonna take longer than it already has, and then I will fucking kill myself, but I'll take you with me, I swear it on your dead mom's name*, I will take you with me and maybe Betsy and her insane husband, too.

"Oh, there was this whole thing," Madison said, looking (Fred would have thought it was impossible) vaguer than usual.

"There was a thing?"

"Mm-hmm, in the papers or whatever . . . I guess all this happened in Minnesota and mama's friends kept her in the loop. Mama's got contacts all over the world."

"Which makes sense; she's had centuries to cultivate them. Go on."

"I guess Betsy's stepmother made like she was dead. Or maybe Betsy was the one playing the prank . . . it was this whole thing a couple of years ago, and everybody was upset"— Madison was making vague gestures that matched her vague expression—"and my mom read about it, or heard about it, or something, and ended up getting in touch with her. All because she thought Betsy was dead."

"She *was* dead."

"Funny how things work out, huh?"

"Hilarious."

"Her stepmother—Betsy called her the Bug, or something— she was pretty bitchy. Maybe she told people Betsy was dead to be mean? Dunno. Maybe Betsy told people she was dead because she wanted to fool the Bug."

"Okay, as far as origin stories go, that was pretty bad." She should have guessed Madison wouldn't have sufficient details. Fred's curiosity was now bing-bonging away like Big Ben. "You know, when this is over, I'd love to sit all the parties down and have a round-table session for the better part of a week."

"Sure," the young woman said dully. "You'll want to talk to my mom, just like the Folk want to talk to you. You'll want to talk to Betsy; my mom will, too. She'll have to; I don't think she's paid tribute, but since the queen's helping me—"

"That remains to be seen. All she's done is use me as her skeleton key and chug smoothies."

"Well. Everyone's gonna talk to everyone else, and I'll just . . ." She shrugged and trailed off.

Exasperated, Fred gently shook Madison's shoulder. "Knock it off, Madison. You're a rich, gorgeous young woman who's probably had a zillion boyfriends while at the same time have never had a pimple. You're not invisible, for God's sake."

Madison just looked at her.

Oh. Is that how it is? Is that's how it's been her whole life? Over-looked in the face of her no-doubt fascinating mother? Doors open because of her no-doubt fascinating mother, but once Madison is inside, she disappears? Again and again and again?

Does she wonder, sometimes, if she can ever stand out? Orphans . . . her dead mother took in orphans. Madison's not the oldest nor the youngest; just one of a crowd of foundlings a dead woman pitied.

Fred quit shaking her. "I'm sorry," she said quietly, and did not let herself look away from the single tear that rolled down Madison Fehr's perfect cheek.

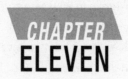

CHAPTER
ELEVEN

Madison pulled herself back together, which was excellent, as Fred had few talents, and comforting crying women was not one of them. So as Jonas and Betsy came back up the stairs, Jonas holding smoothies and Betsy on her cell, Fred eavesdropped. Which was simple, since Betsy's voice had all the hushed modulation of an auctioneer on crack.

"Sinclair, it's the coolest place! We've gotta come here once we get things cleared up; you will *love* it. You can get a smoothie and a lobster roll and a bowl of soup and a salad and a cream puff and licorice and sushi and a steak *in the same building*. Well. *We* can't, but you know what I mean." She held the phone away and called to Fred. "Our Founding Fathers invented the food court! And also democracy."

"Try to stay calm." But again, she couldn't help smiling to hear the exuberant blonde rhapsodize about the city she loved best. *Funny how I had to face moving to the other side of the planet to finally appreciate my home. My true home, with my mom's people.*

She would never have fit in beneath the Caspian Sea, pretending to co-rule the Undersea Folk. And she had never quite fit in on land, either. She belonged to not belonging and, as she had deduced right around the time she killed her father, likely always would. Funny how a realization that had seemed so awful at the time hurt a little less each day.

"—anyway, I'm fine and I'll keep you posted, and listen, do you know anything about this we're-here-we're-mermaids-get-used-to-it thing? Because—what? You do? Well, way to keep me in the loop, dude! We gotta talk about this . . . Yeah, I know I've had other things on my mind, but I could have . . . What? . . . No, I should not watch more news; I get enough bad news from whatever contractor has to give me an estimate on how to fix whatever thing we broke that day. Why would I want to hear about ever more death and despair, and fishing-opener advisories and state fair coverage? 'Tonight on KARE Eleven: people suck.' Pass . . . Sorry, I didn't catch—no I do *not* want to talk to the babies and, as I've mentioned several times before *and* after you went insane, *they are not babies!*" She glanced at Fred. "I gotta go; the mermaid's here and she looks pissed about—no, wait, that's just the way her face is . . . Yeah, that's right, I said *mermaid*, I've been hanging out with one all night and I'm not telling you one other thing. Love you."

"So now what?" Jonas asked. "We could spend hours making the haters list longer, but—"

"I'm not gonna be much help if we're gonna keep on with listing names," Betsy pointed out. "And I want to. I think Madison here got a raw deal, and no matter how unpleasant and awful Fred is, she doesn't deserve this kind of hassle."

"Thank you," she said dryly. "That was your husband, right? He was outside with you earlier tonight. The tall dark-haired man?"

"Mmm-hmm." Betsy fluttered her eyelashes. "Isn't he dreeeeeeamy?"

"I guess. He's a vampire, too?"

"Yep."

"And since you're the queen, that makes him the king?"

"Sure."

"Gosh." Jonas faux sighed. "Boston's soooo lucky! My horoscope didn't so much as hint at any of this today. *Avoid situations with money*, that's what I got. Thanks for nothing, universe."

"Isn't it dangerous to just . . . you know."

"Out ourselves as blood suckers?" Betsy teased.

"Well. Yeah."

"We're trying things different than the last guy. This is the information age, the twenty-first century, and it's time for vampires to actually live in the real world with the rest of the real world. Does that make sense?"

Madison and Jonas nodded; Fred did not.

"Just . . . take my word for it. A different way of running all things vampire was called for, so we're giving it a go. If it doesn't work, we can always go back to the skulking-in-dark-alleys, sleeping-in-coffins way of life. Yawn. And while we're throwing around personal questions, you're engaged, right?"

"Right." Fred glanced at Jonas, a little nervous. She hadn't planned on him showing up but he had. Now she could only hope he'd be so distracted by Madison's woes he wouldn't remember—

"*Which* reminds me."

Fred groaned and buried her head in her forearms.

"The *other* two reasons you're in town this week are to visit your mom, who actually misses you—weird, right? Yeah, but she's your mom, and just like with Cliff Clavin's mom on *Cheers*, nature dictates there be a bond."

"What's *Cheers*?" Madison ventured.

"Old TV show . . . The second reason you're in town is to meet with me and get more wedding stuff done. Now obviously Madison's little strange-men-tried-to-kill-me-and-will-stop-at-nothing-until-Fred's-dead-too thing comes first, but only just. So to answer your question, Fred's not only engaged (again), she's getting married in six months."

"Justice of the peace," Fred said, trying not to cave in to despair. "No cakes. No dresses. No churches. No pastors. A judge and a piece of paper. And then Legal's."

"*No way.*" Jonas turned to Betsy. "She was gonna marry a prince. Artur of the Undersea Folk, right? And have a royal wedding—which she was *letting me plan*—before jetting off to the other side of the planet to live in the Caspian Sea, where she wondered why her Kindle wasn't working. And I was gonna get to plan a royal wedding! But noooo, she decides she's in love with a romance novelist—"

"No!" Betsy gasped, hanging onto Jonas's every (shrill) word.

"—dumps the prince—a perfectly nice guy, by the way—chucks all the old wedding plans, and thinks her mom and I are gonna let her do the justice-of-the-peace thing for fiancé number two."

"Maybe I'll get killed by the guys Madison ran into," Fred said, brightening. "Then no weddings."

"Wouldn't that be great? Dare to dream. But first things first. Madison's mom asked me to come, which I was fine with, since I'm a warm, cuddly, hands-on undead monarch. I've got a responsibility to my subjects, and also apparently their adopted daughters. So devoted to duty am I, I didn't hesitate after I realized where the John Fluevog store was."

"What?"

Jonas's eyebrows arched into blond, horizontal parentheses. "Oh ho."

"Oh ho what?" Fred asked. "What is a Fluevog?"

Betsy's eyebrows were doing their own arching back at Jonas. "I'm betting you know where Newbury Street is, huh?"

Fred snorted. "It's his Graceland." Newbury Street was one of Boston's older streets, crammed with ever more expensive boutiques and restaurants. Wikipedia dubbed it one of the most expensive streets in the world, as it was strewn with shops for Ralph Lauren, Donna Karan, Marc Jacobs, Chanel, and Armani, to name a few. It was beloved by locals as well as tourists. Fred wouldn't go there if someone stuck a gun in her ear.

"I would very much like to see John Fluevog's John Fluevog store. And we've been at this for hours, with no end in sight."

"So we should quit and go look at shoes?" Fred snapped. "Be serious."

"Shoes, wedding gowns, whatever." Jonas shrugged.

"Don't even joke about that!"

"I'd never, Fred. Also, John-John loves my toned blond ass."

"And that's relevant . . . how, exactly?" *Why are you asking when you're afraid of the answer? Why are you asking someone who always answers your questions when you're afraid of the answer?*

"Because I did him the favor of his life not even five years ago. But it's sorta confidential."

"Introduced him to his wife?" Betsy guessed.

"Took a bullet for him?" Fred ventured.

"Got him off marshmallow peeps?"

"Eww, no. I cured him of his dandruff with my own home brew, and he's in my debt forever, or until I decide to quit Aveda and design my own hair products, so he can pay me back by financing my independent shop."

In response to Betsy's puzzled expression, Fred added, "Jonas is a chemical engineer; he designs shampoos and lotions and other smelly stuff for Aveda and now has found the cure for dandruff in shoe designers."

"Wow!"

Fred was pleased Betsy was impressed with her friend, then annoyed to be pleased.

"Are you single?" The vampire plunged ahead when he started to answer. "Because I've got the perfect guy for you. The perfect guy. Really cute, really smart—a doctor. Takes things like vampire roommates and the Antichrist popping over for smoothies totally in stride."

"I'm sorry, but—"

"The zombie thing? We're working on it. With it, I guess. Listen, he can't die because he is already. Dead, I mean. So you'll always have a date! Until *you* die."

"Wow, so, so tempting, but I have to plan Fred's wedding. Not just plan her wedding, Planning Fred's Wedding, Take Two. And then . . . what was it? Oh, right. Get married myself. To a woman. Who I love. Who's alive."

"Oh." Her face fell. "Well, congratulations, I guess."

Fred sighed. "How come the weird ones are always taken?"

Jonas gave Betsy's hand a quick pat. "Well, anyway. Even as late as it is, I *might* be able to arrange for a visiting vampire queen to check out the hippest shoe store in a five-hundred-mile radius at, say, midnight."

"Wait, now we're shoe shopping?" Fred snapped. "Forget it."

"Fine, we'll shop for wedding gowns instead. There's actually a gown shop right next to his store. What are the odds, I ask you? I'm getting chills. The gods want us to go to Newbury Street with our American Express cards tonight! That's what all this is for! And also, saving Madison from killers."

A long silence, broken by Fred's weary, "Fine. Shoes. God help me. But first, Madison, I need to see all the e-mails and online correspondence you had with the would-be killers. Which I probably should have thought to ask for first. And we should all get descriptions of the guys in question . . . the other thing I should have thought of first." Fred wished she could blame the vampire's brain snatch on how amateur her response had been, but the truth was Fred had shaken off Betsy's mojo hours ago. The problem was, too much had been thrown at her in too short a time. Another problem: they weren't cops. They had no lawful authority. They were in over their heads, and not by inches. By entire fathoms. Which reminded her . . .

"Is there a reason we're not giving full reports to the police and having them look into this? Yeah, our little group is made up of things like vampires and mermaids and chemical engineers and rich wards of ancient vamps—"

"Sounds like we could be out in the world solving crimes. I always wanted my own Mystery Machine," Jonas commented.

"—but we have no lawful authority. Do you know how to make a citizen's arrest? I don't."

Betsy shook her head. "If you tell the police even a tenth of the truth, they'll lock you up. You'll end up in a psych ward somewhere with a Valium drip."

"God, that'd be great." Fred sighed, and Madison nodded.

"Of course it would be great, but it doesn't get anything done. And it leaves poor Madison even more exposed."

"And we don't want Madison exposed," Jonas said. Then: "That was less lewd in my head, and more protective."

"So, what?" Betsy spread her hands. "We've gotta go somewhere, but we don't know where, and we've gotta do something, but we don't know what, and we've gotta find bad guys, but we don't know who. Hell, I barely know where I am; I don't know this part of the country at all. I took a cab from our hotel so I wouldn't have to pahk—"

"Don't," Jonas and Betsy warned in unison.

"—the cah in Hahvahd yahd." The vampire beamed. "Don't

I sound legit? Like I've lived in Boston my whole life and for a while after my death? I sound wicked smaht!"

"We *hate* that," Jonas said, and Fred nodded. Her saying she hated something was nothing new; it might make a stronger impression if someone as easygoing as Jonas said it. "Every goddamned tourist in the world thinks it's hilarious, and they all trot it out, usually when we're trapped with them on a subway car. And they're awful at it. And have you noticed Fred and I don't drop our *r*s?"

"I was a little let down," Betsy confessed. "I figured you'd be dropping them all over the place."

Fred tapped the table to direct Betsy's attention to her. "I mean, do *you* guys like it when HBO reruns *Fargo* and half the world thinks everyone in Minnesota talks in this here kind of accent, then? And then when yer talkin' in that there kinda accent and sayin', 'Yah, you betcha' alla time with those big head nods, d'you like that there? Or not so much, then?"

"I'm very, very sorry," the vampire said at once. Betsy was the picture of contrite. "You're right. It's awful. We should all just move to North Carolina, then. They've got that there nice southern accent, like syrup, then."

"Well, all right," Fred said, magnanimous in her triumph. "But we're getting off course, again. Madison, I'll need those e-mails, and also—what did these guys look like? How many were there?"

Madison was again unable to look her in the eye, so she stared over her shoulder instead.

"Come on, it's all right," Betsy said kindly. "Like everyone else at this table—in this building, in this city, even—hasn't gotten in over their head? We all have—hell, over my head is the norm in my part of the world. So how do we find the turds who wanna rid the world of the anti-Ariel?"

"Do *not* call me—"

"Three of them are here now," Madison whispered, still staring over Fred's shoulder.

CHAPTER
TWELVE

"Don't look!" Madison hissed.

Too late. "Oh, what fresh hell is this?" Fred muttered, trying to stare without staring.

"They're here? That's them? Yesssss!" Betsy pumped her fist. "What luck! Let's go get 'em."

As Fred tried not to gape at the vampire with admiration, Jonas shook his head. "Luck isn't the first word that popped into my brain," he said, also trying to look without looking.

"Jonas, please get Madison the fuck out of here right now," Fred said, keeping a smile on her face and projecting *I'm not worried, I'm not worried, what bad guys?* as hard as she could. "Go somewhere safe; do *not* linger."

"Madison, have I mentioned the deplorable state of your split ends? I know," he said, rising and cutting her off before she could speak, "you've had other things on your mind. But accidentally setting up your old boss to be murdered and then getting your mom to send the king and queen of the vampires to town to hang out in Faneuil Hall drinking smoothies is no excuse. So we're off to a friend's salon. Sure it's late, and sure we're exhausted, but your *hair*, Madison, your *hair*. Did I mention the friend's wife is a homicide detective for our fair city? I'm thinking at least three inches off the ends." Jonas unhurriedly strolled with Madison toward the exit opposite the approaching bad guys. Fred had to admire the sheer slickness of the man. She knew he was afraid and she knew he didn't want to leave her. But he also knew Madison was the most vulnerable . . . and the most frightened. *I might only have one friend, but he's a keeper. Better one Jonas than a thousand friends not half as wonderful.*

"He would have been *so* perfect for my dead doctor." Betsy sighed.

"How many brains can you hijack at once?"

"Uh, sorry? Oh. Oh!" Betsy was watching the men approach, looking as unconcerned as Fred was—she hoped. "Mojo, you mean. Um . . . one?"

"That leaves me with two."

"Good work, Dr. Bimm! You're, like, soooo good at math."

"You realize when you talk like that you make my ears bleed, right?"

"I didn't before; I guess it's, like, a bonus."

Fred groaned. *Vampires channeling valley girls. Maybe I'll luck out and these three will kill us. Death can't be worse than this whole awful evening.*

The men approached, taking their time. Dressed, Fred

thought gloomily, for ass kicking: casual pants, pressed polo shirts (one in indigo blue, one in brown, one in black), dark socks, loafers. They all had cell phones clipped to their belts, but Fred could see no guns. Their hair color ranged from blond to brown, and all sported military-short haircuts. Two of them had dark eyes; the shortest brunette (short being relative; they were all at least six feet) had blue eyes. All were trim and muscular; they moved like a team. They had done things together. Probably a lot of things.

Soldiers, Fred realized, feeling her heart drop to her ankles. *Some kind of soldiers; these are not random baddies. Tell me an entire army doesn't want me dead. Bad enough the entire staff at the downtown Y wants me dead . . .*

"We were looking for your friend, Dr. Bimm," the one in the black shirt said politely. *Dark colors to blend at night. And in this part of town, those nicey-nice tourist outfits, that's practically a uniform. No one would look twice.* "What luck to find you, too."

"Super-duper-awesome-great good luck," Fred said without a trace of a smile. *Keep them here and off Jonas.* "Why don't you three go fuck yourselves and leave us alone? And go to hell and drop dead and any other disrespectful thing you don't want me to say in front of your boyfriends. Don't worry. We'll wait. Make a list."

"You'll wait; I don't have all night. Besides, all the food stalls are closed now," Betsy added. "You can't get so much as a glass of milk. What good is Nathaniel Hall without the food?"

"*Faneuil* Hall," Fred corrected her sharply.

"Are you sure? Because that name makes *no* sense."

"Of course I'm sure, I've lived here most of—"

"We've got team members scooping up your friend and Ms. Fehr," the blond, brown-eyed chap in the middle said, soooo politely. "And we know your other friend has been with you half the night, hearing all sorts of things that should never have come out of your big mouth, so she'll need to come with us, too."

"Awwww, you picked me!" Betsy turned to Fred. "This is *so* much better than high school. I never got picked first for Phys Ed. This is like high school with goons and guns."

"Shut your mouth!" Fred wanted to punch Black Shirt as much as she wanted to scream; she indulged in the latter for now. "This woman is not my friend!"

"And now you've ruined it." The vampire sighed. "This part is also like high school."

Brown Shirt's phone buzzed, and he and his two buddies smiled. *It's a signal; they've got Jonas. Fuck.*

"Take them," Black Shirt said, sounding almost bored. "Right now."

"That's just right," Fred began, but stopped when Betsy laid a hand on her arm.

"Don't get your fins in a bunch, Fred. I've got this. Okay, asshats, too bad for you that I'm as badass as I am hot-looking, because now you're in for—"

"Just . . . stop." Fred took three steps, passed Betsy on the right, and in less than a blink had flanked and seized Black Shirt by the collar and twisted. His yelpish bark ("Blaayarrk!") startled almost everyone in their little group. She shoved him back, hard, and didn't have to watch to see he'd gone sailing past the tables and over the railing to crash with a horrid *thud* on the hard floor one story below.

Even now it had been less than a moment, so she had all the time in the world to turn and dodge Indigo Shirt's hand, his fingers stiffened to chop. She grabbed said stiff fingers and twisted, smiling a little at his pained yowl; then she forced his elbow to bend the wrong way, and smiled wider when his howl abruptly stopped as he passed out. She felt a blow land on her left shoulder and kicked back; the last one flew into their now-empty chairs so hard the chairs imploded on impact.

"Whoa." Betsy was staring. "Chairs don't bust up like that except in the movies. Eww, he's got wood stuck to him—in him—everywhere, he's—Oh my God, he's got a splinter in his *eye*! *What* eye, ha-ha. Um, will you think less of me if I throw up now?"

"Stop talking. Must you preface every single thing you do with nauseating endless speculative continual monologues?"

"So, you know, boys," Betsy said, staring. "Let that, uh, be a lesson to you. All three of you. When you wake up. If you wake up." The vampire seemed pleased. "I almost never get saved, y'know? I usually have to do the saving. This trip to Boston, it's like a vacation for me."

"How wonderful for you," Fred snarled, seizing her wrist and dragging her toward the far exit. "Come on, some of their goons have got Jonas."

"I'm guessing all that swimming around in the deep ocean depths makes you ferociously strong as well as ferociously grouchy? You're kind of an effortless badass." Betsy was, thank goodness, allowing herself to be dragged. In fact, Fred was moving so quickly the other woman's feet occasionally left the floor. "It's great."

"What?"

"It's the effortlessness that makes it *really* cool," she said cheerfully.

"I just want this night to end," Fred groaned.

"Not me! It just got interesting."

CHAPTER THIRTEEN

"They underestimated you," Betsy said as Fred flew through the exit door and raced for the emergency stairs. "Not just a little. They underestimated you by yards and yards. I did, too, which was pretty dumb of me. You did sort of make me fly through the fish warehouse with the greatest of ease. And you're smart, too—a doctor! But not a real one."

Argh. She has a natural gift for hitting all of my buttons. Since when does a PhD in anything but *medicine means you're not a real doctor?*

Incredibly, she was still babbling as Fred hurtled toward the stairs. "Okay, sure, you're smarter than me and prettier—maybe a *little* prettier—but—"

"I am not prettier than you."

"Quit it! I hate when pretty girls act like we don't know we're pretty. They don't, is what I meant. When *they* act like they don't know."

Ah! These go down to the street, and Jonas has to be at the end of the street. "Absurd. You look like you fell off a *Vogue* runway. Can you handle a three-story fall?"

"Well, yeah, in the sense that it won't kill me, but it'll still sting like—shit!"

Fred threw her over the railing, grabbed the same railing, and vaulted over. As the street rushed up to them she heard, "You suuuuuuuuuuuuck!"

All the way down.

Fred landed hard and couldn't keep her feet, but managed to roll with the impact. When she stood, her feet and ankles ached horribly but nothing was broken. She'd gotten more from her father than the tail—the strength and the dense bones—for which she was often annoyed but tonight was thankful.

"You are too pretty!" Betsy was flailing in garbage. "And that was a shitty thing to do to a guest!"

"Not my guest," Fred muttered, looking for Jonas. "And once you get the garbage out of your hair, you'll be pretty again."

"That's a lie and you know it."

From around the corner, an aggrieved shriek: "You're both hags! Shut up!"

"Wow." Betsy had climbed to her feet and was brushing coffee grounds off her clothes. "He's almost as bitchy as my zombie."

"What?"

"My doctor, I meant. He gets shrill when he's tired, too."

"Your doctor zombie." Fred sighed. So many questions. But maybe she should keep some to herself. At once she felt shame; proximity to the vampire queen was turning her into a mental and moral coward with all this I-don't-want-to-know and keep-me-out-of-it nonsense. And even knowing that, understanding that, did not make her want to discuss zombies with the fanged blonde.

She shook off the thoughts and raised her voice. "Be right there, Jonas!" So he hadn't been picked up by the baddies . . . that was good. He hadn't sounded under duress, which was better—not in imminent danger of being shot or plummeting three stories. She assumed Madison was also all right—Jonas was, at heart, a gentleman, and wouldn't leave a lady in distress if someone kneecapped him with a ball peen hammer. "Idiot."

"Yeah, these bad guys . . . sooo rude. They could at least call first if they're gonna show up and beat their chests and then let you go through them like a band saw through a hot dog."

Heh. "I meant Madison. She's the reason I'm—we're all—in this mess. And for what? Because she doesn't get enough attention at home? Christ."

"Aw, come on." Betsy was wobbling, then her steps became more sure. Fred had no idea how, but the blonde had managed to kick off her beautiful shoes during her shrieking plummet to the street, then find them again (in the dark—the closest street light was a block south) and slip them back on, and was now keeping pace as Fred hurried through the alley. "She's just a kid. Just like you were once and just like I was once—Shit! These cobblestones are a bitch."

"She's a grown woman, she's been the legal drinking age for years, and even if she wasn't, I'm not her mother, and even if I was, *she's a grown woman.*"

"I need to meet her mother," Betsy said in the tone of someone making a mental to-do list.

"Yeah, and Madison's mom, frankly, should be the one getting jumped in Faneuil Hall and mind-raped in the Aquarium."

"And my husband should still be sane and every member of the Kardashian family should be indicted, arrested, and executed. It's not a perfect world. She's your responsibility, and bitching about it won't help."

"She's not!"

"Come on." Fred's eyes had quickly adjusted to the dark—another genetic gift from the Folk, as it was pretty damned dark at the bottom of the ocean. So she could see Betsy's wry expression, and was startled at how pale she was—even for her. "She's in this mess because she looks up to you."

"She's in this mess," Fred said firmly, "because she's an idiot."

Betsy was getting still paler. Fred had a sudden suspicion that she was one of those people who went white when they were pissed. *If she's dead—undead—how does her blood even circulate? When she's pale does it mean she's mad or hungry or what? I've killed at least one man, maimed two others, and am now jogging down a dark alley with a hungry vampire I might be pissing off. I have a genius for getting into these situations.*

"How often do you need to fe—"

Betsy cut her off. "Again: you've got to help her fix it. You. Not Jonas and not her mom—though I think she could have come to town in addition to asking me to come, but that's a chat for another night. No matter how much they annoy you, no matter how big a pain in your ass they are, you're in it, Fred."

"They?"

"Sure."

"Oh ho. It's like that?"

The vampire made a gesture; half shrug, half frustration.

"Do you think I came back from the dead overjoyed to discover I was responsible for thousands and thousands of people, whether they were awful and needed to be stopped, or victimized and needed my help? Or just minding their own business and sucking on stray cats and not bothering anybody? Come on. God's got a wicked sense of humor, putting me in charge. But I'll tell you what I learned, Fred; what I'm still learning. Bitching and moaning about it just makes everything take longer." She paused. "If you meet my husband, never tell him I said that."

Fred wasn't moved to laugh. If anything, she wanted to cry. "I didn't want any of this. I didn't ask for *any* of this!"

The queen's eyes went wide. "You think that's relevant? That you didn't ask for this? Christ, it's the least relevant thing ever! It doesn't matter that you don't want it and it doesn't matter that you don't deserve it and it doesn't matter that you don't have the time or the authority or the willpower; *you have to fix this.*" Suddenly realizing she'd been almost screaming, Betsy cleared her throat and walked faster.

Fred hurried to keep pace. "Is it possible you're projecting on me, just a little?"

"Oh, sure," she admitted. "Also, I'm a flaming hypocrite."

They trotted in silence for a few seconds. "They're really counting on me to get them through this, aren't they?"

"Yep."

"Why? I'm not—look at me! When I don't have a tail, I'm not special. Frankly, now that the Folk have outed themselves and the world knows there are millions of people with tails, I'm not special all over again. I—I kind of liked that." Ironic: Madison only wanted to be seen. Fred wanted anything *but* to be seen.

Betsy shrugged. "The people around you would disagree. I've been telling the ones around me that I'm the poster child for Ordinary Citizens Who Happen to Be Dead, but they won't listen. I know we should be glad they see us as heroes, but I find it scary, sometimes."

"Scary," Fred said, "is the exact right word."

"Uncanny, right? No matter how much I fuck up, the people who love me see me as important and competent and non-fuckup-ey. It's so weird and sad."

Fred snorted a laugh through her nose; she couldn't help it. Then they rounded the last corner and found Jonas and Madison in the custody of four more Polo Shirt Gangsters.

"Oh, look at this," Betsy said, trying to comb something black and viscous out of her hair with her fingers. "It's a whole rainbow of bad guys. The Skittles Gang."

"The prof advises police and ambulance are rolling," Green Shirt said, putting his phone back on his belt.

"Those are the magic words. Let's go," Red Shirt replied.

"What about our guys?" Other Red Shirt said.

"Fuck 'em. They were warned about the hybrid; if they were dumb enough to jump her without neutralizing her from a distance, they deserve all the months of traction."

"And also, the morgue," Fred said demurely. She'd said it to gauge their reactions, and was rattled when none of the Skittles Boys so much as made a sad face. *Great. Not just soldiers; committed men who value the team as a whole, not the individuals in the team. Maybe we'll really, really luck out and they'll be religious fanatics as well!*

"Are you okay?" Fred murmured to Jonas, who had the beginnings of a black eye.

"Sure. There *were* five of them."

"That's my boy."

"And you or Betsy or I should definitely kill both Red Shirts," he added darkly, glaring at both Red Shirts. "To let them live is spitting in the face of decades of sci-fi television fantasy tradition."

"Aw, man. Are you sure you're straight and happily in love with a live woman?" Betsy asked. "Because, seriously, you would *love* my zombie friend."

"Tempting," Jonas commented with a wry look at Fred, "but I'll pass."

"Not that I'm complaining, because I'm glad you're both alive, but why didn't you . . . uh . . ." *Signal there were bad guys around? Or run? Or scream for help so we wouldn't have just blundered right into you? Or something?*

Through long acquaintance, Jonas knew what she was truly asking and shook his head. "You wanna go where they wanna take us, Fred, and right now. Trust me."

She sighed. "More bad guys?"

"And a doomsday device."

"What?" Fred nearly screamed.

"Yeah, you heard me, an actual doomsday device. What's that black stuff all over your shoes? Toner from office garbage?" he asked Betsy.

"What?" she nearly screamed.

"Yeah, you heard me."

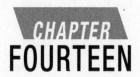

CHAPTER
FOURTEEN

The Skittles Boys marched them silently and efficiently back to the NEA, not answering their questions or rising to their taunts. Since Jonas and Betsy were gold-medal taunters, that was something Fred found most ominous of all. Despite the balls-up at Faneuil Hall, it bespoke of the men's (and where were the Skittles Girls?) professionalism.

As it was late, the area was nearly deserted. There were a few—a very few—people on the street, mostly coming late to the nearby hotel. Fred considered, and rejected, screaming for help. Doomsday device? Mermaids, vampires? Polo Shirts? Bad guys dressed like Skittles? *If* someone heard their cries and *if* someone took them seriously and called a cop and *if* Dispatch sent a unit, they'd all still be inside the NEA by then, and nobody would be able to stop the bad guys, or save the good guys, in time.

Besides, Fred suspected what was happening inside was private Folk business. And possibly private vampire business.

Betsy's thoughts (such as they were) must have been along the same lines, as she suddenly piped up, "Wow, it's like a buddy movie crammed with the supernatural."

"This is *not*. For one thing, we have no lawful authority. For another, we live half a country apart (for which I will always be thankful). Also, I loathe you. Not buddy-movie loathing. I loathe you like famine. I loathe you like war."

"No, you don't," the vampire replied with grating cheer. "Your bitchiness is purely surface bitchiness. Inside you're like a big old gooey . . . I dunno . . . jellyfish? Help me out, marine biologist. A big old gooey glop of caviar? A big old—Where'd you get that?"

Betsy's sharp digression startled everyone, but Other Red Shirt slid the key card through the lock without pause, and opened the door.

Jonas turned to Madison, who'd been silently (thank God) crying during the last of the walk. Orange Shirt (Betsy also referred to him as Sunkist) had impersonally collected their phones, and Madison, frightened at the thought of losing the line between her mother and herself, had clutched it for a few panicky seconds. Jonas had gently coaxed her into giving it up and had been holding her hand and murmuring comforting things like, "As fast as tech moves, it's actually gotten outdated since suppertime and you need to get a new one." Betsy had surrendered hers with a bit more grace: "But how will I know what the weather is in Istanbul? Or when my FB stats get updated?

Or which restaurants deliver after midnight? Or how much Plymouth Rock weighs? Also, I occasionally use it as a telephone."

Now, watching the bad guys deftly get through the electric lock, Jonas cocked his head, puzzled. "I thought you got your purse back."

"I did." Madison sniffed. "Just the money was gone."

"Let's see." Betsy started counting off on her long fingers. "Bad guy conspiracy, check. Henchmen, check. Funding—obvious from the uniforms and your cute matching phones—check. Doomsday device, whatever the fuck that is—check. Plan to steal NEA employee's key card without her knowing that's what you're doing—check. Tech to copy keycard and return purse to further confuse said employee—check. Plan to keep said employee and anyone she might call away from the fish warehouse—check."

All night. We were sitting around all night making a list, *for God's sake, when we could have been here, maybe putting a stop to this shit well before the bad guys expected us to show up.*

"I like you better when you're ditzy," Fred muttered, following her into the building.

"You're the only one," she admitted.

"You mean they didn't want to kill me? They just rilly, rilly needed my ID and stuff to get in?"

"Check," a new voice said, and they all looked around, and then down. "As if we could mistake the Fehr heir for a talking sardine."

A white man in his midsixties, sitting painfully straight in his wheelchair, rolled quietly toward them. He had long gray hair pulled back in a ponytail that, if free, would have reached down his back; his beard was short and carefully shaped, covering his upper lip and chin but none of his neck. He was wearing a crisp white dress shirt, black slacks rolled to show both legs were missing below the knee, and a navy blue tie embroidered with bright red peace signs. On the left armrest of his chair was a shiny green sticker: "Whales are people, too!"

"Oh, good God," Betsy groaned. "Save me from aging hippies."

Fred, whose mother was one, said nothing, but smiled a little.

"My name is Hedley Ran and I don't know you," he told Betsy, and Fred noticed his back never touched the back of the wheelchair. "Or you, sir." Dismissing Jonas with barely a glance. "I know you, miss, through your insipid letters and lies. And I know your friend."

I'm not Madison's . . . grrrr.

"I will not speak with the fish," the old man said. "So you tell her for me, girl, tell her she and her school of friends are done. Because of me."

Jonas cleared his throat politely. "Sorry, just to clarify here so Madison can correctly pass on your message, did you mean *school friends* or *school of*—"

"It's a fish insult," Fred explained. She rolled her eyes at Hedley Ran. "He probably thinks he's being subtle. And so he is, compared to any of us. Which is still pretty unsubtle."

"Tell the fish I'll use her coworkers and her research and her beloved NEA to destroy her 'people.'"

"The fish can hear you fine, and is fluent in English," Fred informed him. "You really think you're special, huh? You are not. You're just another bigot. There's a zillion of you: blacks, Asians, Native Americans, Folk, you've always got somebody to fear and then to hate." She turned to her friends. "I've actually run into this before. Some of the idiots we're stuck sharing the planet with think that because the Folk have tails and scales, we're not human and, ergo, can be treated like pets instead of citizens. There's been talk of rounding us up and dumping us into concentration lakes."

Madison's eyes went wide and Jonas said, shocked, "You never told me that."

"Why would I? It's awful enough that I know it; I'd never bring you guys down with it."

"This isn't about bigotry," Ran insisted. "It's about the survival of our species."

"Um, technically that could be construed as bigotry, depending on how you define *survival* and *species*," Betsy began, but he cut her off.

"Before they flaunted themselves before the world, I knew her kind of old. They were smarter to stay hidden, to be the monsters in our nightmares, the kind we think aren't real in the light."

Fred very carefully did not look at Betsy, who *was* a monster of nightmares people thought weren't real in the light.

"I was born with two legs and when I married my wife I had two legs. Now I have none and my wife is dead and my unborn son with her."

"Oh my God!" She stared at the man, horror-struck.

"Truly," he agreed, allowing himself a small grim smile. "You didn't know what kind of monster you took to friend, did you?"

"I can't believe what I'm hearing! Fred, you bitch, what have you done?"

"Huh?" Fred asked, having no idea where Betsy was going with this.

Betsy shook a finger beneath Fred's nose and asked, as stern as a spinster schoolmarm, "Did you kill his wife and unborn son?"

"No."

"Do you *promise*?"

"Yes."

"Look, Fred, we're in kind of a bad situation here." Betsy slung an arm around her shoulders and led her a couple of steps away from the group. "Listen, this is serious. This poor guy's got a real problem. We owe him the truth, so just tell it straight, okay? I promise, whatever you did, we'll deal with it. So. One last time: did you kill this man's wife and unborn son?"

"I did not. I've never seen him before tonight."

She sighed in evident relief and turned back to Hedley Ran, whose smile had dropped off like it had been slapped away. The Skittles Boys were helpless in the face of severe vampire sarcasm. "There, see? It's okay. Everything's gonna—We can absolutely work through this. You don't have to worry: she's *not* the one who killed your wife and unborn son. Thank God, right? Total relief! Because that would have made for a super awkward work environment."

Fred was trying to lock the laughter in her throat, which was why she sounded like a water buffalo. Drowning.

"Is that supposed to be your idea of a jest, young lady?"

Quick as thought, Betsy dropped her bantering tone, and when she spoke, there was so much ice in her voice it made Fred shiver.

"Of course it's not a jest, you bitter pathetic asshat. Fred's right, you're not special. You're just another bigot sitting around chanting about race wars and revenge because your life is shit and you don't know why so the plan you came up with was to hate people you've never met. I don't know what's more amazing—that you can fool yourself in the face of simple common sense or that you can infect other people with your insanity." She flapped a hand at the Skittles Boys, disgusted. "Boston sucks."

"Don't blame the town!" Jonas yelped.

"She's right, though, it's stupid to blame an entire race for something one person did." Fred spoke quickly, the better to get Ran's attention back on her and off Betsy (and so as not to dwell on the irony of Betsy doing what she denounced Ran for). She didn't know what the vampire was going to do, but assumed her rant was part of a plan. "If one of my people was even responsible."

"All of your people were responsible!"

Fred blinked. *Mission accomplished. His attention is definitely back on me.* "Care to elaborate? No, don't bother. I don't care, is the thing. I really don't."

"Are you being this argumentative on purpose?"

"Count on it," Jonas said with a vigorous nod.

"If you're trying to stall because you think people can find you via your cell phones, or if any of you think to slink away and call for help—"

"Oh, hell no," Betsy said. "As a feminist, I hate calling for help. Plus it'd ruin everything. I've got a rep to consider."

"We're not stalling." Fred was pretty sure that was true. "We're also not impressed. This—whatever this is"—she waved a hand, encompassing Ran and his henchmen and the NEA building—"it all goes back to you thinking you're special. Not like anyone else. And see, it's a lie. *I'm* not like anyone else."

"Well, I'm not like anyone else, either," Betsy whined.

"Not now, Betsy. You—you're just an aging hippie with a superiority complex."

He opened his mouth but Fred cut him off. "Admit it. You think you can make decisions about hundreds of thousands of people because *you're* so uniquely superior. It's bad enough you really think you're special; what's worse is it's for the dumbest reasons imaginable. Because you're old but you have long clean hair. Because you need a wheelchair but you won't let yourself slump in it. And because in the sixties you thought unprotected sex meant you were deep, and bragging about a three-day booze-pot-shit fest in a field in New York State meant you actually did something. And you did do something: got high, and fucked in the shit. Not the mud. The shit."

"Woodstock was the defining moment of—"

"Of shit. They ran out of food, they ran out of water, they ran out of places to shit. Okay? Three days of starving and shitting. Women had miscarriages there, do you get that? *Babies died at Woodstock* but you're all still bragging about it like it was a plan. Like it was a good idea. You were right about one thing, though: Woodstock absolutely did define a generation.

"You Baby Booming idiots did one thing, *one thing*, to get yourselves noticed: a whole bunch of you got born between 1946 and 1964. And . . . that's it. That's what you did. And it's not even what *you* did. Your parents came home after driving Hitler to suicide and they all had simultaneous sex and then you guys were born. You've been coasting on your parents having simultaneous sex for going on *seventy years*."

Fred was starting to see little black spots blooming before

her eyes, evidence of a Type Three Shitfit. She staggered a little and Betsy reached out to steady her. "Are you all right?"

"My mom . . . was at Woodstock . . . and is a hippie . . ."

"I'm so sorry."

"You don't know . . . you just don't know how awful it was . . ."

"I do *now*. You should write children's books. *L'il Foxy and Friends Catch STDs While Fucking in Woodstock Shit*. Like that."

Hedley Ran had simply waited in his chair through Fred's rant, his pale cheeks getting more and more flushed. His posture improved, which she hadn't thought was possible. The Skittles Gang stood around waiting for orders, and Ran, when he saw she was done, obliged: "Kill her friend."

"Madison . . ." *Is not my friend*, Fred was about to say, when Red Shirt Two produced a pistol from somewhere and shot Betsy in the chest.

CHAPTER
FIFTEEN

Fred had never been prouder of her friends in her life (except Madison wasn't her friend). Their eyes widened, yes. Madison sucked in a breath; Jonas leveled a long stare of contempt at Ran. They didn't scream. They didn't cry. They didn't beg for their lives.

So, of course, she took her example from theirs, and simply looked at Hedley Ran the way a picnicker looks at a line of ants marching toward Potato Salad Hill: annoying, but no real threat. To Fred's intense pleasure, *Ran* was the one who seemed shaken and shocked.

The Skittles Boys were worse off, pale and sweating and their gazes darted here and there; none of them could settle on any one thing to look at. Betsy's crumpled body? Noooo. Madison's pale, sorrowful face, Jonas's contempt? Her own scorn? No and no and no.

"Oh, starting to sink in?" she asked. "It's real, boys. This isn't Final Fantasy XXXVVIII. That?" She pointed to Betsy's body. "The state of Massachusetts calls that felony murder and they get pissy about it. That's life without parole, and it's on all of you. I assume you've all got good lawyers on retainer? A cheap one in this town charges five hundred an hour." She had no idea what a lawyer, cheap or otherwise, charged, but five hundred sounded pricey. Their blanched expressions told her the shot had hit, hard. "I'm sure Ran here will happily foot the bill. Get it? Foot the bill? Because, in case you can't tell, he's got no feet."

"You see," Ran said quietly. "It cares nothing for its friends. It's not human, and it's wrong to treat it as one."

"You're the one who isn't human," Madison said quietly. She had cried silently, helplessly—but had stayed with them. Hadn't run or begged. Hadn't flinched away from the shot, from Betsy going down. "She didn't even know me and she wanted to help. You won't ever understand that kind of thinking. My mother tried to tell me about people like you." She shook her head. "I'm not a good listener."

"Shut up, cunt."

"Hey!" Fred seized Madison's wrist and pulled her behind her, shoving a pissed Jonas back with the other hand along with an I've-got-this glare. "You've got us all here, you're getting what you wanted. There's no reason to talk to her like that when you could be calling *me* a cunt."

"Yeah," Jonas spoke out, still hovering protectively near

Madison. "Fred's used to it; call her the cunt, the whore, the bitch, the shrew, the witch, the tart, the twat, but leave Madison alone!"

"Thank you, Dr. Bimm. And, uh, Jonas."

"My *friends* call me Fred, so you'd better start, Madison. There. There! You see what you've done to me?" she cried to the man in the chair. "You've made me befriend Madison Fehr! You evil bastard!"

"Enough of this." If Ran had been rattled earlier, he was getting himself back under control now. "We need to do the test and get rid of the witnesses, then move the device. In that order."

"That would be the doomsday device?" Fred asked. "When you're not blaming strangers for your wife's death and committing felony kidnapping and murder, do you sit around in your wheelchair watching old spy movies? Doomsday device. Christ."

"It will work," he insisted, answering Fred but speaking to Jonas. "Tell it to have no fears on that account."

"Fred, Ran says his machine's gonna work and not to worry about it or anything."

"I have tolerated its presence here long enough, hers and the other fish she takes to mate. Now is the reckoning I promised my wife, and *it* isn't the only one who will suffer."

"Fred, Ran says he'll get you, and your little dog, too."

She could have laughed to see confusion chasing anger across Ran's face. *He can't understand. He's got guns and thugs and a doomsday device and he's sure we're in his power and he can't understand why we will not take him seriously. And he never ever will. And that's the funniest fucking thing I've heard all day.*

"You won't laugh when it works," he hissed, rattled into speaking directly to Fred. "Doubting my design is a mistake."

"Oh, I'm sure it'll work, Dr. Ran. I'm absolutely certain your Doomsday Device will work. No problem there; your dooms-day device is going to be a mechanical marvel. That's not the issue with your doomsday device. I'm not worried about whether or not the doomsday device you've no doubt spent years build-ing will work. I'm concerned about your doomsday device because it's . . . you know. A *doomsday* device."

"It can make all the mockery it likes," Ran began.

"Thanks. You look embalmed. What's worse is I suspect this is actually a good day for you. And you still look wretched. She's dead." Pointing at the "corpse." "And she looks a lot better than you do."

"Oh, that." Ran looked down. "Throw that in the tank."

"Which one?" Fred asked, honestly interested. *Let's see, there are over seventy separate tanks on the main level alone, not counting—*

"The big one, of course. The one we need for the test."

Fred didn't like the sound of that at all.

CHAPTER
SIXTEEN

Betsy's dead body went in with the inevitable splash, and they all watched it sink. Fred thought she certainly looked dead, and from Jonas and Madison's expressions, they thought so, too. Pale, blanched. Blood-stained shirt. Eyes frozen open and staring, drifting down and down and down. *Please be alive, you Minnesotan blond bloodsucker; I would be losing my shit for real if I thought you were truly as dead as you looked.*

"Get on with the speech."

"What?" Hedley Ran asked, again startled into answering her directly.

She folded her arms across her chest and shook her head. "Oh, come *on*. You haven't gone to all this trouble, making nice with Madison to trick her out of her key cards and rounding us all up in here and dropping sly little hints you think are subtle about your doomsday device and going on about how I'm not human and will pay the price, blah-blah, you haven't set all this up to *not* tell me all about your evil genius plan and how we'll rue the day we killed your wife, except no one in this building, and I'm betting no one in this state, had anything to do with that, but what are mere facts to a mad scientist?"

Ran ignored *mad scientist*. "We needed your friend, yes. When my research was complete and the device was built, we needed a test site. The NEA was perfect for a number of reasons."

"It's a miniature ecosystem. It's a small, controllable version of what you want to do on a large scale," Fred said glumly, "so it's the perfect test site."

"Well, yes," Ran said, taken aback.

"Whatever you've built is going to do something to the oceans that won't thoroughly wreck the planet. Poison that doesn't affect landers, or high-secrecy sound waves, or . . . anything that will kill the Folk without killing the planet for who's left." She rubbed her forehead. "But you don't dare just unleash it on the world. Not without testing it first. Test it here, make sure it works the way you want, and at the same time you can destroy the building which housed the evil fish bitch who killed your wife and unborn son, except I didn't."

"Well, yes."

"Also wiping out all the witnesses."

"Well." Ran shrugged modestly.

Fred stared into the tank. For years, those fish and reptiles and mammals had been her responsibility. She kept a close eye on them, gauged their health, kept track of what they ate, noted any illnesses or unusual deaths. Yes, they could be a pain in the ass. Yes, she knew they disliked her and thought she could be more accommodating to their needs for '80s glam rock. But they were living creatures, they had feelings and fears and, if they had to live in captivity, she could at least make sure they were safe.

No matter how much they annoy you, no matter how big a pain in your ass they are, you're in it, Fred.

Great. Now she was hearing the vampire in her head.

"Hey!" she shouted, startling Ran so much that he slumped for a second. "Nobody kills off those little jerks but me! And since I wasn't planning on it, you don't get to, either."

"You can't stop it," Ran snapped. "The device is wired into the building's power grid. I control the device, and my men control—"

Even though Fred had been expecting something, her heart still lurched when the lights went out.

CHAPTER
SEVENTEEN

There were muffled sounds of a struggle, and she wasn't sure where the gun was, and Fred had less than a second to decide. So she dived at the source of all evil, and knocked Madison Fehr out of what she feared would be harm's way. *This only happened because we have an intern program at the NEA. Interns are the source of all evil. I have decided.*

She'd expected the shot but was still aghast at their stupidity—she could barely see, so she knew damned well Ran and his Skittles couldn't see *at all.*

And their decision is to shoot? They could just as easily hit each other!

"Just stay down," Fred said, and heard Madison's affirmative gasp. Not that the poor girl could move; Fred was sticking to her like sand on feet, reasoning that she could tolerate a bullet far better than Madison. Hell, she hadn't known fiancé number two even a month before he'd had to dig a bullet out of her shoulder. *Betsy's right: getting shot sucks. Maybe if we stay flat enough, I won't be.*

Fred's eyes had adjusted, though she knew the others were still blind. Jonas had somehow gotten to a Skittles Boy in the dark and incapacitated him, but now was standing, uncertain and trying to see.

"Get your ass on the floor!" she hissed. Stupid brave dumbass gentleman! These were just the sort of people who could get her killed. *"Down, down! All the way down, FLAT! Now don't move!"*

He obeyed at once, knowing she could see, but being Jonas, it wasn't in him to let the screaming go by. "Say it, don't spray it," he muttered to the tile, and Fred snickered.

Then she saw what was coming up behind Hedley Ran, and the laugh stuck in her throat.

It was Betsy, dripping wet and *pissed*, Betsy who had somehow swum up the side of the tank after floating along the bottom for fifteen minutes. Betsy had not only swum to the top unmolested by the sharks, but had slithered up and out of the water and over the side of the tank *without making a sound*, which Fred would have thought impossible, because moving water made noise. Still, the vampire had done it: she'd not only gotten out and gotten down, but she came up behind Ran, jerked him out of his chair, bent over him, and—

Ran screamed.

Once.

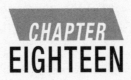

CHAPTER
EIGHTEEN

*The power came back on with non-dramatic ease. No flicker-*ing, no fumbling. No sinister bomb countdown. One second, they were trapped in the dark with a vampire, and then they were trapped in the light with a vampire.

He said the device was tied to the power, but someone cut the power. Now the lights are back on, which is either wonderful or terrible.

Betsy was standing over Ran's body, his blood smeared from her lips past her throat, her blood all over the front of her shirt. Ran looked like a pile of trash someone had crumpled and tossed.

"You guyth okay?"

"Depends," Fred muttered, rolling off Madison and stand-ing. "What's wrong with your voice?"

"Nothing. I thwear!" At Fred's glance, she shrugged. "My

fangths come out when I feed, thmell blood . . . like that. Taketh a minute to go back."

Fred started to laugh. A tension releaser, for sure; it had been a stressful evening. "But that's so absurd! It's the least suave sexy cool thing I've ever heard! TV vampires don't lisp!"

"That'th not my fault. Don't laugh, it'th a real problem," she complained.

"Sorry," Fred gasped between giggles. "So sorry!" She steadied herself and snorted one last giggle. "Sorry. Ask me how much I needed that."

"Say it twice. I'm not gonna lie." Betsy's eyes were bright and her cheeks flushed. She looked beautiful, despite (because of?) the blood. Vibrant. *Alive.* If there was still a bullet hole in her chest, Fred couldn't see it. The tear, yes. The hole, no. "I've been dying to do that for the latht half hour."

I laughed because it's one thing that makes her seem less sinister. It's okay. She's a good guy. If she wanted us dead, there were only a million opportunities. She saved us. It's all right.

"I'm pleased you are pleased, my own."

Fred screamed. She'd had no sense of the man, *no* sense. But he was there, as if conjured by a wish. Some of the most intense fight-or-flight impulses lit up her nervous system and she realized she'd jerked back from him without realizing she'd moved.

"I beg your pardon," Betsy's insane husband said, and inclined his head in a polite nod. "I meant to reassure, not startle."

Startle? I'm startled when I stub my toe. You did not startle me.

"Perfect timing, babe," Betsy announced, stepping over Ran without looking.

"The timing was yours, Elizabeth." Betsy's insane husband went to her and dropped a light kiss on her blood-splattered cheek. Casual as the kiss was, he was looking her over with care, as if to reassure himself she wasn't hurt. "As we decided, if you didn't call me at a certain time, I was to create a diversion."

"No wonder you didn't care if they took our phones." Jonas hadn't screamed, but he was very pale and kept his distance from both vampires.

"See?" Fred cried, looking around the room. Two of the Skittles had killed each other in a cross fire. Jonas had knocked the other one out. Sinclair must have tackled Sunkist on his way in; Orange Shirt was unconscious, and his left eye was blowing up like a bike tire. Betsy, of course, had rid the world of Ran. "This! This is why you don't fire a gun *when you can't see anything*. Idiots!"

"Lucky for us," Jonas said.

"*Lucky?* It could have been one of us."

"Like I said. Lucky."

"Can I just say," Betsy began, wiggling from her insane husband's embrace, "how awesome *there's no reason to talk to her like that when you could be calling me a cunt* was? I also like how you told him he looked embalmed. Tomorrow it'll really be true." She threw back her head and laughed. Her insane husband watched her with a fond smile, but Fred noticed Madison and Jonas didn't find it quite as hysterical.

"Thank you for helping us, sir." Madison came forward and held out her hand. While they shook, she continued. "We owe you and Betsy more than we can pay back."

Fred was impressed; she might have been able to say the words, but probably wouldn't have sounded so unrattled. "She had you tucked up her sleeve, Mr. . . . uh . . . Other Vampire?"

He smiled. His devastating good looks almost made her

forget her momentary terror. He'd seemed large and forbidding outside on the sidewalk. Here at the top of the Giant Ocean Tank, he was a dark giant. Suit, shoes, eyes: deepest black. "My queen occasionally finds me useful."

"You didn't think I'd come to town with the king and not have him skulking nearby? Also I didn't have a choice; he was gonna do that anyway. I've spent years trying to get him to quit with the protective skulking. Finally I just started to use it to my advantage.

"My love is a quick study," Sinclair replied, and Fred could hear the laugh lurking in his voice.

"Later for you, buster." Betsy glanced back at the corpse she had made of an elderly cripple. "So the doomsday thing won't work?"

"Not after what I did to it." Another thin smile. "I am a layman at best when it comes to science, but it was clear to me he was onto something. I'd like to call in some experts to have a look."

"Or we could smash it to little bitty pieces of doomsday," Fred suggested. She had no idea what it would have done or how it would have worked, and never wanted to find out. Whatever it was, it needed to disappear. Today. Forever.

"As you say. And if the queen agrees."

Oh ho.

"I bet it would have worked. Like Dr. Bimm said, that wasn't the problem. It was one thing to assume he was nice because he wrote nice e-mails and then find out he's bad," Madison said, lower lip trembling. "I'm not that stupid; people lie. They lie all the time; that's something my mama never had to tell me. But he had all these great ideas. He couldn't lie about the science, and he had these rilly, rilly smart ideas . . ."

"Yeah, he did. But intelligence and goodness don't always go together. Just ask any of my friends," Betsy added with a smile.

"You are too modest, my own."

"He's really got that tall, dark, and mysterious thing down, huh?" Jonas commented. Fred was amazed; it hardly ever took him that long to rejoin a conversation.

"Hey." Betsy pointed at him. "If you're going to be into any-one I know, you're gonna be into my zombie friend. We've *talked* about this, Jonas!"

"Having found such utter bliss in her own marriage, my queen tirelessly seeks to foist marital bonds on others."

"Do not." Betsy took in the carnage again. "What are we supposed to do with this mess? Tell me nobody could hear the shots from outside."

"No chance." Fred shook her head. "The place is as good as soundproofed. But we should talk about calling a cop. Or some-thing."

"Not at all. Of course my queen and I will attend to this; why should you and yours be further inconvenienced?" Sinclair said it so smoothly, it was obvious he was used to hiding commands inside questions. "The police will be of little help but will incon-venience and/or incarcerate everyone in this room." Another sliver of a smile. "We have schedules to keep. All of you do, I'm sure."

Jonas and Fred looked at each other. "We're breaking the law if we don't," she warned.

"Yep. But Tall, Dark, and Terrifying has a point. What can

the cops do except make it more complicated and awful? It won't be the first time we've all agreed to keep something quiet."

Jonas had her there; he was referring to her murdering her father, and a few other things he was too tactful to bring up in front of strangers.

"You have people who can take care of this?"

"You've heard of cleaners? Our cleaners have cleaners. They do great work; they'll treat the NEA right."

"Then . . . I guess we're done." Was it possible? It was too much to hope for.

"Perhaps not quite. Come here, dear." He crooked a finger at Madison and she took a slow step forward. "I cannot pretend to understand the ordeal you have endured, but I can promise—"

"Don't! *Please* don't spell me." Madison had thrown her arms over her face and backed off. Alarmed, Fred started to go to her but stopped when Jonas grabbed her arm and shook his head. *Wait*, he mouthed, and she did, but if she had to get between Madison and the guy capable of stealing her mind, she would. The thought of enduring another brain invasion left her cold and shaking, but the thought of standing by and letting Madison endure one was unthinkable.

"Child, I meant no—"

"Of course I want to forget," Madison said to her arms. "I'd give almost anything to forget, and people *died*! And people I rilly care about almost died because I'm stupid. I'm gonna have bad dreams about tonight forever. About Betsy getting shot and dumped in the tank, and Dr. Ran, and Fred squishing me in the dark so she'd get hurt but not me, and being squished knowing you were all in danger and that it was my fault. And I'll dream about Betsy drinking Ran's blood, too, and you, too, sir, I'm sorry, but I will, I'll have nightmares about you. You're *scary*." She slowly lowered her arms and gazed up at him. "But I earned those nightmares. We lived through this and it was terrible and those memories are *mine*. It's—it's not for you to decide it's too much for me."

Whoa. Fred's own eyes were wide; never had she respected Madison so much, nor been so ashamed of her own petty snobbery. *Again: Who's the actual idiot, Fredrika?*

Sinclair took a courteous step back. He was probably unaware, but it had seemed as if he'd been looming over Madison. "My apologies, child, I only meant to reassure. Of course they're your memories and your dreams; I am not a thief. Pass that on to your lady mother, if you will."

Madison kept darting quick looks at him, then glancing away, then back. Fred realized she'd probably learned Vamp Etiquette 101 from the cradle. "Th-thank you. I didn't mean to say you were a thief. I'm . . . not handling this well. Dr. Bimm will tell you I'm not very—"

Fred shook her head. "Not true, Madison. Not even a little bit true. You're handling this better than me, that's for sure. And it's Fred, dammit."

The younger woman beamed, all fright forgotten. "I'll never forget that you helped me, Dr. Bimm. You would have taken a bullet for me. You squashed me to save me!"

"Sounds awful; don't ever save me, Fred," Jonas said with fervent relief. "Isn't she both heavy and weirdly bony?"

"Shut up."

"It's almost like we're rilly, rilly sisters!"

"We are not! Just knowing you is awful. We're friends, and I am horrible to my friends, just so you know."

"She speaks the truth," Jonas added.

Madison beamed. "I know you're exaggerating, just like a real sister would."

"A real sister couldn't be worse, now shush."

"Sisters *are* worse," Betsy muttered, and Sinclair chuckled. "Don't get me started."

"Yes, I'm sure yours is the embodiment of all evil and despair." Did the vampire queen have to try and one-up her on every little thing?

"Well . . ."

"Shush." Fred was gratified to see Betsy hush. She held out a hand for Betsy to shake. "I'm grateful for what you did. What you both did. We are all, I'm sure." She glanced around; saw Jonas and Madison nod. "Yes, you're terrifying and spend far too much time talking about shoes, and *you* tend to appear out of nowhere like death in a designer suit, but it's all worth tolerating."

"Awww. I feel all soft and mushy inside now."

"I myself less so. Still, your sentiments are appreciated. Perhaps we could meet again in a more official capacity?"

"You mean an official meeting of Undersea Folk and vampires? Stranger things have happened. Especially tonight. Look, I just want to get home and draw myself a nice bleach bath and scrub myself bloody and then get drunk and have the first of many nightmares about tonight."

"That sounds good to me, too," Jonas announced. "Madison, come home and crash with me. We'll get to whatever's left to square away tomorrow. Barb won't mind."

"Really?" Madison was shyly thrilled. "That'd be—you won't mind?"

"'Course not. After what we've endured? Vampires and Fred and doomsday devices and Fred and Ran and Fred and Skittles attacks and Fred?"

"I hate you both," Fred announced, and saw at once they were unmoved by her pronouncement. "And I'll get back to the hotel and take my bleach bath. But Betsy . . . a personal question? Please?" Even after what she had seen that night, she still couldn't fathom how such a thing could have happened. "How exactly did you get to be queen of the vampires?"

"Aw, it's boring."

"Come on."

"It's a long story, and I come off shrill and bitchy in it."

"So? Pleeeease? I never wheedle. You've got to tell."

"Bottom line, the vamps were ready for a change. And the change was me. Took me a while to see it, though. Anyhoo, they were talkin' 'bout a revolution—"

Fred groaned. "Is that Tracy Chapman? Or The Who? And it's *generation*, not *revolution*. If it's The Who."

"Hey, you asked for the gory details; don't cry about it when you get them. So like I was telling you, we—"

"We?"

"Sinclair; he wasn't insane then, he didn't go insane until a few months ago."

"Responsible pet ownership is not insanity," the king announced in a tone that scared everyone but Betsy, who flicked her hand like what he said was a fly. "Anyway, we decided the old king sucked, got a bunch of rabid vampires to eat him alive, and then had sex in the deep end of a pool and emerged victorious fanged monarchs. To sum up: the king is dead. Long live . . . me."

"Oh," Fred said in a small voice.

That nice smile again and there was the midwestern easy-going blonde who said *bar-er* instead of *bar* and *hey there, then!* for *hello* and *such a deal!* for *that's a good price.* "You asked," the nice blonde killer reminded her.

"I did."

"Only the really bad guys died."

"Then I guess it worked out."

"Oh, it did. Aren't you glad for me, Fred?"

"Sure."

"You don't look glad," she teased.

"You're a little terrifying sometimes."

Betsy laughed. "You'd be amazed how often I hear that these days!"

"I wouldn't, actually."

CHAPTER NINETEEN

"We just . . . left them."

"Yeah," Jonas said.

"We knew what they would do. They're vampires, for God's sake. And we just left them there. To be eaten—the two still alive." Fred took a breath, forced it out. "To be killed."

"Yeah."

"It's bad that I don't mind more," Fred worried. "I know I should feel shitty. I should be wringing my hands and wishing we'd put a stop to it. But I can't make myself get upset over it. They shot Betsy—they had *no* idea she'd get up again. They were going to kill all of us. And then all the Undersea Folk. I'm—I'm *glad* they're getting eaten!"

"So we're on the same page."

"We're going to hell," Fred predicted with a sigh.

Jonas slung an arm across her shoulders. His other arm was around Madison, who was so tired she was almost sleepwalking. Occasionally he'd steer her around a post or street light. "At least you'll be burning for eternity with people you know," he teased. "And at least you've seen the last of the vampire queen. Unless you decide it's time to bridge the gap between the Folk and the undead."

"Don't joke about that. Bad enough to put up with two of them. I'm so glad this night's over . . . I'm so glad they're going home."

"C'mon. They weren't—Okay, *he* was fucking terrifying, but she was pretty cool."

"I didn't say she wasn't pretty cool; I said I'm glad they're going home. I kind of like her," she said with reluctance. "All most people want to do when they find out who I am is stare and ask silly questions about mermaids granting wishes or how I deal with pruned fingers. Betsy's so self-involved, she doesn't care about any of that. With her it's all *cut to the chase so I can go home and catch the Macy's sale.*"

"So you like her because she's self-involved?"

"Really self-involved. To an astonishing degree. It must be one of her powers."

Jonas shook his head. "No, I get the feeling she was like that in life, too."

"Yes, but I think in un-death she hides behind it a little. She's not as ditzy as she seems. I . . . guess that's a good thing."

For her? Or for us? Fred didn't know, and was too exhausted to care. But when she'd slept a while she'd give the matter more thought. Betsy Taylor had been the most terrible wonderful person she had ever met. Or the most wonderful terrible person. It wouldn't do to let such a person slip off her radar.

Not at all.

Incomer

Incomer (n):

An outsider who moves to a community or a place, as used by those who consider themselves to be its original inhabitants.

One who comes in.

—WIKTIONARY, WIKI-BASED OPEN CONTENT DICTIONARY

Cape Cod: small peninsula off Massachusetts that sucks money out of tourists and retired millionaires to survive, since the traditional fishing industry is slowly dying . . . basically we hate tourists but without them we'd be totally impoverished . . . the winters are horrible and in the summer tourists are everywhere.

—URBAN DICTIONARY

A dream is a shadow . . . of something real.

—CHRIS LEE, *THE LAST WAVE*

"I just killed my best friend!"

"And your worst enemy."

"Same difference."

—VERONICA SAWYER AND JASON DEAN, *HEATHERS*

Worry (v):
1) to torment oneself with or suffer from disturbing thoughts; fret. 2) to seize, especially by the throat, with the teeth and shake or mangle, as one animal does another. 3) to harass by repeated biting, snapping, etc. 4) to progress or succeed by constant effort, despite difficulty.

—DICTIONARY.COM

"It's anxiety. Jenna's been away too long. She's a goner, I'm sure of it. She's probably choked on a piece of LEGO or something."

"She's just at work!"

—RYAN AND WILFRED, *WILFRED* "HAPPINESS"

Well, you know, Lois, you mean a lot to me. I mean, things you say and things you do resonate with me in a big way. When you drive away to go to the market, I just don't know what to do with myself. And then when I hear that car coming up the driveway, I just go berserk. I mean, you know, half the time when you go to the market, I just assume you're leaving forever, and when you get back, I realize I have no idea how long you've been gone, and I . . . well, you know what, I'm— I'm rambling.

—BRIAN GRIFFIN, *FAMILY GUY*

Author's Note

Some writers use their work to put forward their own agendas, be they moral, political, religious, educational, pro-life, pro-death penalty, pro-can't-we-all-just-get-along, pro-if-you-don't-like-it-move-to-another-country, pro-why-do-you-hate-America, and the like. And I'm going to do that, too. I've got an agenda. Okay, it's not so much an agenda as it's an open letter to a woman who has been my archenemy for over a decade.

There's a part in the story coming up about a mom hollering at her son, Curtis, on the beach. She's yelling at him to come back for more sunscreen, and he's ignoring her. And rather than get off her ass and go get him and haul his bratty butt back to their blankets, put him in a choke hold, and slather him crown to toes with sunscreen, she just stays on her towel and yells his name. And yells it. And yells it.

The kid never comes over, and why should he? He knows she won't get off the towel. We all know she won't get off the towel. The entire frigging beach knows she won't get off the towel. Eventually Curtis gets hungry and wanders back for Goldfish crackers, and while he's munching, she squirts him with sunscreen.

I know I'm sliding into a rant, but this happens to me every time I go to the beach. I swear this woman and her brat are following me around the world. In Australia her kid's name was Christopher, in Florida his name was Mike, in Massachusetts it was Curtis . . . uncanny. (And it's always a boy. I guess girls come back to the towel. Weird.)

Anyway. Anonymous lady with no real control over her offspring: stop following me. Barring that, get your ass *off* the blanket if the kid doesn't come when you scream his name two dozen times.

Thank you, anonymous lady! It feels so good to get that off my chest. Oh, and thanks for buying my book.

CHAPTER
ONE

TEN YEARS EARLIER

She was happy she was born during the worst winter Massa-chusetts had seen in decades—since 1994, the old-timers claimed. It wasn't an absolute, but a cub's first Change usually happened around their birthday. Which meant that in the thrill and passion and danger and chaos of her first Change, she didn't have to worry about running into any of the three million three hundred thousand tourists who flocked to Cape Cod in the summer and fall. Tourists didn't have much interest in Massachusetts in mid-January, even the ferociously rude ones.

More clams for meeeeeee, she thought gleefully, digging so hard the sand flew ten feet and hit hard enough to scratch glass (if there had been a glass sheet in the middle of the beach in the middle of January). The moon was full and soared above her, fat and white. The wind whistled off the Atlantic and chilled her, but not as much as it would have if she was down there in her tender pink skin and her pale hairless hands and her pale hairless feet.

She wasn't! So that was good! There was a time for hairless hands and a time for efficient strong paws, and this was paw time.

Excited beyond words (literally), Lara dug and dug for her dinner, the hole already so big if she wasn't careful she'd slip on shifting sand and topple into it. She was not known for her grace, on four feet or two. Wouldn't *that* be a funny thing for her Pack mates to see! *Here is your future alpha leader, the one whose hairy butt is sticking out of that hole.*

Ha!

Even if she didn't get her teeth on the clams, in the clams, the act of hunting for her dinner was intoxicating. *She* would decide when and what to eat! Not Mother! *She* would decide if it was clams or rabbit or both or neither! Not Mother! *She* would blow off erosion concerns and decide how many holes to dig on the beach! Not the Woods Hole Oceanographic Institution! She was thirteen; she wasn't a baby cub anymore. Those decisions *should* be hers, but her mother was sooooo stubborn. She was even stubborn about being stubborn. Double stubborn!

She can't even Change, she'll never Change, but Mother decides? It's wrong-bad.

But that was awful; worse, it was disloyal and mean. Her mother hadn't been born to the Pack, but that was okay. She and Lara's father had met on an elevator, and conceived Lara on that elevator, and that was okay; that was life in the big city. Her mother was the alpha female and, thus, the full fat moon of Lara's days, if not her nights, and that was . . . sorta okay. Lara would owe Mother respect all the days she was the alpha female, and all the days after, when Lara herself was. And she wouldn't be for years and years and years and years and years, and it would be years-long, it would be years-forever before she would lose her.

Thoughts for thinking later. So many smells. Salt and wet and grass and rot and fish and cold and wood and a thousand others, each one begging to be followed to its source, each one calling her like chimes bringing her to church. She would keep digging for supper. No, she would run down the dead fish up the beach. No, she would dig. No, she would flush rabbits from the deep green lake of grass. No, she would dig. Why was she digging again? Oh. Supper-food.

A seagull who thought he had dibs swooped above her and dived, then pulled up at the last instant. He soared above her and dived again, all the time scolding, scolding. Lara lunged straight up and her teeth snapped shut a bare inch from the gull's left leg, startling it in midcall: *Khee-khee-kheeaa—kheeaaaawwwwppp!*

Almost got you, gull-bird! More of that if you get too close! Might get you next time, might! Why was I digging—oh. Right.

There had never been a more wonderful night in the history of forever.

She was a lucky, lucky cub. She lived in a magnificent stone castle with a red roof, a castle with a mile of grass in front and a bazillion miles of the Atlantic behind. There were hundreds of windows she could peek out of, windows so big and wide that no matter how little she was, she could stretch up and peek out: at two, at four, at five, at seven, at ten, at twelve, now.

It had many outdoor rooms where she and her Pack could eat or rest or eat, and even cook in the rooms and then eat in them, outdoor rooms protected from all but the yuckiest elements, outdoor rooms—

She knew that was wrong; groped for the right word. She remembered almost everything on four legs that she'd experienced on two, but interpreted the events differently. So it took her a few seconds for the association to—porch! The castle had many porches. And three little oceans inside. Pools!

If she couldn't be in her wolf form all the time, it was nice to have a castle to run amok in the rest of the month. And the castle was stuffed with people, generations of relatives and friends and friends of friends; the Pack always tried to live together if territory would tolerate the numbers. Solitary living was death-pain for them.

Then she saw him, and was glad.

She wasn't sure why watching the inlander watch her made the night even better. They weren't friends; they didn't know each other except to nod hello. They couldn't: his litter was made up of people who *chose* to live far from the bulk of the Pack; she didn't know how they bore it.

He'd know who she was, of course, but the poor cub couldn't Change. *Horrid* legacy from the witch. Not his fault, but the other cubs disagreed. On wonderful, wonderful nights like this, he could only watch; never join. It was a sad, unlucky thing.

She was sorry for him but glad for herself. All her good luck—the castle, the rank, the Change—made his bad luck, his inlander luck, seem worse. She was selfish enough to be glad it wasn't her, and sorry enough that it was him.

She was glad he was there now. She thought she'd want to go through her first Change alone, and until that moment, she had. But being able to share the experience, even for a few moments, made it better. *Did you see I almost got that noisy-stupid-smelly gull? Do you see how wide and wonderful-deep my hole is?* She felt they had a connection, she and this neighbor she rarely saw and did not know.

They stared at each other across the beach for a second-hour-eternity, and then he raised a hand to her and continued on his way, and she went back to digging for her supper.

The clam was so sweet and delicious she didn't mind the sand in her teeth.

CHAPTER
TWO

"You're mad I'm not dead, aren't you?"

Lara Wyndham, Pack leader of the Wyndham weres for nineteen hours, groaned and rubbed her eyes. Her toe throbbed from where she'd stubbed it before sitting at the table. "Of course not, Dad."

"Really?" Michael Wyndham shook out his newspaper. His actual newspaper, paper and ink and circular ads and everything—how quaint! *"I'd be mad I wasn't dead."*

Given that her father took the Pack to avenge the murder of *his* father, that was something to think about. "You're such a nutter." She stared down into her bowl of grits with butter and four slices of crumbled bacon. Normally she'd be unable to resist such a soupy, bacon-ey, buttery delicacy, but the thought of wolfing (heh) anything besides a cup of tea brought on faint nausea.

Which was, she knew, stupid. It was also a huge giveaway to her folks that something was wrong. So she seized her spoon and started to eat.

Her mother slouched into the kitchen, yawning and going straight to the sideboard to grope for a coffee mug. She was dressed in her even-though-it's-Thursday-I'm-dressing-like-it's-Saturday-morning outfit of jeans and a long-sleeved flannel shirt, although the temp was supposed to hit thirty degrees that day. With the Atlantic in their backyard, her mother often went around shivering.

Jeannie Wyndham's curly blond mass was streaked with gray ("Battle scars, right up there with stretch marks."), and the laugh lines around her blue eyes had deepened over the years, but there was no way around it: her mother was, as several of her friends, male and female, had pointed out, "so mega-hot she's absolute zero." (Thank God, *thank God* that when the remarks got back to her mom, she had no idea what they meant.) Back in the day they'd have called her a *cougar*. Lara preferred *Mother* or *You make me so . . . arrgghh!*

She stirred her hot chocolate and thought again that it wasn't easy, having a legend for a mom. Oh, and one for a dad, too. Definitely to be filed under "Things To Deal With: Not Easy."

"So, big day." Jeannie was heavily creaming and sugaring her coffee, which she'd poured into a mug the size of a flower pitcher. "Feel any different?"

"Tired." She had not slept well; she hadn't for days. She didn't mention this to her parents. The thought of the chat that would ensue ("Mommy, Daddy, I've been having nightmares; I'd like a nightlight and for you to tuck me in with lullabies and toast. Lots of toast. A bed isn't a bed without crumbs. Also I keep dreaming about Derik's son even though I don't really know him.") made her shiver.

"I'm not sure it bodes well, if you're already tired," Michael teased. He, like her mother, was aging well. Unlike her mother, he was Pack, and Pack always aged well; it was written into the genetic code. There were grandfathers on the Cape who occasionally got carded. ("We card everyone, though," was not reassuring to a species trying to stay beneath the radar.) There was no gray in his deep brown hair, and not many lines on his face. Only his eyes changed with age: their startling gold color—like Baltic amber, like old coins—deepened each year. Her mom good-naturedly complained it was like staring into a road hazard sign.

It was a good life, and her parents were smart enough or humble enough to know it. They looked great, they were rich, they had decades ahead of them, their cubs were grown ("Note we didn't say *out of the nest*, because they'll never leave."), and so Michael and Jeannie Wyndham were doing something no alpha couple in the two-million-year history of the Pack had done.

Retiring.

CHAPTER
THREE

SIX YEARS EARLIER

"But we don't do that. Alphas don't retire."

"We *can*. We just haven't."

"Mike—"

"I hate when you call me Mike."

"—I say this with love and respect and as your best bro and as someone who has killed for you and would probably die for you, probably: you're out of your fucking mind."

"I also hate when you come into my house long enough to raid my larder, tell me I'm insane, goad my daughter into ever more juvenile delinquency, speculate on whether you'd die for me or not, and then . . . whoosh! Off to cause chaos somewhere else. You're like a blond Loki."

"Completely thoroughly *out* of your *fucking* mind. Do I smell brownies? And when's Lara get home? I might die for you. I'm almost positive I probably would."

Lara nearly tripped over one of the benches for joy as she came in through the mansion's east entrance. It was her favorite, because that side of the mansion saw high traffic. The people who lived there—her parents, her little brother, herself, other Pack members, assistants, cooks, and people who worked there (cleaners, drivers, gardeners, etc.)—avoided the north door because of the incredibly polished (read: slippery) front hall and intimidating (read: old, four-foot-circumference, about eight-thousand-dollars-per-prism) chandelier that loomed overhead.

Thus the east entrance was cluttered, with muddy floors and dirty windows and boots in winter and tennies and sandals in summer and things hanging on hooks and beach towels laid out on benches to dry and a half-full bag of birdseed slumped in a far corner (though they had no bird feeders), a partially deflated basketball, two bottles of plant food, a small baggie filled with Phillips Head screws and a flat-head screwdriver, and sand every-where, *everywhere*. "It's too big to be a mud room," was the general joke, "so it's the mud wing."

Though her father was on the north side of the mansion, she could hear and smell him, and better yet, she could smell Derik Gardner, her father's best friend and worst enemy. So she dumped her overstuffed backpack on a bench that was already groaning with beach towels, swim shoes (heedless of damage to paws on all fours, Pack members were oddly fastidious about getting their pink hairless feet dirty), and umbrellas (though it hadn't rained in three weeks). Then she unslung her purse from around her neck, tossed the purse by the backpack and the car keys on the purse, and wasted not one more moment.

She hurried through the long halls, past enormous windows overlooking the grass ocean and wood so old and tended so long it was black with age and polish buildup. Her home smelled as it always did, a delightful mishmash of Pack members and food and furniture polish and dust and hunger and love.

She burst into the main hall beyond the north door and instantly slipped. Both feet went up in the air, but from long experience, she tucked and saved the back of her head from a teeth-rattling rap. A startled grunt ("Nnnnff.") was forced out of her, but that was okay because Derik heard her coming and—

"Jeez, how many times, Lara? Seriously. Before you get bored or die?"

—knew she'd be sprawled on the floor. "Hiya!" she cried, holding up a hand. He pulled her to her feet with an effortless tug and she threw her arms around him. "You never call, you should have said you were coming, you never do and I could have skipped school!"

"You couldn't, actually," her father said from the doorway to the north receiving room, but he was smiling.

"Why would you assume I'd have any interest in spending time with you?" His hug belied his words. "And I didn't know myself we were coming."

A lie. But one told in kindness. Derik had alpha tendencies, but the Pack already had one. Rather than give in to instinct and tradition to fight his best friend to the death, orphan his children, and make a widow of Jeannie, Derik had left the Cape. Sometimes he came back and stayed for months; sometimes he dropped in for an overnight and was gone by dawn. At no time did he courteously call ahead. It was a deliberate slight to the Pack leader, but Derik was so well loved, Michael let it go and would hear no words against his friend. "We have forty bed-rooms. We have a kitchen so large it can feed a small country, and the food supplies to go with it. What's the problem? Are you afraid he'll have to sleep on a couch and hose himself down in the side yard, and eat crackers for breakfast? Or fall over the kitchen cliff when he's looking for the bathroom in the middle of the night?"

(The kitchen cliff was the steep bank about thirty meters from the kitchen porch, which due to the design of the mansion and the placement of the Atlantic ocean, led straight down to the water. So if you hated what was on the breakfast menu, you could theoretically walk out the kitchen door and kill yourself.)

"Why d'you think Dad's out of his mind this time?" She fol-lowed them into the receiving area, a large room splashed with sunlight and furnished with sofas and chairs that were as com-fortable as they were elegant. The hardwood floor gleamed (thus the slipping) and the many rugs, supposedly hauled over on the *Fortune*, which landed at Plymouth Colony about a year after the *Mayflower*, were Savonneries and worked in deepest blues and golds and greens.

"I'd tell you, except it's so weird you won't believe me."

She nodded. "Is it the retirement thing?"

Derik sighed and glanced at Michael. "Unless he's discussed the subject with his heir like a sensible madman."

"He's for sure sensible. If Dad retires and I'm Pack leader, can you come back and live here for good?"

Derik's blond brows arched and her father frowned. "Lara. Absolutely none of your business and inappropriate besides."

"Okay, but can you?" She knew she could push things with her father; he expected her to be aggressive and not easily backed down. They all did. But she also knew there were limits. "Derik? And your wife and cub, too?"

"I . . . don't know, hon. I hadn't thought about it. Your dad just now sprung this on me." He glanced over her head at her father. "I hope—Michael, I hope that wasn't a factor in you coming up with this idea. The problem's mine, not yours. The Pack's yours until you're dead; we all know."

"It's just something Jeannie and I have been kicking around. She's got fresh perspective, something I lack."

"Oh, that's not all you lack," Derik said cheerfully, his momentary concern gone with the wind. Derik's moods were weathervanes, and it was always windy. "But I don't have that kind of time; you'll have to think up your many thousands of shortcomings on your own. Meantime, you and Jeannie want to join Sara and me for dinner? No kids, though. I can't stand yours, and mine can't stand me."

Another lie, Lara figured—hoped, at least. Derik's son was so quiet and introspective—a radical departure from both parents—it was hard to picture him hating anyone.

"Speaking of," Michael said, his head cocked to the left in what her mother teasingly called his Petey the Dog expression. They all heard the polite one-rap knock, and then the door opened and Jack Gardner stepped into the entry.

He saw them at once and inclined his head. "Sir," he said to her father. "Miss." To her. "Captain Weirdo." Derik.

"This is why I knocked up your mother?" Derik mock bitched. "To be hung with humiliating nicknames?"

"It would be nice"—Jack sighed—"if we could go one entire day without you saying *knocked up* and *mother* and *hung* in the same sentence."

"It's Michael and Lara," her father said, "you're practically family, Jack; you must know it." His tone was light, but Lara knew he was a little taken aback at the teenager's formality. And maybe a little hurt, too; none of the Wyndhams saw as much of the Gardners as they would like. To be treated as a stranger by the son of the man he considered a brother was hard. "My God, you've gotten huge."

"I was gonna tell Lara the same, but simple self-respect prevented it," Derik said. "It's so embarrassing; I hear myself saying all the stupid things that annoyed me when adults said them to me: Look how you've grown. You're a young man already. When I saw you last, you were only yea big. Don't eat that; I dropped it on the floor."

"The golden days of childhood"—Michael sighed—"gone forever. And you still eat things off the floor."

"Don't judge me." Derik sniffed. "Floor jerky is perfectly good, as is floor bread and floor yogurt. We don't all eat off gold plates, y'know."

"It's nice to see you," Jack soberly told her. "You get prettier all the time, which I always think is impossible, and then you top yourself." All said in the tone of a boy reading a computer printout.

"It took you that long to think of something to say?" Lara teased. Often he didn't speak at all after nodding hello.

"I was just waiting for a break in the Michael and Derik show."

"Ooooooh, torched you! That's my cub," Derik said proudly. "Always so—hey! Mock him, not me."

Lara had been studying Jack since he'd come inside. She knew he was a couple of years younger than she, but he had such a serious mien he seemed older. The fabulous gray eyes helped; they seemed to change given his mood: from smoky fog to dirty ice, depending. His hair color came from both parents, dark golden blond with rich red lowlights, thick and lustrous; it fell across his forehead in waves, almost into his eyes. He had his mother's milk-pale complexion; not a freckle in sight. Jack was that ghostly hue all year around, which, when he visited, caused no end of teasing ("Hey, Jack, I can see you, and when I close my eyes, I can *still* see you.").

Yes, he'd always been a cute kid, but adolescence was giving him something . . . she didn't know . . . presence? She wasn't sure, but assumed she found him so striking because she didn't see him very often. She figured it was because she saw him with fresher eyes as opposed to the other boys, who, if they didn't live in the mansion, lived within five miles of it. They rode buses together and went to the same schools together and got along and fought and argued and pranked together. Jack seemed above it all because he was apart from it all; it was refreshing.

What the . . . Pull it back, Lara! He's only fifteen! He's just a kid, she thought with the worldly wisdom of a nineteen-year-old girl. *It's a little creepy to find him sexy.*

She should leave. Quickly. Packers lived, fed, fought, fucked, and died on their instincts, all their instincts. Even though the poor guy couldn't Change, he might have some or most or all of the other senses. He might be able to pick up on her (inappropriate) interest.

"Well, I—"

"I have to leave now," Jack murmured.

"Yeah, me, too, but it was—"

"It was nice to see you again, Lara. I'll wait for you, Dad."

"Okay, bye!"

"Good-bye."

Jack practically ran back to the front door, while Lara lurched through the entry, trying not to slip on the shiny floors. The last thing she heard before she got clear was Derik's, "What the hell?"

She could almost hear her father's shrug in response. "Teen-agers."

CHAPTER
FOUR

Michael Wyndham, former Pack leader now embarked on his first full day of retirement, stared down at the shredded bat at the kitchen entrance and thought, *This does not bode well.*

His mind ticked over the possibilities.

1) Some cat (or dog or possum but likely a cat because cats were weird) got ahold of the bat, somehow, ripped it up a little, then got bored with it and left it on the front porch because it had pressing business to be weird somewhere else.

2) Some cat (or dog or possum but likely a cat because cats were weird) got ahold of the bat, somehow, ripped it up a little, then left it on the front porch as some kind of

sick-ass present, the sort of thing weird cats got off on when they weren't shitting in boxes.

3) A Pack member was sending a message.

4) A non-Pack member was sending a message.

5) The bat, fed up with the state of the world, killed itself by flying through a fan or food processor or whatev y'like and then managed to drag all its bits and pieces to the kitchen step, a sort of, "Woe, mankind and Pack, let this be a warning; the bell tolls for thee!"

Michael rubbed his eyes, eyes people alternatively found fascinating or unsettling, and thought, *Oh, please let it be number five.* But of course it couldn't be. The idea was absurd: if the bat truly wanted to kill itself, it would have folded its wings and dived over the kitchen cliff.

He raised his voice—it was after breakfast, Sean would finally be up but Lara would be out and about, and Jeannie had another meeting of her No, Really, Erosion Is Erasing the Cape! Club. "Son? C'mere and give me a hand."

"Argh," was the reply, muffled because the speaker was no doubt into his second pound of bacon. "It's the crack of eleven thirty, Dad; let a guy get his eyes open, will ya?"

"Now, Sean."

"Nnnnf. Gnnff. Rrowwllff."

"There's no need to—" he began, but his son had appeared in the doorway leading to the steps. "To eat all the bacon at once; it'll still be there after you help me."

"That's a lie and you know it," Sean Wyndham informed

him. His mouth was actually shiny with bacon grease. "I take no chances ever since BaconGate. And what's the—oh." Sean looked down at the pile o' bat shreddings. "Jeez, Dad, I feel bad. I didn't get you anything."

"Just hush and help me clean this up."

"Whatever the bat did to piss you off, I'm sure it's very sorry now. It was between you and the bat and it's over. You need to put it behind you. I think it's inappropriate to bring anyone else into your and the bat's private business."

"Shut up, boy." He sighed, alternatively wanting to hug and throttle his only son. "And help me."

"I can manage one of those," he decided. "Shutting up or helping. You pick."

"Sean . . ."

"Plus the new guy—Len? Lenny? He's starting today, right? I almost tripped over him on the way out here. He's looking for something to do."

"*Sean.*"

Sean bitched good-naturedly through the ordeal, as Michael had known he would. But he was a cheerful helper, lightening an unpleasant task with his constant stream of witticisms, as Michael had also known he would.

There were times he caught himself staring at Sean, amazed that someone so unlike himself could come from . . . well . . . himself.

It was repulsive to compare children to one another, mentally toting up their faults and fine points like they were living ledger sheets. But sometimes he couldn't help it: Lara was like him—and his father—in so many ways, and in what few ways she wasn't, she was like his beloved Jeannie. It meant the three of them had frequent arguments and power struggles, which only increased as Lara got older, and occasionally there were threats of death and mutilation (not necessarily in that order) when, say, report cards came out, or Lara decided there was no need to wreck the car *and* tell her parents. *I can manage one of those* was practically a Wyndham family slogan.

The retirement announcement, Derik and his family returning to show their support, and the tension were all relentless reminders that his whole experiment would not have been possible without Lara . . . and Derik. And the truth was, he had starting mulling over the possibility two decades ago.

CHAPTER
FIVE

TWENTY YEARS EARLIER

Michael Wyndham stepped out of his bedroom, walked down *the hall, and saw his best friend, Derik Gardner, on the main floor headed for the front door. He grabbed the banister and vaulted, dropped fifteen feet, and landed with a solid* thud *he felt all the way through his knees. "Hey, Derik!" he called cheerfully. "Wait a sec!"*

From his bedroom he heard his wife mutter, "I hate when he does that . . . Gives me a flippin' heart attack every time," and couldn't help grinning. Wyndham Manor had been his home all his life, and the only time he walked up or down those stairs was when he was carrying his daughter, Lara. He didn't know how ordinary humans could stand walking around in their fragile little shells. He'd tried to talk to his wife about this on a few occasions, but her eyes always went flinty, and her gun hand flexed, and the phrase hairy fascist bastard *came* up, and things got awkward. Werewolves were tough, incredibly tough, but compared to Homo sapiens, who wasn't?

It was a ridiculously perfect day outside, and he couldn't blame Derik for wanting to head out as quickly as possible. Still, there was something troubling his old friend, and Michael was determined to get to the bottom of it.

"Hold up," Michael said, reaching for Derik's shoulder. "I want to—"

"I don't care what you want," Derik replied without turning. He grabbed Michael's hand and flung it away, so sharply Michael lost his balance for a second. "I'm going out."

Michael tried to laugh it off, ignoring the way the hairs on the back of his neck tried to stand up. "Touch-ee! Hey, I just want to—"

"I'm going out!" Derik moved, cat-quick, and then Michael was flying through the air with the greatest of ease, only to slam into the door to the coat closet hard enough to splinter it down the middle.

Michael lay on his back a moment like a stunned beetle. Then he flipped to his feet, ignoring the slashing pain down his back. "My friend," he said, "you are so right. Except you're going out on the tip of my boot, pardon me while I kick your ass."

This in a tone of mild banter, but Michael was crossing the room in swift strides, barely noticing that his friend Moira, who had just come in from the kitchen, squeaked and jumped out of the way.

Best friend or no, nobody—nobody—knocked the alpha male around in his own . . . damned . . . house. The other Pack members lived there by his grace and favor, thanks very much, and while the forty-room house had more than enough room for them all, certain things were simply . . . not . . . done.

"Don't start with me," Derik warned. The morning sunlight was slanting through the skylight, shining so brightly it looked like Derik's hair was about to burst into flames. His friend's mouth—usually relaxed in a wiseass grin—was a tight slash. His grass green eyes were narrow. He looked—Michael had trouble believing it—ugly and dangerous. Rogue. "Just stay off."

"You started it, at the risk of sounding junior high, and you're going to show throat and apologize, or you'll be counting your broken ribs all the way to the emergency room."

"Come near me again, and we'll see who's counting ribs."

"Derik. Last chance."

"Cut it out!" It was Moira, shrieking from a safe distance. "Don't do this in his own house, you idiot! He won't stand down, and you two morons—schmucks—losers will hurt each other!"

"Shut up," Derik said to the woman he (usually) lovingly regarded as a sister. "And get lost . . . This isn't for you."

"I'm getting the hose," she warned, "and then you can pay to have the floors resealed."

"Moira, out," Michael said without looking around. She was a fiercely intelligent female werewolf who could knock over an elm if she needed to, but she was no match for two males squaring off. The day was headed down the shit hole already; he wouldn't see Moira hurt on top of it. "And, Derik, she's right, let's take this outside—ooooof!"

He didn't duck, though he could see the blow coming. He should have ducked, but . . . he still couldn't believe what was happening. His best friend—Mr. Nice Guy himself!—was challenging his authority. Derik, always the one to jolly people out of a fight. Derik, who had Michael's back in every fight, who had saved his wife's life, who loved Lara like she was his own.

The blow—hard enough to shatter an ordinary man's jaw—knocked him back a full three steps. And that was that. Allowances had been made, but now the gloves were off. Moira was still shrieking, and he could sense other people filling the room, but it faded to an unimportant drone. *Derik gave up trying for the door and slowly turned. It was like watching an evil moon come over the horizon. He glared, full in the face: a dead-on challenge for dominance. Michael grabbed for his throat, Derik blocked, they grappled. A red cloud of rage swam across Michael's vision; he didn't see his boyhood friend, he saw a rival. A challenger.*

Derik wasn't giving an inch, was shoving back just as hard, warning growls ripping from his throat, growls that only fed Michael's rage—

(Rival! Rival for your mate, your cub! Show throat or die!)

—made him yearn to twist Derik's head off, made him want to pound, tear, hurt—

Suddenly, startlingly, a small form was between them. Was shoving, hard. Sheer surprise broke them apart.

"Daddy! Quit it!" Lara stood between them, arms akimbo. "Just . . . don't do that!"

His daughter was standing protectively in front of Derik. Not that Derik cared, or even noticed; his gaze was locked on Michael's: hot and uncompromising.

Jeannie, frozen at the foot of the stairs, let out a yelp and lunged toward her daughter, but Moira moved with the speed of an adder and flung her arms around the taller woman. This earned her a bellow of rage. "Moira, what the hell? Let go!"

"You can't interfere," was the small blonde's quiet reply. "None of us can." Although Jeannie was quite a bit taller and heavier, the smaller woman had no trouble holding her back. Jeannie was the alpha female, but human—the first human alpha the Pack had known in three hundred years. Moira would follow almost any command Jeannie might make . . . but wouldn't let the woman endanger herself, or interfere with Pack law that was as old as the family of Man.

Oblivious to the drama on the stairs, Derik started forward again, but Lara planted her feet. "Quit it, Derik!" She swung her small foot into Derik's shin, which he barely noticed. "And, Daddy, you quit, too. Leave him alone. He's just sad and feeling stuck. He doesn't want to hurt you."

Michael ignored her. He was glaring at his rival and reaching for Derik again, when his daughter's voice cut through the tension like a laser scalpel.

"I said, leave him alone."

That got his attention; he looked down at her in a hurry. He expected tears, red-faced anger, but Lara's face was, if anything, too pale. Her eyes were huge, so light brown they were nearly gold. Her dark hair was pulled back in two curly pigtails.

He realized anew how tall she was for her age, and how she was her mother's daughter. And her father's. Her gaze was direct, adult. And not a little disconcerting.

"What?" Shock nearly made him stammer. Behind him, nobody moved. It seemed nobody even breathed. And Derik was standing down, backing off, heading for the door. Michael, in light of these highly interesting new events, let him go. He employed his best Annoyed Daddy tone. "What did you say, Lara?"

She didn't flinch. "You heard me. But you won't hear me say it again."

He was furious, appalled. This wasn't—He had to—She couldn't— But pride was rising, blotting out the fury. Oh, his Lara! Intelligent, gorgeous—and utterly without fear! Would he have ever dared face down his father?

It occurred to him that the future Pack leader was giving him an order. Now what to do about it?

A long silence passed, much longer in retrospect. This would be a moment his daughter would remember if she lived to be a thousand. He could break her . . . or he could start training a born leader.

He bowed stiffly. He didn't show the back of his neck; it was the polite bow to an equal. "A wiser head has prevailed. Thank you, Lara." He turned on his heel and walked toward the stairs, catching Jeannie's hand on the way up, leaving the others behind.

Moira had released her grip on his wife, was staring, openmouthed, at Lara. They were all staring. He didn't think it had ever been so quiet in the main hall.

Michael was intent on reaching his bedroom, where he could think about all that had just happened and gain his wife's counsel. He didn't quite dare go after Derik just yet—best to take time for their blood to cool. Christ! It wasn't even eight o'clock in the morning!

"Mikey—What—Cripes—"

And Lara. His daughter, who jumped between two werewolves with their blood up. Who faced him down and demanded he leave off. His daughter, defending her dearest friend. His daughter, who had just turned four. They had known she was ferociously intelligent, but to have such a strong sense of what was right and what was—

Jeannie cut through his thoughts with a typically wry understatement. "This can't be good. But I'm sure you can explain it to me. Use hand puppets. And me without my So You Married a Werewolf *guide . . ."*

Then he was closing their bedroom door and thinking about his place in the Pack, and his daughter's, and how he hoped he wouldn't have to kill his best friend before the sun set.

CHAPTER SIX

Though the memory was years old, it still had the power to astonish him. From her earliest beginning, Lara had been as protective as she was aggressive; the only thing she feared was failing in her duty. Nothing else had the power to frighten her: she was too young and vibrant to understand death, never mind fear it, and she had been born into privilege and would never fear poverty or deprivation. Getting caught in a mistake or, worse, letting someone down . . . *that* had the power to make her tremble.

Sean, now. Humans said *cut from a different bolt of cloth* and the Pack said *came from the wrong litter* and both sayings summed up how you could adore and cherish someone not at all like you while also being utterly puzzled by them.

He would kill or die for Lara because she was just like him. He would kill or die for Sean because he wasn't.

SIX YEARS AGO

"Hey. Move."

Sean raised a hand to shade his eyes. He'd wandered over to Nauset Beach; public beaches were a pain, but this one had waves today, which, for New England, was pretty much unheard of.

"S'up?" he asked the three shadows. The sun was at their backs, and with the ocean racket and hollering little kids and squealing teenagers and bellowing moms ("Curtis! I said don't go back in until you've put on more sunscreen! Curtis! Do you hear me, young man? Get back over here right now! Curtis, do you hear me? You are gonna be red as a lobster and I'm not gonna—Curtis! You get back here! Get back here now and get some more sunscreen on! Curtis! Curtis Daniel Graham, you get back here! I am talking to you, young man! You get over here right now! Right now, I said! Curtis! If you don't get over here right now, Curtis, you will—Curtis! Curtiiiiiiiiis!"), he'd never heard them come up. From their lack of neck, he assumed they were Riley, Jeff, and Geoff from the middle school football team. At twelve, Sean had no use for football teams or football players, and not much use for middle school. "Are you trying to loom?" He yawned. "I'm guessing you're going for loom."

"You've got a private beach, Wyndham."

"That's true," he admitted cheerfully. "But today I want the luxury of my private one and also the pain in the ass of this public one. Go away or I'll end up with a tan the exact shape of your head and shoulders, which will be weird for all of us—pphhhmm."

He'd said "pphhhmm" because Riley had—yep, he really had—kicked sand in his face. The smallest of the looming trio, Riley had small, fast feet. "Really?" he complained. "You don't feel like a bad ad in a seventies comic book doing that?" He spat out several grains. "I know how this goes. All I need is a bikini'd babe to lose respect for me because I didn't engage, and then I'll storm home and secretly embark on a weight-gain, weight-lifting regimen, and come back years later to find you and kick your ass. I dunno. That sounds like so much work."

"So how about you get the fuck outta here?"

"But I just got comfy. See?" He pointed to what he was lying on. "It's my tanning secret: an authentic President Eastwood beach blanket circa 2016. Note his squinty expression, like Popeye with a kidney stone. His squint says, 'I'll keep you safe and will blow up any country that dares mock the U.S. of A., punk.'"

"We never know what the fuck you're talking about," Geoff whined. Sean could tell by their tone and scents that they were frustrated bordering on bored; their body language just hadn't caught up. Their stance and scent broadcast their confusion: they were being all kinds of aggressive and Sean didn't much care.

Yep. He didn't. They'd get bored and leave, and he didn't care; he'd go back to sunbathing. They'd stick around and harass him, and he didn't care; he'd dish it back. (And nobody could outtalk Sean Wyndham.) They'd step up the harassment and get physical, and he didn't care; he'd hold his own, or decide they weren't worth physical exertion and go back to his private beach.

He. Didn't. Care.

It made bullying Sean Wyndham a nightmare.

"Is it true your grandpa and your uncle both died of cancer this year?" he asked with honest curiosity. Packers didn't get cancer. Geoff

hadn't taken a break from snapping bras, handing out wedgies, or rolling up on beaches to pick fights with smaller kids, so it was hard to tell if he was in mourning or not. "Because I'm sorry if it's true." And he was. Cancer sounded just awful. It was like hearing someone died of bubonic plague—it was nothing you or yours had had to worry about for centuries, but it was still pretty bad news.

Geoff's hands, which looked the size and texture of catcher's mitts, balled into fists. "You shut up about that."

"So, yes?"

"Faggot," Geoff said, desperation clear in his tone. So: no sympathy today; all bullying activities will continue as scheduled. You had to admire the boy's stoic endurance.

"Careful, or I'll tell my boyfriend on you and he'll kick sand in your urethra." Sean yawned and lay back down. "Don't you guys have date-raping skills to bone up on? Get it? Bone?"

"You—" Jeff broke off and, even though his back was to the parking lot, Sean was downwind and knew why. "Uh."

"Now you'll be sorry, A, B, and B-minus."

"What?" Riley asked, just as Sean's father reached their little group. "What's going on?"

"Heeeeeeere's Daddy!"

His father glanced down at him. Sean waved up at him from his Clint Eastwood towel. "I love that movie, The Shining," *Sean said, apropos of nothing. "The third remake was the best."*

"Your mom's been looking for you."

"Probably because I stole her towel," he agreed.

"At least you're willing to confess your crime." His father stared across his son's sprawled tanning body at the would-be bullies. Even in faded, paint-stained cargo shorts, a T-shirt from Cap'n Frosty's, and

bare feet, his father cut a formidable figure. And Dad was old. Almost forty. He'd prob'ly need a cane soon. "Is there a problem, boys?"

"Uh—"

"No, sir."

"Nuh-uh, Mr. Wyndham, we were just hanging out with Sean."

"Mmmm. I don't think I know any of you."

"That's A," Sean said, pointing to Riley. "That's B." To Jeff. "That's B-minus." To Geoff. "B-minus had recent deaths in the family, so we're being nice to him. Right, B-minus?"

"What?" his father and B-minus asked in unison.

"They're exchange students," Sean explained. "From a land far, far away. Their real names are too complex for my feeble American brain, so I've given them letters."

"Sean—"

"Thanks for stopping," he told the three boys, who were retreating as quickly as they could while trying to make it look like they weren't. "See? All gone."

"Sean—"

"No, Dad," he said kindly. "I'm not giving you their names. I handled it. It's fine. No need to pull a Godfather."

His father squatted beside him, yellow eyes intent on his face. "You've got sand all over your mouth."

"I got hungry while lying on Clint's face."

"Sean! They rolled up on you, kicked sand at you, crowded you."

He put his sunglasses back on. "I know the short-term memory of a preteen boy is horrifically short, but I did manage to remember the events of the past forty seconds, Dad."

His father pulled the sunglasses off to maintain eye contact. "They were challenging you for territory. People will do that your whole life and it's okay, it's how things are. I can help you with that. You've got to—"

"What, Dad?" Sean propped himself up on his elbows. "I'm three times as strong and five times as fast as they are. They only made the football team because I didn't bother to try out. Same with basketball, same with every organized sport ever. They think they're stronger than me and we know they aren't. So, what? Show them they're wrong? Put them in the ER for the rest of the afternoon? For what? To prove they didn't scare me? They didn't scare me." He wondered how to politely ask his father to keep lecturing him on the other side of his pilfered towel, where he wasn't blocking the rays. "Besides, karma's gonna get them."

"You have to make your own karma, Sean."

"I'm not sure you actually understand what karma is, Dad."

"Sean, you can't let people like that—"

"Kids. Kids like that. Actually, asshats like that."

"Asshats?" His dad sighed. "You've been talking to Betsy Taylor again."

"Only because you weren't home to take the call. Oh, and because she's an honest-to-God vampire! It's weird that I think she's so smokin' she's absolute zero, right?"

"She's been eligible for Social Security for years, so, yes, it's weird."

"What's Social Security?"

"A program President Fey had to—we're getting off the subject."

"Are we? Huh."

"Nice try. But still," his father persisted, and Sean stifled a groan. The old man had the worst time letting go of a bone. Any bone. "You've got to stand up for yourself or—"

"Or they'll think I'm a chicken? Do not care, Dad. At all. Or you will? I'm not a coward, Dad, and it's enough that I know that. I don't

need to waste one moment proving it to anyone, even you." Sean sighed and laid down, then sat back up. "All this—it's the same again."

"I don't understand."

"We're different. What all this means is, if someone did that to you, you'd have to prove you were El Alpha Supreme-o and kick their asses and send them to the ER in garbage bags. And that's fine. But I'm not you. I don't have to prove anything. Not even to you." Maybe, *he thought, thinking of his big sister, who would not have been able to walk away from A, B, and B-minus,* especially *to you.*

His father looked at him for a long time—well, probably only a few seconds, but it felt like a long time. Finally he shook his head. "Sean, I don't understand you."

"That's okay, Dad. I understand you."

And he smiled, not bounced out of countenance by anything that had happened in the last ten minutes. Or the last ten years.

And his father shook his head once more, and smiled back.

CHAPTER
SEVEN

It had been a long day, Lara's first full day as leader. And it had gone all right, she thought. Well. She had no frame of reference, but no one died, no one wanted to fight, no one even wanted to raise their voice.

The full moon was three days away, and the Pack's territory was bursting. Often people who lived in other parts of the state/country/world would travel to the seat of power for their Change. Pack members who hardly ever got to see each other could kick back, relax, chase some rabbits together, maybe make a new friend and fuck on the dunes . . . good times. The moon, so enticing when she was full and fat, always went back on her crash diet, and Pack members back to their day jobs as accountants and Democrats.

Those who lived too far from Cape Cod, or didn't feel it necessary to fuck on dunes, would absolutely show up this moon of all moons to inspect a new Pack leader. So Lara's day had been filled with meeting and greeting and (she hoped) assuaging anxiety with her serene, responsible demeanor. Or at least a demeanor that said, *Hey, things will be okay under the new regime, probably, I'm pretty sure . . . Steak tartare, anyone?*

("Confidence," her brother had teased her hours ago, "thy name is Lara." Sheer self-respect demanded she put him in a head lock until their mother began shrieking that they'd punch through the wall or stair banister again and threatened to go for her Beretta.)

Thank God for Sean. She knew her little brother's disinterest in all things aggressive, forceful, or hostile disconcerted their father and amused their mother to no end, but she'd never been more grateful for their differences than this week. An Armageddon-esque comet could be rocketing toward Massachusetts, and Sean would swipe Mom's Clint Eastwood towel and lay out on the beach to watch it come in and kill them, possibly sucking down Bloody Marys by the barrelful.

"How can I have sired a beta male?" her father had wondered once, years ago, when he thought Lara was farther away than she was. He'd only dared bring it up when Sean was several states away on his annual camping trip with BabyJon Taylor, the vampire queen's brother/son hybrid. Who wasn't a baby, but that was by far the least weird thing about the Taylor pack. *By far.*

"You mean, how come your son isn't a raging, testosterone-stuffed, date-raping jackhole like his papa?" her mother had asked with aggravating cheer. "Not that we were even on a date when we first met, Mikey, if you'll recall correctly, and I can see by the way you suddenly can't look me in the eye that you do.

Nothing like *Wham, bam, sorry I knocked you up, now you gotta move to the Cape and raise cubs with me . . . What was your name again, ma'am?* to liven up a girl's evening. What a romantic you were, my love!"*

"Argh. You made your point." Lara could hear the ruefulness in his tone, knew he was scrubbing his hands through his thick hair and, yes, avoiding eye contact with her mother. They would both kill or die for each other, but her mother maintained the lifelong right to tease her father about their first "date." "Okay, so, of course, betas aren't *all* bad."

"I think you mean"—Lara sucked in her breath, hearing the warning (and if she could pick up on it, her father could, too)—"betas aren't bad at *all*."

"Yes. Of course. That's what I meant. Yes. Yes. We need them, obviously. The Pack wouldn't survive without them. If it was all alphas—"

"You'd be fighting."

"Yeah."

"All the time."

"Well, yes."

"You'd be fighting about when to fuck, or fighting about who to fuck, or fighting about where to fuck who and when, and in the meantime the rest of the Pack would have starved to death. It'd be just, *aarrggh, we're so hungry, please stop fighting for just a little while so we can take five minutes to hunt for*—gaakkk!"

"Yes." Michael choked back a laugh. "That's just right."

"So, what? You've got an alpha. You've got something else.

---

*The sordid details can be found in *Secrets: Volume 6: Love's Prisoner.*

At least you and Sean can be in the same room without wanting to set each other on fire after twenty seconds."

"That was an accident," he corrected her, "and it had nothing to do with the Miniskirt Battle of 2020. And the firemen were able to save most of the wing."

"I'm gonna indulge my inner Trekkie for a minute—"

"*Please* don't."

"—and remind you of the IDIC. Infinite Diversity in Infinite Combination. Translation: you're a fortunate man in all things, if everyone was the same, it'd be a nightmare of boredom, so shut your jackhole and kiss me."

"It sounded different when Spock explained it," he'd replied with a sigh, and then they weren't talking anymore, and Lara went back outside without her mom's Clint Eastwood towel, so they wouldn't know she'd heard.

No, she didn't understand Sean's way of seeing the world, but she appreciated it. He was a blast of freezer air in August—different and refreshing and weird. He tolerated things she couldn't: bullies and bullshit. And knew things she didn't—how to go along to get along. Not for nothing did he graduate Best Storyteller and Best Shoulder To Lean On. He put up with a lot, and she didn't understand it but did respect it.

(Also, she'd tracked down every cowardly stinking shit-mouth bully who ever dared touch her brother and kicked their asses, from Dennis Linderman in preschool to Jeff Pedermahn in middle school to Maureen Chowton at high school graduation.)

Tonight, she knew Sean would rather be in Boston with their folks but had never so much as hinted at the possibility of making the trip with them, or meeting them later. She appreciated that, too.

So Lara meeted and greeted and her parents were not at the mansion, were deliberately not at the mansion. They'd spent the afternoon and evening in Boston, doing their own meeting and greeting with Dr. Bimm and l'il Dr. Bimm. Knowing how much Sean enjoyed l'il Dr. Bimm's company, she made a mental note to invite Fred's pack to swim and sun and eat with them before summer disappeared completely. Once things settled. Because they would settle. They'd *better*.

Dr. Bimm had to kill her own father to not *take the Pack. So things could be a lot worse.* She still wasn't quite sure what had brought such calamitous events about, had never gotten the whole story. Dr. Bimm would never talk about it, and l'il Dr. Bimm hadn't even been whelped when it had happened. If her parents knew any of the deliciously gory-sounding details, they'd never shared.

She gave herself a mental shake to get back to the present. Anyway. Her parents weren't there, but not because they doubted her. They'd gotten themselves gone because they didn't want to be cornered for endless rounds of, "Say, you're alive! So you could still be running things. We're glad you're not dead and no offense, Michael, but *what the fuck were you thinking*?" Not that they could avoid it completely. But not being available for consultation on Lara's first day sent a powerful message.

("Lara's agreed, I've agreed, my mate has agreed. The decision has been made," her father said. He didn't add, *And that's it*, because this wasn't the movies, it was the Pack. *And that's it* was understood, and thus unnecessary to verbalize.

In other words, that's how it is, and if you don't like it, howl at the moon somewhere else.

"The other Wyndham family motto," Sean decided.)

She'd expected to spend the day without her parents but with several Pack members, many she'd never met. She had not expected to miss three: Derik, Sara, and Jack.

Okay, the truth: she'd missed one.

Where is he? she'd wondered, shaking sweaty hand after sweaty hand. (She was almost positive the sweat wasn't hers.) *This is kind of Pack history in the making and they haven't visited in two years. I know they're here now; they'd never miss this. Why wouldn't they come over on my first day?*

She didn't know. And suddenly being the leader wasn't such fun after all. Not that she'd expected fun. She hadn't. But she'd expected something.

CHAPTER
EIGHT

Lara stared down at the dead fish on the kitchen stoop and thought, *This does not bode well.*

She went back inside, stubbed her toe on the doorway leading to the kitchen, and while absently rubbing her sore toe had a quiet word with Lenny, who promised to have a quiet word with Kara, the head of the kitchen staff. Then she scored the last cup of hot chocolate and sat back down at the breakfast table. *That will teach me to wander down for a bite, think,* Hmm, what smells like a dead fish? *and then go find a dead fish.*

Question: How did a kitchen full of Packers not smell a dead fish?

Answer: the Atlantic Ocean is about sixty meters from the kitchen door.

Funny how this was one of her favorite rooms, even when her folks were out of town. The room was big and bright, with lots of windows and light blond wood on the walls and the floor. The table was small, but the sideboard was almost as big, and groaning with food. Even though her folks weren't here, Sean *was*, and the kitchen staff planned accordingly.

She hadn't slept well, again, and was sure it showed: sweat pants, battered T-shirt, hair that had yet to meet a brush that morning. Her eyes felt like sand traps. Who cared? If Jack hadn't bothered to come around, what was the point?

Argh. That is not *what I meant. I meant, a leader shouldn't spend enormous amounts of time wondering if she's pretty enough to receive. She just receives. Or not. Sweat pants or a Gucci gown, it's all about the girl wearing the clothes, not the clothes wearing the girl.*

She pulled her iPad out of her robe and unfolded it until it was about 210 mm by 230 mm: the size of a standard piece of printer paper. Not that anybody used printers anymore. Some people liked to show off by not unfolding it any larger than a pack of cards, but Lara had never been a fan of eye strain.

Data immediately began to stream across it, but she had no interest in current events. She was stuck in the past, and wasn't sure why. Pack members weren't prone to introspection.

She was surprised she could be lonely in a household full of at least twenty people, day or night.

Is my father lonely, even with my mother?

He *must* be. And before now she had never wondered. She had never even thought of it. *What else haven't I thought of?*

Lara wasn't surprised she'd had another stress dream last night. She'd been having them on and off since her father had proposed his terrifying, unprecedented idea. Werewolf (oh, that silly name, but it saved time because everyone knew what it meant) dreams and stress dreams had two things in common: the dreamer wasn't aware they were dreaming until they awoke, and they were stressful. There was, of course, good stress and bad stress.

Guess which one I keep getting?

No, the surprise wasn't that she'd had a nightmare. The surprise was that Jack Gardner was in it, was always in those dreams.

She had dreamt of him from earliest childhood; strange! She *still* didn't know him well. She didn't know him and . . .

. . . she was afraid of him. And again, had been from earliest childhood.

You're thinking about this to avoid thinking about your new role, about the dead fish, about the dead bat Dad didn't tell you about. It's chickenshit. She knew it. She wouldn't hide from it. Because it was also a matter of fear, and hiding from that? Also chickenshit.

She dreamed of him, but told no one—not even Daddy, who she could tell anything. He might not love her as much if he knew she was a stupid scared cub.

She wasn't alone in that, either, which should have made her feel better but didn't. Some of the other cubs, they'd expressed fear through anger and she wasn't sure they knew it.

When the adults were out of sight and smell, the other cubs would pick on Jack and bully him, and he'd either hold his own—he had their strength, if not their other gifts—or retreat. Then he'd be gone again, no one knew for how long, and it was funny how that just made the other cubs more afraid.

Their parents had a name for Jack Gardner, a name said with such distrust it sounded like a swear word: incomer.

She'd never heard the word before. And they'd almost . . . they'd almost *spat* it. Like it was a swear, a really bad one.

So she borrowed her mother's old iPad, a clunker that didn't even fold, and looked it up. The definition didn't seem terrible. An incomer was someone who moved to a place he wasn't born. Heck, her mom was an incomer. So was Jack's mom. And Jack's dad, *her* dad's best friend. Derik had to take off and live entire months—sometimes years—in places her dad *wasn't*. Or they'd kill each other. Not in the silly play-fights humans were so fond of ("I can't stand that guy, I'm gonna kill him, he took the last donut!"). In an I'm-afraid-I've-killed-your-husband-but-I'll-make-sure-you-and-the-cubs-are-taken-care-of way.

That wasn't especially scary; that's how things were. Alphas were rare, and they didn't live together for long. Couldn't. So Jack being an incomer, that was okay. It wasn't scary or weird. Lara was so, so thankful her brother had zero interest in running the Pack, that she was the only alpha of her generation.

So Jack was an incomer: so what? She looked up the antonyms, too; she knew from Miss Berrin, her least favorite English teacher, that antonyms could help you figure out strange words. So she checked out related words, and some of those were fine and some of them were scary, a little.

Refugee. Relocatee. Foreigner. Those words made it sound like an incomer had things done to them, things they couldn't help. Things that made *her* want to help *them*. Those words made her mad that the other cubs were being mean about Jack.

Migrator. Pilgrim. Pioneer. Those words made her proud that Jack was (sometimes) a neighbor. Lara had grown up less than thirty-three miles from Plymouth Rock. *Pilgrims* sought new challenges, wanted better lives for their families. *Pilgrims* braved hardship that would kill those who had stayed behind. *Pioneer* wasn't just a good word, a *pioneer* was brave and sought new territory so they and their cubs could have better lives; *pioneers* were to be respected and revered.

Exile. Illegal. Alien. Those were scary. Those made Jack sound like he wasn't just different, but that he could do things to them. Pol Pot and Idi Amin were exiles. (Cubs learned early what humans were capable of doing to their own packs. If she hadn't seen the footage, she would never have believed they were capable of such utter insanity.)

Illegal made it sound like Jack was doing bad things, breaking Pack laws and other ones, too. And *alien* . . . that made it sound like he was strange and frightening and could do things no one else could.

Like his mother.

The sorceress.

The Pack was afraid of her, too, but that was a whole other thing, and it had nothing to do with why the Gardner litter had to move around so much.

Usually when Lara researched something, even when she found out bad or scary things, she felt better for *knowing*. After looking up incomer, she felt worse.

"This is gonna sound weird given that if you fall out the right door in this place you're actually in the ocean," her brother announced, slouching down the stairs, "but what smells like dead fish?"

Firmly back in the present (for the moment), Lara watched him come, amused enough to almost cheer up. Only Sean could make slouching an *active* verb. He was so laid back he almost came down the stairs lying down.

"You're right," she replied, "it sounds weird. Is this the part where I pretend you're not down here to check on me because you and dad found the bat? Thanks for telling me, by the way. I know why Dad didn't."

"Yeah, he's weird like that, what with loving you and not wanting you to worry on your first day and hoping it was some dumb coincidence. He mentioned his suicide theory, and I have to say, I was skeptical. I'm pretty sure that bat was murdered."

"Makes two of us." She stared into her cocoa. "I guess whoever it is left it on the kitchen stoop because there are a zillion scents around here at any time, especially the kitchen area, and it's the busiest part of the house. It's risky because someone might catch you sprinkling bat bits on the front stoop, but if no one does see you, it's not likely to be discovered right that second so you'll have time to . . . I don't know. Get away? Get back to work? Is it supposed to scare me? I'm more annoyed than afraid. I told Kara I'd take care of the fish but she said not to worry about it. And I'm really not."

"That's the spirit. And to answer your question, no, this is the part where I pretend you're not drinking the last of the cocoa, you heartless bitch. What?" he yelped, scanning the sideboard. "You scarfed all the juice, too? Green tea? *That's* what's left? Why don't I just drink a nice cup of dirt? Huh? Is that what you want, Lara? For me to drink a cup of dirt? Will that make you happy?"

"Nice try, but I'm not distracted. Not much." She sucked down more hot chocolate with a loud slurp. "Ahhh! Nectar of the gods."

"Don't blame you. People like us—"

"Here we go."

"—who turn into wolves once a month and rut and poop on beaches and dig through the garbage dump are not known for our subtlety."

"That's true." Lara smiled at him over her cup of delicious, delicious hot chocolate. "We're not."

"So who's doing it? And why?"

"Extrapolate, Holmes."

"No more word-of-the-day toilet paper for you. Listen, if somebody's pissed about you running things, they can just roll on up and Challenge you. Now is the best time: you're still feeling your way around, but you're the boss now. If someone wants your throat, Dad can't stop it. In fact, if someone wants your throat, and tears it out, Dad not only can't stop it, he's gotta pay fealty to the new Pack leader. Instead of leaving grotesque hope-you-fuck-up-the-new-job-bitch! gifts on the back steps, they should be kicking the door down and wanting to make with the rumble."

"Rumble?" She almost laughed.

"Watch an old movie. Just once. That's all I ask. Once. And you know I'm right; you know a Challenge works way better than a gut-laden welcome mat. You're still thought of as an annoying little kid even though you're an annoying adult. So what's with the dead pets? It's so dumb."

"Not pets. A bat and a fish."

"No, Lara. A pet fish and a pet bat."

Shit. "I didn't think of it like that."

"That's okay." He yawned, grabbing a double handful of bacon from the sideboard. The breakfast room was splashed with so much sunshine Sean's eyes were almost closed in a squint. He'd worn sunglasses every day for a month until their father had had enough and banned them. "You know we don't keep you around for your great big brain."

"So . . ." She pushed her mug over to her brother, staring at her iPad while he gulped the last three scalding mouthfuls. "Do I call Dad first, or them?"

Sean didn't say anything, which she should have guessed. He'd tease, they'd banter, he'd make pointed remarks about her dreadful clothes or morning breath or lack of boyfriends, but for a real question? He knew it was her call. Literally her call.

She opened her mouth to make it, but cut herself off.

He's here!

"Lara?" Debbie, one of the kitchen staff, poked her head around the corner. "We got that mess on the step cleaned up—sorry we didn't catch it."

"Never apologize!" Sean's voice was muffled with bacon. "You had two hundred bacon strips to fry. That comes before *everything*."

Debbie laughed at him; she'd been working in the Wyndham kitchens since their father was Sean's age, and feared none of them. "Listen to you, boy. Slow down! Lara, hon, Jack Gardner's here to see you. And, Sean? We can put on a new pot of cocoa if you like."

"No, my sister's backwash dregs are all I'm gonna need. So it goes for Pack peons. Hmm, I might have to start a club. The PPs. We'll need a kicky slogan, though. Wait, what? Jack's here, finally? Lara, that'll put a smile on your hideous ugly face! I know you were wondering why they didn't stop by yesterday."

He was coming. She couldn't hear him, but she could feel him. "Lara?"

She hoped dead pets and Gardner's arrival were only coincidences. She had no taste for what she'd have to do if they weren't.

"Hellooooo?"

Almost there. Almost there. Almost there. She was on her feet and had no memory of moving. When had she stood? Had she always been standing?

A polite rap on the doorway (there was no actual door, just an open space that led from the kitchen hallway) and he was there. He was *right there*, filling her senses, her world. She could *hear* him filling her—or was that just the thrum of blood in her ears, the call of hers to his?

Someone was speaking to her, but their voice was tinny and fading. A tall, broad-shouldered shape and fog-colored eyes and her-his-their instant desperate need, that's what she saw and felt.

"Hi, Jack! Great to see you! I know it's been a couple of years—are your folks here?"

Had she always been waiting for him to return to her life?

"Are you okay?"

Yes. She had. When had the world gotten so small? It was her. And it was him.

"Jack?"

That's all. That's all the world was, now.

"Oh my God."

I can't be feeling like this unless he is, too. Impossible. Impossible. Oh, I'm not lonely anymore . . . and now I know why Dad isn't, even if I never noticed, or thought to ask.

"Oh my God! Don't! Don't do anything yet!" She could *almost* hear the sound of furniture being knocked over in Sean's haste to leave. "Look, I'm going, I'm going! Jack, move out of the doorway and I will leave, I promise. Jack! Move so I can flee! Jaaaaaaack!"

At last, at last, at last, Jack was moving, and he took the quickest path to her, he took two steps and then stepped on the chair and then used the chair as a stepladder to the table and plates crashed and broke and glasses shattered as he walked through bacon and broken crockery and a plate of scrambled eggs and stepped in the butter and knocked over the vase of sunflowers and plodded through the plate of sliced tomatoes to get to her and it was all taking so *long.*

Why, he's been walking through breakfast looking at me for days and days! And who is screaming?

"Please wait until I get clear of the building, for the love of God! Yuck! Yuck! No, Deb, do *not* go in there, for your life. Or at least your eyes. No one go near this room for the rest of the day! Do we have any crime scene tape?"

CHAPTER
NINE

By the time Jack reached her, he was pulling at his shirt and she had torn hers off (though it was so ancient it hadn't needed much force). She tried to step toward him and tripped; he caught her before she went sprawling.

Then he was kicking out of his dark brown boat shoes, their bottoms caked with bacon and butter and glass shards—

(maybe he should leave them on)

—and she was trying to help him with his jeans, and her hands felt like they'd grown extra fingers, and none of the fingers could hear her brain's commands; she was clumsy at the best of times, and now she was almost paralyzed.

While she was puzzling the intricacies of his belt—

(shiny thing equals buckle, buckle must be pulled on until prong is released equals jeans down equals jeans off equals sex)

—his mouth came down on hers in a kiss so scorching, she felt the jolt to her toes.

(Buckle must be destroyed equals jeans off equals sex.)

She could feel his hands on her waist, her thighs, pulling, and then her (beltless!) sweat pants were reduced to a few sad tufts of faded cotton and she finally defeated her ancient (or so it seemed; how long had she been battling the fucking thing?) nemesis, the belt buckle, and yanked at his zipper and jeans hard enough to jerk him forward. Then he was laughing into her mouth and she could see the funny side to their insane urgency. Not so funny they'd be willing to stop and discuss how amusing it all was, but, yeah, still funny.

"Hate your—nnf!—jeans."

"Let me—agh!" He slipped in butter or bacon grease and winced; she smelled blood and realized he'd cut his foot on broken glass.

"Dammit . . . dammit! Come here." She grabbed his forearms and pulled; he skidded with her. She glanced down at the side-board to take inventory—

(candlesticks, bread basket, biscuits, more butter, pitcher of orange juice, three juice glasses, pile of napkins, several clean forks, I hate orange juice!)

—and then swept it all off—

(Kara's gonna kill me)

—and hopped up. She realized she still had her panties on and hopped down and yanked and then hopped back up. A clever man, Jack had caught on and put his—

(warm, strong, ummmmmmmm)

—hands on her knees and spread them, dropped his pants—

(screw you, belt buckle! You have no power now!)

—and surged forward and put his arms around her lower back and yanked her to him, and he slid into her warm wetness like a knife through butter (like the kind he was standing in and she was sitting in). He'd barely seated himself inside her when he pulled back, and she opened her mouth to groan in protest. *(Was the belt buckle having the last laugh after all?)*

His next stroke forced the air from her lungs in a gasp, something that, if she'd read it in a book, she would assume had hurt.

It didn't. She hooked her ankles just above his ass and held on tight, clutched his shoulders, and bit his ear so hard blood squirted in her mouth and he shuddered. "Never stop," she hissed, her words slurred with so much desire she thought she might die of it, and his blood was in her and his cock was in her and this was the secret, this was how it was supposed to be. "Never stop, Jack."

"Never," he said, and bit her back, and her orgasm was on her like a breaker.

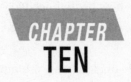

CHAPTER TEN

"Okay. That was . . . buttery."

Jack, who'd sort of slumped to the floor after his explosive orgasm, had just enough strength to laugh. "Exactly what I was going for."

Lara, still sitting on the sideboard, studied him, this man she'd dreamed of for years, had feared for years without knowing why. Now she knew. It made her no less afraid, but the fear changed nothing. They were supposed to be together. They were mated long before they had fucked. Her other self, the self with four legs and fur, the part many Pack members thought of as their true self, had known.

"You know, when we were younger and you'd come to visit, I'd have to—"

"Leave the room so you wouldn't pick up on how badly I

wanted you." He'd staggered to his feet and was gingerly picking the remains of his clothes from the mess of butter/sugar/broken glass covering at least a third of the floor. "You were always beautiful. You always seemed so far above me. I didn't have the courage to let you see how badly I needed you."

"Don't worry," she cheerfully confessed, "I was a big chicken about my desire, too."

"Relief! Ouch." He made a futile attempt to wipe the bottom of his foot clean. "I wonder that our fathers never picked up—ouch—on it."

"We should just stop moving except to find the door." Lara pushed some broken glass out of their path with her big toe. "And maybe they did but never discussed it. Or maybe they didn't, because they're our fathers and will always see us as children to be protected. Not adults who—" She cut herself off. *Who should be doing the protecting.* The bat. The fish. And what next? And why?

"It's ours to protect," Jack told her. His arms were scraped and scratched, like her back, like the bottoms of their feet. Every step was a crunch and a wince.

"Stop that."

"What?"

"Reading my mind."

He didn't smile; he was studying her. The color of his eyes was somehow sharper as he took her in, all of her. She let him look; it was the first time someone had stared at her that she hadn't taken as a challenge. After a long while—or so it seemed to her, but it may have been only seconds—he said, "I dreamed about you."

"Oh, yes," she said, and went to him, and stood in his warm

embrace while butter oozed between her toes. "We have to get the hell out of this room."

He laughed again, and she realized, in all the visits when they were children and teens and young adults, she'd never seen him laugh.

He's complete now, too.

Why had no one told her what it was like?

Likely most people don't know.

That was a worse thought than the bat and fish "gifts."

"Come on, then, Lara." He scooped her up in his arms and tossed her over his shoulder in a fireman's carry. She clutched his waist, then his ass. "No need for you to cut your feet more than you have."

"You can . . . heal like Pack, right?" She'd never had to ask. She'd never thought to ask. Not that it mattered. It wasn't about what Jack could do; it was about what he was. She closed her eyes; staring at his ass was making her forget about glass, cleaning up the mess they'd left in their lust, and dead fish. And breathing regularly.

"Yes. I can heal like your father, like my father." There was a pause as he picked his way across the room. "Everything but run around on four legs. You've never asked me that before."

She shrugged as best she could, upside down. "I'm probably going to be asking you lots of things I haven't."

"Please let that be some odd Wyndham euphemism for *have more sex until you can't feel your legs*," he muttered, and she laughed so hard he had to tighten his grip so as not to drop her.

After threatening the kitchen staff with death and mutilation if they went in the breakfast room with so much as a paper towel to start cleaning, she and Jack went to her suite and cleaned up. This led to more delights in the shower, and then on her bathroom floor, and then in her bed. By the time they were clean and dressed, they were also exhausted and it was long past lunchtime.

"Too bad," she said, elbowing Jack so he'd move over on the bed. He groaned and halfheartedly rolled a few inches. She flopped down beside him. "We've gotta get the breakfast room cleaned up, and I've got to make a phone call. Two calls, actually. And we should eat more. I don't think you ate at all."

"Not eggs or bacon, certainly." He gently touched her bitten ear. "Is this about what you've been worrying all morning?"

Lara had to smile at *been worrying* as opposed to *been worrying about*. Jack used it the way dogs would worry at a sore place on their paw.

"Yeah, which reminds me, you haven't left dead bats or fish on my kitchen stairs, right?"

"Uh . . . no. I thought I'd try flowers."

She snorted. "Sure you did."

"I might have eventually tried flowers." He caught her hand and pressed a kiss to her palm. "I've been waiting to return to you for a long time."

"Return to implies we were together and you left."

"Only in dreams," he said, his eyes far away. "I dream about you all the time."

She nodded.

"We'll mate and have cubs, then."

She nodded again.

"And should probably mention this to both our parents."

Hmm. That could be interesting.

"Your brother, I suspect, is aware."

She slapped her forehead. "Sean! Ah, God. He might be traumatized." Pack members weren't as hung up on sex as Western humans—who was?—but still. When your sister and someone you barely knew started boning away in the breakfast room where you were happily eating bacon mere moments before . . . "Ah, God," she said again, because it was all she could think of.

Jack gave up trying to keep a straight face and burst out laughing, actually clutching his stomach and rolling back and forth on her bed. "He was trying to leave the room and screaming like a witch, and my only focus was—well, it wasn't on him."

"All right. Dress first. Clean breakfast room. Apologize to traumatized brother. Make phone calls. You promise you didn't bring me a dead fish before you came over?"

Jack sobered and sat up. "No. And I can tell it's bothering you more than you're letting show. Let me help you."

Lara studied him, this man she barely knew who would be in her life through death and further. She still couldn't grasp how he had become so vital so soon; she had no idea how she would explain this to her mother. (Her father would bluster but, she suspected, would also know what she was talking about. He just wouldn't want to apply that knowledge to anything having to do with his daughter's sex life. Especially since pre-Jack, the answer to that would have been, "What sex life?")

"A few years ago my dad had the idea of retiring, not dying."

"Excellent plan."

She slapped his leg. "You know what I mean—so I could learn from him while leading. There'd be a young Pack leader and the old one would still be alive for advice and such. And after he talked about it with my mom, he talked to your dad."

Jack nodded. "I remember. Everything changed after that visit."

"Right. Well, we talked about it for years, and finally agreed. And yesterday was the big day, and first thing in the morning, before my folks left for Boston, my dad went out and found . . ."

CHAPTER
TWELVE

Kara and Deb asked and asked, and the third time Lara refused their help in the breakfast room, she couldn't take Jack's pleading looks any longer. "It's our mess," she said again.

"Of course it is." He'd gotten dressed in the jeans and the hated belt, but had to borrow one of her dad's old T-shirts, since his had been ruined. They'd gotten all the gunk off his shoes. "But they keep coming in wanting to help, and we keep sucking at cleaning up."

"It's true," Kara called from the kitchen.

"You're not helping," Lara called back.

"And they said they have extra help this week, a new kitchen guy."

"That's true!" Kara called.

"Enough! Both of you. Let me think." Lara puffed a lock of

dark hair out of her eye. They'd wiped and swept and mopped and hauled out bags of garbage and broken glass, and it still look like they'd barely started. "I guess . . . if you guys insist . . . really insist . . ."

"Thank God," she heard Deb mutter. Kara, Deb, and at least four other cleaners descended on them so quickly Lara realized they'd been waiting patiently in the kitchen for their turn. "*Thank* you," Deb said as the others scattered around the room and got to work. "Appreciate you wanting to take responsibility. Your folks—your mama especially—she didn't want a couple of entitled jerks for kids." Lara nodded; when they were cubs, the quickest way to get in trouble with their folks was to make a mess and then put on let-the-servants-handle-it attitude. "But you're not cubs. And you're in our way. And you're terrible at this. And don't you have more important things to be doing, Pack leader?"

"All right, all right."

"Besides, these things happen." Deb was giving Jack a long look and Lara caught the sharp scent of her interest. "And probably will again, I'm betting."

"Also, when you tell your folks what happened, can you do it when we're all around and can hear the whole thing? What?" Kara asked when Deb rolled her eyes. "My Cloud cable's out."

"You and you!"

Lara had been so consumed with the work—and the odors— she hadn't heard or scented Sean's return. He was standing, arms akimbo, in the doorway, giving her a Level Four Death Glare—until then, only her mother had been capable of generating that level of wrath from eyes alone.

"Hi, Sean," Lara said, so meekly everyone else stared.

"Ah, Sean, we just—" Jack began.

"Shut your cake hole, fornicator! You and you . . . let's go upstairs and talk."

Fornicator? Jack mouthed at her as they followed Sean up the stairs. She shrugged, pointed at Sean's back, and mimed a look of utter contrition.

"I can hear you, you know," Sean said, which made *no* sense, but they dropped their hands and followed like a couple bound for the gallows.

"Okay, first? Gross, and gross. And walking through bacon? I don't know what kind of degenerate jungle you grew up in, Jack 'I Think I'll Bang Your Sister Right This Second' Gardner, but if you're gonna be living here, which I assume because of the banging you are, you're gonna have to treat bacon with a whole other level of respect, *all* the *time*. Oh, and be a good mate to my sister and a good dad to your cubs and stuff."

"Respect bacon." Jack nodded. "Good mate, good dad. Yes."

"And you!" Sean jabbed a forefinger at Lara, who watched it warily. Rarely had her brother gotten so frothy. Of course, he had cause. But it was still odd to see him genuinely irked. "I get how alpha-ness is a curse of loneliness and no one can understand the depth of your sad pathetic forlorn-ness, blah-blah-blah, but take ninety damned seconds and get a room. There are twenty bedrooms in this house! There is no need to harm the bacon, ever!"

"Yes, Sean."

"I mean, I understand why you couldn't resist. You've gotten nailed—what? Five times in the last five years?"

"Really?" Jack asked, unable to conceal his delight and surprise. "But you're so beautiful, and you could have any—"

"No one's talking to you, Jack-in-the-penis!"

"Yes, Sean." *What sort of toys did this boy play with as a child?* "Sorry, Sean."

"Anyway, I get why you were slaves to your grotesque animal urges, I'm just saying leave the bacon out of it. Okay?"

"Okay, Sean."

Jack was still nodding. "We're very sorry, Sean."

"No, you aren't, Jack, but when my dad decides to beat you to death, you'll both need an ally, so I'm officially forgiving you gross weird fornicators."

He hangs around waaaaay too many humans. Fornicators?

"You leave humans out of this," Sean retorted, still pointing. He collapsed into the nearest chair; they were in one of the game rooms, so there were plenty. "Now. The fish? The bat?"

"Jack says no."

"Which means no. And speaking of humans and hanging out with them too much—"

"If a Packer was doing those things, we'd smell it on them." Not so much the bat and the fish, but the deceit. The guilt. Packers couldn't lie to each other, not about real things.

"Well, yeah. I was thinking about that while you two were— while I was trying really, really hard to think of something else. So who's the human leaving you grisly love notes, and why? What does any human care about Pack stuff?"

It reminded her of the old childhood joke: Q) Why did the human cross the road? A) Why do humans do anything they do?

There were humans on the Cape—all over the world—who knew about the Pack. Sure there were. There were inter-Pack/

human matings and friendships, of course, starting at the top with the then-alpha and his mate. When Jeannie moved to the mansion, she hadn't given up her human ties, her human friends. And in the near-mid-twenty-first century when the world was aware there were mermaids and vampires, the need to keep all things Pack a deep dark secret had never been *less* vital.

"So any number of humans could have left the bat and the fish," Lara summed up. "Who'd want to, though? And that's a queer kind of courage, walking into the wolves' den to leave that stuff. In front of everybody—in broad daylight, even."

"If you knew who, you'd know why," Jack said.

"And speaking of why, I'd better call now."

"All done having sex for a while?" Sean asked snidely. "Ready to get back to the boring business of Pack leadership? Swelleriffic." She ignored his jibes, but wouldn't much longer. Sean must have sensed her tolerance was coming to an end, because he moved from scolding to brisk. "Who first?"

Lara sighed. "You know who."

"Double swelleriffic!"

Jack was looking from brother to sister and back again. "This is why I'm glad I was an only child . . . You two practically have your own language."

"It compensates for bacon brutalization. When I close my eyes I can still see it . . . It was like you *raped* my *bacon* . . ."

"Little brother, *please* shut the hell up. This is hard enough. I almost hate to do it. But it's irresponsible if I don't." She shrugged, then raised her voice and said to the air, "Call: Betsy Taylor."

As they waited for the call to go through, Jack said, "The vampire queen?"

"Friend of the family."

"Yes, I know—the whole Pack knows—but I thought her name was Elizabeth."

"It is, only there was some famous old-timey movie star who had the same name, so she went by Betsy to avoid confusion, and it stuck."

"A little respect, please!" Sean yelped. "*Old timey?* Elizabeth Taylor, circa 1932 to 2011. Jeez. You guys."

"That's of course her prerogative," Jack said, puzzled, "but it's a kid's name."

Lara shrugged. "She's gotta be . . . let me think . . . fifty? No. Almost sixty." It was hard to tell, because Betsy always looked the same. "Could she be almost seventy? My dad would know . . . maybe . . ."

He raised a dark brow. "So you're calling an old woman who isn't Pack for advice?"

"Respect!" Sean yelped again, picking up a cork coaster and lobbing it at Jack. He ducked and it sailed harmlessly over his head. "Please!"

"I'm not calling for advice. And you'll like her."

"No." Jack smiled. "*You* like her. So you assume everyone else will."

"—for one second, Sink Lair! You know the rules: if you use up the last of the strawberries, you have to buy more *yourself.* No fair leaving the empty—"

"Betsy?"

"What? What did you—*No,* that's not Tina's job, and you're not delegating, you're just being more of an asshat than usual."

"Betsy?"

"Yeah? What? Sinclair, can you hear—Oh, shit . . . Am I on the phone?"

"Yeah, this is Lara Wyndham. Calling from the Cape."

"I hate—wait. I've gotta start talking slower; the tech has trouble understanding if I talk fast—Okay, just—it's nice to hear from you and all—Am I still on the phone?"

"Yes."

"You can hear me?"

Um, obviously. "Yes."

"Oh. Okay." A gusty sigh, which made Lara roll her eyes. Betsy didn't have to breathe, so the sighs were solely for drama. "I miss my iPhone. So much!"

"What's an iPhone?"

"Shut up."

Sean clapped both hands over his mouth to squash the giggles. Where once there were Clouds for online storage, to keep data and e-books and files of enormous size, phones had gone the same way. From wire to wireless to Cloud, once the area in question was tech-prepped, people just had to raise their voices and say the right thing and/or the right numbers, and the Cloud would connect the call. No big clunky fifty-millimeter-by-one-hundred-millimeter phones; their voices were all the hardware they needed.

"What's going on? I haven't seen your folks in forever."

"Yes, they're fine . . . Betsy, there might be trouble headed your way. Something's happened here."

"Aw, what? Jeez, you've been the PIC for, what, thirty hours?" Sean leaned forward. "PIC?"

"Hi, sweetie! Packer in Charge."

"How'd you even know—" Lara slapped her forehead. She'd likely bruise soon, if she didn't get smarter. "My dad told you."

"He gave us a heads up, yeah," Betsy admitted. "He didn't anticipate any problems, it was just an FYI."

"A what?" Sean was always interested in old acronyms.

"The worst thing about how there aren't phones anymore is that you're always, fucking *always*, on speaker phone," the vampire fumed from fifteen hundred miles away.

"What's a speaker ph—"

"Shut up."

Sean stuck his tongue out at the air, and nearly bit it when Betsy shrilled, "I heard that!"

"Spooky," he muttered.

"Listen, it's not that I don't find it flattering that a gorgeous young werewolf with her own Pack to run amok with is taking time out to chat with an old lady, but why are you calling really?"

"There's not a whole lot to tell," Lara began, "since we're not really sure ourselves what's going on. And my parents aren't here, so—"

"Are you in danger?" Betsy asked sharply, all playfulness gone from her tone. "Lara, it is not weakness to ask an old friend for help, okay? There are ways to get me to visit that don't involve letting your mom know you're worried you're in over your head."

"How—" She looked at her brother and Jack, both sitting calmly, two of the six people out of billions she'd show uncertainty to. "What makes you think I think I *might* be in over my head even though nothing too terrible has happened yet?"

Betsy made an impatient noise and followed it with, "Because you're not a raging sociopath. Anybody would be in over their head. You're barely cloning age and you're responsible for thousands. Or millions. However many Pack members are running around peeing on fire hydrants."

"Oh, *Betsy*," she groaned. "That's awful. You're awful."

The vampire laughed and laughed. "Gotcha. Totally worth it; I bet that's the first time you've smiled in days."

"The third or fourth, actually," she said, looking at Jack and ignoring Sean's feigned vomiting. She explained what happened, and was a bit piqued to hear Betsy's (overly dramatic) sigh of relief. "Excuse me?"

"A dead bat? That's it?"

"I was concerned it was a symbol you or yours may be in trouble," Lara said coldly, "and wished to take the time to inform you of same. So sorry to have bothered you."

"Lara, wait." A short silence, mercifully sigh-free; they could hear her murmuring to someone, probably the dead-sexy vampire king. "I did that badly. I'm sorry I said it the way I did, and I don't mean to make light of your problems. I'm glad you called and I'm truly sorry you're in difficulty. It's just—trust me, I was afraid it was something else, something I thought I fixed. Something I'm pretty sure I *did* fix, so don't worry. About that, I mean. Believe me, the world could be in much, much, much, much, much, much, much, much, much, much, much, much worse shape than it is now, even after the Kardashian Massacre. Those idiots—taking over every television network with their insipid 'reality' shows wasn't enough? They had to try for the entire Eastern Seaboard? All because Kim lost the election to Tina Fey?"

This is the problem with the elderly; they love their tangents. Lara rubbed her eyes; low on sleep rations, exhausted from hours of astonishing sex. *All right, there are worse problems.*

Betsy's ramble was coming to an end. ". . . anyway, take my word for it: worse things might have happened, and now won't, and so as terrible as things are right now, it's not a tenth as bad as they might have been, so chin up, l'il werewolf."

"This is one of those mysterious vampire things, isn't it?"

"Yeah, hon, it is."

She swallowed a yawn. "I hate when you call me l'il werewolf."

"I know."

Lara wasn't sure whether to be relieved or irritated. She opted for the former. "You'll tell me the whole story some day? Assuming I live through this?"

"Well . . . all right, but in one version I come off really evil and ancient and dress in truly ugly gear, the version that will never come to pass."*

"I'll try to be brave throughout your torrid tale of ugly gear," Lara promised. "You're sure everything else is all right?"

"Everything else is hunky-dory. You have no idea what that means, do you? Sean will tell you."

"No, I won't," he called.

"Don't make me come out there," the vampire threatened.

"I would *love* it if you came out here."

She laughed. "Perv! I'm old enough to be your . . . um . . . big sister."

"What bullshit," Lara said.

"Come on, you haven't visited in forever," Sean whined. "It's only twenty-four hundred kilometers."

"Stop it! Stop using the metric system."

---

*Gory details in *Undead and Unstable*.

Lara winced. Another pet peeve of the elderly. "Betsy—"

"I hate the goddamned thing! We shouldn't have agreed to the switch and we shouldn't be teaching it to our kids!"

"Hey, hey," Lara soothed. "Come on. Canada really helped us out during the Kardashian riots. The least we could do was adopt the metric system and help Quebec gain independence and be its own country. In lives saved alone, it was worth it—you've got to admit."

"I don't have to do anything except stay hot and not turn evil," she snapped.

"Well, you've done at least one of those things," Lara said with evil intent, knowing the vain vampire would spend the rest of the night wondering which one she meant. "End."

"Oh, now that's just ru—"

Heh. *Got the last word in, anyway.* Betsy hated the new phone tech, and half the time chattered five minutes after the call ended. It was comforting: it was one of the few ways the vampire queen acted her age. It could be jarring to be with someone who looked thirty but was close to a century old.

"I'd like to meet her," Jack admitted. "I think."

"No, you would—I told you, you'd like her."

"And she loves my sister," Sean said. "It's so annoying. I should be the one the dead queen loves! Why do dead queens only love stupid Lara?"

"Come on," she replied, embarrassed. "You know she likes all of us."

"She likes me. She likes Mom and Dad. She likes Jack's folks—so, yeah, Jack, you should definitely meet her. But she *loves* Lara."

Jack smiled. "Why wouldn't she?"

"Do you have several weeks? My list is lengthy."

"She *likes* me because she's a vampire queen who's not afraid to get her hands bloody or shitty. That's all."

"Oh, well," Jack teased. "If that's all."

"The first time she came out here, she took me to the playground and I got into a fight with a local kid." Lara shrugged; it was a story she remembered only because other people liked to tell it. She herself had no real memory of the incident; she'd still been a cub, and such power tussles were far more frequent for cubs than human children. "Apparently I made the turd my beta bitch and Betsy saw the whole thing and loved it. We were pals after that. And my folks liked her, once they got to know her."

"Yeah, mine, too." Jack smiled, remembering. "My mom liked how Betsy never held *your* mom shooting her against her."

"Mom put three in her chest." That she *did* remember, though she'd been even younger than at the time of the playground incident. "It just made Betsy mad. It . . . made an impression." One way to put it. "But I'm just talking because I'm putting off what I don't want to do."

"I know it's not starting to have sex while a your brother's in the room . . . You sure didn't put that off . . ."

Lara didn't smile. "You know. The easy one's done." She raised her voice. "Call . . . Fredrika . . . Bimm."

Jack's eyebrows—the most eloquent brows she'd ever seen, frankly—arched again.

"Oh, yeah," Sean said, noticing. "It's a party around here allll the time. After we call the mermaid, let's call a fairy or a banshee or something."

"Actually, that—" Jack began, but just then the mermaid answered, and whatever he said was cut off.

CHAPTER
THIRTEEN

"Yes, hello?"

"Dr. Bimm. It's—"

"Lara and Sean."

"And the fornicator to be named later," Sean began, but Lara whipped a soft pillow at him, which hit right between the eyes, and the resulting dust cloud incapacitated him for several seconds.

Lara raised her voice to be heard over his wheezing. "Dr. Bimm?"

"What is it, Lara?" Dr. Fredrika Bimm, her generation's Cousteau, had a phone manner identical to her manner in person: brisk and borderline unfriendly. "Someone giving you trouble already? What's it been, thirty hours?"

"Unbelievable," she muttered. She described the bat and the

fish and the condition both had been left in. "So my questions are—"

"Are the Undersea Folk, aka Mermaids on Parade, sending the Wyndham Pack a message in a deliberately vague, careless, and sloppy way?"

Somewhat taken aback, it took Lara a few seconds to respond. *Funny how hearing my dad deal with Dr. Fred was funny as hell. Actually having to deal with her, less so.* "No, I was concerned you—"

"Because we're not. The Undersea Folk have nothing—not one single thing—to fear from your Pack. And if we did, we'd send a message you would find unmistakable in its threat."

"Well, that's good." *I guess.* She thought about it, then mentally shrugged and asked, "Why not?"

"First, our territory is about fifty thousand times the size of yours. Second, we've got corresponding population to match. Third, the Folk have two-thirds of the ocean to wander in; the Pack has . . . Cape Cod. Which is sinking. Into the ocean."

Silence. Even Sean had lost his smile.

"Fourth, even if Orleans and Barnstable and Yarmouth don't become Atlantis II, III, and IV, you're losing more territory each year and will eventually have to make nicey-nice—more so than your father already has—with the Folk. Or declare war, which you'll lose, so you'll have to play nice. I'm not sure about the vampires, but you can be sure *they're* wondering about it, even if Betsy thinks you're just too, too adorable to take seriously yet.

"Fifth, if I had a problem with you, Lara, you'd know it. Your family would know it. My family would know it. There would be no puzzled ruminations followed by vague phone calls to fish, no pun intended. You would know, and you and I would work out our problem, or we wouldn't."

"You're welcome to my home anytime to work out anything you like," Lara said pleasantly, ears pricked forward. Thinking: *Come on, come on, come on.* Thinking, *An actual fight would be terrific as opposed to ruminating followed by phone calls. She'd come and we'd go; she'd likely get a few licks in and then I'd eat her cold, cold heart, problem solved.* "Really, Dr. Bimm. Anytime."

Fred chuckled, a short sound full of warm humor—the only warmth she'd shown during the conversation so far. "No chance, Lara. You like to fight. I think you need to; I think you're almost as bad as the humans that way. You'll always be better at it than me because you like it, and I don't. You might actually get the upper hand, and that would be inconvenient for me."

"We sure don't want to inconvenience you, Dr. Bimm."

"Fred, for God's sake, I've been telling you to call me Fred for over a decade. Lara, it's not us—I think I've made that clear—"

"As clear as the clearest piece of glass in the clearest window in the world," Sean added.

"Shush, boy. As I said, it's not us—but if you're in trouble, if people are moving against the power shift already, the kids and I can be there in six hours."

A good trick, from the bottom of the Caspian Sea. But Lara knew she meant it. Dr. Bimm got off on pretending she didn't give a shit, while secretly giving a shit. *Not one of my parents' friends are normal. This is significant, probably.*

"I shouldn't care what you guys are doing on your puny little sand bars, but I do. It's one of my many flaws," Dr. Bimm admitted. "Do you need help holding one of your puny little sand bars?"

Aww. I may cry with gratitude. "We can handle it," she replied, looking at Jack, who'd been listening to the entire thing with an expression made up of astonishment, irritation, and admiration. "But if not, you'll be the . . . thirtieth or fortieth person I'll call."

"Ouch," the mermaid said with mild reproach. "End."

"Dammit," Lara muttered, slumping back in her seat.

"Now you know how poor Queen Betsy feels when you hang up on her." Funny how, though there were no phones anymore, the phone slang persisted. Nobody really *dialed* anyone, either, but they sure said they did.

"That's not all I know. It's good they're not having any trouble on their end. But it doesn't help us figure out what's going on *here.*"

"Bat, fish. I suppose you've already thought of this," Jack said, standing, walking around Lara's chair, and leaning down to rub the tension out of her shoulders. "But perhaps a guard for the kitchen steps. All the steps?"

"Of course I've thought of that," she lied, and his shoulder rub turned into a pinch. She yelped and slapped his hand. "All right, busted, I haven't. But, yes, absolutely. I'll watch the damned kitchen steps myself as many nights as I—"

Her brother cut her off. "You're not thinking like a boss, Lara. You've got people to do that stuff. Dad wouldn't stand guard. But he'd make sure it got done."

"True enough." She thought another few seconds. "If the theory is our 'pets' are in danger, what's after the bat and the fish? Would humans count?"

The three young people all looked at each other, and Lara knew in that moment they were afraid, too. "Look, Mom is with Dad." Sean's voice cracked in his anxiety, and he cleared his throat and continued, stronger: "She's safe. Even if she was alone, nobody could roll up on her. But, yeah, maybe that's where these cowardly fucks are going. So we definitely need to post watches tonight. Nobody needs to trip over a dead body in the morning."

"All right, that's good. The folks are due back by sundown anyway, so I'll brief them about what's been going on, and Sean's theories." She shot her brother a look of pure gratitude. "Have I mentioned how glad I am you blew off the Boston trip?"

"And how am I repaid? With bacon rape. I think we'd better starting looking around before tonight. I'll go down and ask the kitchen gang who's been running around here—any strangers— like that. Oh, and check for a dead body on the steps while I'm at it. After I get a sandwich."

He left and Jack bent and dropped a kiss to the top of her head. "Insatiable," she remarked to no one in particular.

"Well, I thought it would be in poor taste to seduce you in front of your brother again."

"You've got it backward; I was the one who put my gear in Seduce." She wasn't in the mood for love-banter—and she was awful at it during the best of times—and got to her feet and began to walk around the game room, circling the pool table and occasionally picking up balls and clicking them together before dropping them back on the felt. Jack sat in her chair, and watched. "Y'know, Dad had straightforward challenges to his authority. Fights, people trying to murder him—there's no gray area there, nothing to ponder. You fight and the winner is the winner. The end."

"The good old days," Jack agreed, and she knew he was try-ing not to laugh.

"I know how that sounds." She managed a half smile. "Dumb thing to wish for, or envy, huh?"

"You're too hard on yourself—and always have been. Even when I only had cameos in your life, that much was obvious. My father says you and yours are the same—you only fear being caught in a mistake."

"And being caught by Sean during sexual shenanigans."

"I now fear that, too," he replied so solemnly she snickered. "I'll watch the steps, Lara. It wouldn't be the first time."

"Oh?" She was a little startled at the topic change, then realized it wasn't a change at all. "What are you talking about, the first time?"

"The reason we didn't pay tribute yesterday, officially meet our new leader. We were here, prowling the property," he told her. "Your father told mine when he left for Boston. My father and I kept watch all around, all day and all night. Once that first twenty-four hours was up, with no obvious trouble, we let off the watch." He rubbed his forehead. "That was our mistake— looking for obvious trouble. A Challenger wanting to eat your heart. A declaration of war. Nothing like what happened yesterday morning and today. So no one saw who left the fish."

Lara nearly squirmed with dueling emotions: *That's so sweet, you chauvinist dolts!* "Well, thank you. I think. That was very . . ." Condescending? Thoughtful? Annoying? Wonderful?

Before she could cough up something not completely insulting, he added, "My mother was also standing by."

Lara nearly vomited in terror. Morgan LeFay's odd sorceries were nightmarish even when she was on your side. Not that Sara Gardner was Morgan LeFay. She was the *reincarnation* of Morgan LeFay. Instead of magic, she had luck. All the time.

Low on cash? Sara could buy a lottery ticket and win.

Bad guy shooting at her? The gun would jam and the bolt would blow back and through the shooter's brain. Or the floor he'd been standing on would crumble beneath him and he'd fall screaming to his death. Or his left ventricle would blow like a spare tire and he'd drop dead with blood in his mouth.

Sara couldn't control it, that was the terrifying thing. Her magic, her luck, was unquantifiable and unpredictable and unconscious. So Sara might take a dislike to you and then . . . oops! Your cat got run over.

"That was . . . thoughtful." She tried to get a grip on her extreme trepidation. The woman was *on their side*. She was practically family. Hell, as of their morning mating, she was Lara's mother-in-law.

She and Derik really were made for each other . . . he can't stay here without wanting a piece of Dad, and people end up terrified of his wife . . . Humans are so frail, she's probably killed several without meaning to. She's never killed Pack. We're a little better at landing on our feet. Or her power—her sorcery?—understands at all levels that the Pack is no threat to her. The opposite of a threat, in fact. Maybe all this time they've been waiting . . . we've all been waiting . . .

"I'm grateful your family was watching our home." She went to him, took his hands, looked up at him. His ear had healed, as hers had. It made her want to draw blood again, and do other things, too, but she forced herself to focus. "I'm grateful your family will be in our lives now. I want your father here—I'm next-gen alpha, he'll have no issue with my status. And of course he couldn't come without his mate. Your mother; our cubs' grandmother. You're all welcome here."

"That almost sounds like a speech," he said, giving her a soft kiss.

"It's not a speech, I think—I didn't practice. It's just what I felt. All kinds of things I knew without knowing I knew are coming out. You know, other Pack leaders really should have written a manual or a book on this stuff, would that be too much? Don't laugh, I'm serious!"

"I'm not laughing at you," he lied, and kissed her again. "A how-to, by Lara Wyndham-Gardner, it'll be just what our cub needs. But not for fifty years at least."

She kissed him back and felt his urgency, dropped her fingers to his jeans and traced his thickening length. But quick as thought, she jerked her hands away when she heard her brother's pounding footsteps.

"We weren't—" she began, but stopped when he darted into the room.

"Somebody had the same thought we did. About the next dead pet being human. And that maybe we'd catch on to their timeline and post a watch." There wasn't a trace of a smile on her brother's face, which got Lara's attention more than anything he could have said. "Better come see."

"Don't tell me."

"There's a dead human on the kitchen stoop."

CHAPTER
FOURTEEN

"I have had enough!"

Lara stood over the body, that of a man she guessed was her father's age, face down on the stoop. It was nearing the dinner hour, so the kitchen was bustling with several people a few feet away with too much to do and too little time to do it. No one had needed to go out on the step (Packers didn't smoke) so no one knew there was a corpse waiting for—what? The first course?

"Yuck," was her brother's comment. "What's the opposite of an *amuse-buche*?"

"I'm serious, no more old TV for you."

"Back off, skank. You're not the boss of me. Except I just remembered you are."

"Skank?" Jack, she could see, was having trouble following them. She and Sean did have their own language, the language of bitter sarcasm. Not only did it come out more when they were under stress, they were fluent in it.

"It's an old-timey word for woman, like dame or broad," Sean explained. "It can be affectionate or not, depending on usage. And the user. And the skank in question, I guess—Oh, shit!" Sean scrambled back and nearly fell into the bushes on either side of the sidewalk and kitchen steps. Lara would have laughed—*she* was the family klutz, not him—if she hadn't been so startled. She'd barely started to look around when Jack stepped up, hauled Sean out of the bush by the back of his neck like a mother cat with a kitten, and thrust the smaller man behind him.

"Wow," Sean said from behind Jack, who was almost looming over the scene. Lara noticed Jack was standing very straight, unconsciously trying to make himself look bigger. If he'd been on four feet and furred, he'd be fluffing out his fur and his hackles would be up. "I feel so treasured and safe. My hero!"

"Sorry," Jack muttered, blushing red so quickly Lara worried he was headed for an aneurysm. "I—don't know why I did that."

Lara did. Beta males looked after the cubs—and the younger siblings. There were no cubs to look after yet. But something had scared Sean and instinct had kicked in, and Jack had acted without analyzing.

"If there wasn't a dead body here, I'd kiss you," Lara vowed, earning a snort of disgust from her brother and a look of surprised pleasure from her mate.

"Ah, thank you, Lara."

"There isn't a dead body, you dim skank."

She bent over the body. "Hey!" She could have sworn—

"Yeah. He's alive. That's what freaked me out. What does it say about me that I was less traumatized when I thought he was dead?" Sean peeked around Jack's shoulder. "See? He's breathing. He was so still before, and, um, a little stinky, so I—"

"This is good," Lara said firmly. She climbed the step, popped open the screen door, and called for Kara to come. Then she shut the door, turned, and knelt by the "body" and touched his shoulder. "A dead human who isn't dead is a terrific improvement . . . Sir? Are you all right?"

"Yeah, are you comfortable on the cement steps all sprawled out like that? Can we get you a lemonade?"

"Shut up, Sean." Lara sighed.

"Ow," the body moaned, stirring. When he moved, Lara got a stronger whiff. Yeesh. She completely understood Sean's error. The man *stank*, which hadn't surprised her when she thought he was a corpse. He didn't need a shower; he hadn't soiled himself. He smelled like . . . like death and poison poured into the same bag of skin. "Stupid chemo—Wha' happen?"

Lara helped the man sit up. He'd gotten a nasty scrape on his cheek when he'd fallen, and his forehead was trickling blood. Sean was hanging back, still spooked, and not just by the smell. Jack, by contrast, was crowding, his knee touching her shoulder as she knelt beside the bod—the man. "What happened to you?"

"I—You!" The man, bald except for a few gray wisps decorating the skin above his ears and the back of his neck, jerked away from her touch; he looked up and saw Sean and recoiled. "And you!"

"Wait." Sean snapped his fingers, blue eyes narrowing. "I know you. The beady eyes, the furtive expression, the catcher's-mitt-sized hands perfect for snapping bra straps—Geoff's dad!"

"What?" Jack and Lara said at once.

"You leave my boy out of this!" The man was struggling to stand but was so weak and smelly he was making no progress. It was like watching a dazed turtle on its back struggling to turn over. "He's not part of this!"

"Jeff's dad?" Jack asked. "Is that what you said?"

"Not Jeff, Geoff. Okay . . . Lara, you know how Dad has two stories about us he uses as prime examples of our basic personality types, and how he uses them as examples or points of discussion *ad nauseam* and we were sick to death of both of them before puberty?"

"Yeah."

"Well, for my story, the day on the beach—"

"Jeff, Geoff, and Ryan!" Lara looked at the man with new interest. "Huh. What are you *doing* here?"

"I think your emphasis is wrong; I think it's *what are* you *doing here*?"

"Wait," Geoff's dad said, squinting up at them. "How do you even know my boy's friends?"

"Family lore; it's boring, never mind. Yeah, this is his dad, I recognize the—that's why you smell!" He turned back to Lara. "Geoff's uncle and grandpa died of cancer when we were in middle school. He's got it, too! He smells like cancer and chemo!" He actually hopped a little in the joy and relief of solving the puzzle. "Yay!"

"*Sean.*"

Her brother flinched back from her and she was sorry to see it—and glad. Because she loved him and would die for him or kill for him, yes, of course, one of those things that went without saying even though people said them, but at the end of the day, she was his leader and some things were unacceptable. She knew he hadn't meant what he'd said, or how it had come across. She also knew reparation was owed, regardless of the man's motives.

Sean turned at once to Geoff's dad, who was staring up at him. "I'm so sorry. I didn't mean it like that; I was worried about what's been happening around here and was glad I recognized you, *not* glad you've got cancer. I'm so sorry. You—you don't have long, do you?"

"No, I do not," Geoff's dad said with touching dignity. "Which is why I'm here. You and your weird dog-people-werewolf-guys have to get out of here and my friend's gonna make sure you do."

"Friend?" Sean blinked and looked around, as if expecting to see someone crouched in the business.

"Is the friend a weird dog-people-werewolf-guy?"

"Well, of course," Geoff's dad replied as if the question—and answer—were stupidly simple.

"Which means you've been scattering dead fish and bats around."

"Yeah, Len said he couldn't do it or you'd all know, but it'd take you a while to figure it was me. Even if you caught my scent, with the chemo and all, you might not know what you were smelling."

"Wait, I'm lost," Jack said, spreading his hands. "Who's Len?"

This time Sean and Lara were both happy to have figured it out, and said in delighted unison, "The new kitchen guy!"

"Aw, shit," Lenny said from behind them.

CHAPTER FIFTEEN

"Oh, hey, you're here," Geoff's dad said, relieved. *"I fell waiting* for you and they got me. So, y'know. Protect your evil henchman. Or something."

Lenny, a male about Sean's size—five-eleven or so—with short wiry limbs and big dark eyes, stared down at the dying human with no expression. That changed when he looked at Lara, and couldn't stop his lip from curling back. "You. This would have been on you."

"Would have been?" Sean looked down at Geoff's dad. "Do you know what he's talking about, Geoff's dad?"

"I have a *name*," he replied, exasperated. "Is . . . is anyone going to help me up?"

"Oh. Sorry. We should explain." Lara shook her head; how thoughtless. "Yeah, Lenny here was going to kill Geoff's dad.

He really was supposed to be the dead human, the third pet, found late tonight or tomorrow morning, which we probably wouldn't have been able to hide like the bat and the fish. Outside law enforcement probably would have gotten involved. Very embarrassing at best, and potentially lethal for a bunch of us at worst."

"What?" Geoff's dad yelped. "Stage two lung cancer's not getting rid of me quick enough for you weird dog people? You gotta speed it along?"

"What do you care?" Lenny's brown eyes snapped with fury. "You're a dead monkey too dumb to know it. When you're all the way dead, you'll be one of billions. Who'll care?"

"Plotting his murder is one thing, but watch your mouth," Lara warned.

"Huh?" Geoff's dad huh'ed.

"Monkey is to human what nigger is to African American: the polar opposite of cool."

"But some of my best friends are African Americans."

Lara was beginning to doubt the man's intelligence, or sanity. She turned back to the new guy, Lenny, who'd started that very week. Who hung around the kitchen. She'd spoken to him about telling Kara about the mess she and Jack made. He'd helped clean it up!

"So use Geoff's dad—"

"I have a name!"

"—to leave your nasty little managerial hints, then kill the messenger to leave a nastier message."

"Dude." Geoff's dad was shaking his head. "Not cool."

Why are they all talking like it's 1995? She shook off the wondering. Lenny was not especially bright, his plan was idiotic, and he'd do something stupid(er) any moment. She just had to pick her moment. Or his. "So we'll probably fight to the death now, but I was wondering if you'd tell me why first."

Jack looked a little startled at her matter-of-fact prediction of how events would unfold, but she knew he was unwavering in his support. He wouldn't interfere when she killed Lenny. If Lenny seemed to be getting the upper hand, Jack would pitch in. If Lenny won, Jack would lose his sanity and eat Lenny's heart, fur or no fur.

Sean, who knew her best, dropped his eyes and muttered to the sidewalk, "Lara, I'm so sorry you got stuck with the alpha card. It so sucks that you have to do this your first week."

She was sorry, too, but wishing it was otherwise was no solution and a time waster, besides. She was getting off lightly and she knew it; most leaders came into their Packs after a murder or two. It was the natural order of things; she dared not complain.

Worse: she wasn't at all sorry for Lenny. Just herself. She supposed she wasn't a very nice woman.

But she wanted answers, dammit. She didn't think that was too much to ask, and if it was, let the cowards sit in judgment.

"Why?" Lenny's tone was so filled with loathing she imagine she could almost see his words oozing like poison gas from his mouth, his lungs, his body, his *self*. "You're that much of a dumb bitch? Hmm, let's see if I can put my finger on the detail . . ."

"Can't you just tell us and quit with the sarcasm?" Sean asked. "And even as I asked you that, I became aware of the irony."

Lara laughed in spite of herself.

"This is why my son never liked you," Geoff's dad said with odd piety. "Nobody ever knows what you're talking about."

"Because you and yours **are freaks**!" Lenny burst out. Lara had the impression he'd wanted to make that statement for some time. Years? "In one generation, your sire tore through centuries of tradition! We used to keep to ourselves; we used to let the monkeys be monkeys and the Pack be Pack."

"You forget," Lara said mildly, "I'm half monkey."

"We both are." Sean stepped up, then leaned over and whispered to Geoff's dad, "I'm so sorry about how we keep saying the M-word, we don't approve at all, but I can't let my sister swing out there by herself."

"Forget? None of us can forget! Your sire is dumb enough to get stuck in a city hours before his Change, fucks your monkey mom, then brings her home! Where, after she whelped you, she then set about fucking with the natural order of things, a way of life that went just fine for thousands of years without *her* input, thanks.

"And if all that wasn't treacherous enough—"

Lara nodded encouragingly. *Now we're getting to it. Finally.* Thank goodness bad guys always had the need to rant, a quality she had never understood (it wasn't enough he hated her family; he had to explain his hatred. Just kill her and be done!), but was grateful this once.

"—then she and her useless mate make friends with vampires and mermaids—*leeches and fish*, for God's sake, like they can ever be one of us!—and they're raising you to be just as inefficient and weak."

"If I was a raging vamp-o-phobe and mer-o-phobe, I'd be mad, too," Sean admitted.

"He's made you think the Pack is run by committee." Lenny was so furious he was actually spitting while he raved. "And you'll teach your born-to-be-useless cubs the same. So it's not just him. Just killing *him*, although it would be really fucking *great*, won't solve the problem. The seeds have to go, too."

"Huh. Seeds." She thought about that. "I promise you this: one of us has to go." She turned to the man on the sidewalk. "Where do you come into this the-world-has-changed-around-me-and-I'm-too-chickenshit-to-adapt ideology?"

"Oh. Lenny and me—" Geoff's dad jerked a thumb in the smaller man's direction. "He used to be the custodian at CCH and we met up and got to talking."

The hospital. Of course. "You understand him meeting and befriending you wasn't a coincidence, right, Geoff's dad?"

"I have a—what?"

"He went hunting. He needed a very sick human to leave his love notes. Like you said—even if we caught you in the act or smelled you or both, it'd take us a while to catch on to what was really happening."

Geoff's dad said nothing, just looked at Lenny with reproach.

"He, uh, doesn't see you as an equal. You're a pet. Like a bat or . . ." Sean shrugged. "You know."

Geoff's dad looked downcast, then rallied. "Yeah, well, Len told me about that. About how you're friends with vampires and sea monsters and stuff. Where's a human supposed to fit into any of that? It's *our* planet! And you're all faster and stronger and—where are *we* supposed to go? If you guys are teaming up—"

"We're not, we're just—" Sean cut himself off when Lara shook her head.

"—what's that leave for regular people? Huh? Six months from now, I won't be here. Where's that leave my boy? And his boys, if he has some? And theirs?"

"So you helped Lenny because you thought that would lead to helping humans?" Jack asked. He'd been quiet so long, if Lara hadn't been conscious of his every movement, every breath, she would have forgotten he was there.

"Don't try to make sense of it," Sean warned. "You'll talk yourself straight into a migraine. If Packers got them."

"You poor idiot," Lara said, and meant it. Fear led people to do the damndest things. She suspected she would spend the rest of her reign being surprised all over again by that. "We've been sharing the planet since your kind were hiding in caves and ours were howling at the moon. Come to think of it, we're still how—"

"Will you pay attention, you giddy bitch?" Lenny nearly screamed. Lara politely pulled her attention from Geoff's dad and gave it back to the villain. "The part I can't stand is you were really going to do it. And nobody was gonna stop you! You were going to betray every last one of us."

"Betray? How—"

"By showing the world our throat! You think it's a coincidence that we've been around for thousands of years?"

"It's longer than that," she said dryly. Ah, a true super villain: he never glanced at a history book. "So have the mers, and the vamps, and the humans."

"It's monkey see, monkey do with you, isn't it?"

"That's *enough*," Jack snapped, moving forward, but she put her hand on his chest and he stopped.

"Okay." Len had lost the power to hurt her, if he'd ever had it. She had zero respect for him, so what did his taunts matter? It was like listening to a recording of swear words: they were words. Without something significant behind them, they were gabble. "Keep going."

"Well—" Lenny lost a little steam. "I'm done, I think."

"Fine. Have you even met a vampire? Or one of the Folk? They visit pretty frequently. You've had the opportunity."

"I don't have to meet a worm to know it crawls."

She managed—just—not to roll her eyes. "So you haven't. If you'd ever taken a break from your hatemongering, you'd find they're like us."

"*They are not! You're* not even just like us, you and your father and that mother of yours."

Sean shot an apologetic look at her. "That's fair, Lara."

She shrugged. "Okay. But I think what I said was fair, too. If Len had bothered to—"

"Yeah, well, people who grow up with cobras spend a lot of time thinking venomous reptiles aren't dangerous. That doesn't make them right. It makes them stupid. You're stupid. You grew up with them, you visited them, they came crawling out here . . . You're used to it, but that doesn't mean they're not dangerous, that we should tolerate them."

"It doesn't matter because—"

"Why were you late?" Sean asked suddenly, noticing Len was getting into froth mode again. He had no idea why Lara was stalling, just that she was, and wanted to help. "Geoff's dad was supposed to be dead by now. You said you didn't get here in time."

"Because I had to help clean up the disaster your sister made in the breakfast room with the *other* freak," Lenny cried, waving his hands in impotent rage. "It threw the whole schedule off! Bombed the whole day! Broken glass and juice and bacon fucking everywhere!"

"Don't talk about the bacon," Sean hissed.

"I feel better now," Jack said to Lara. "I was wondering when he was going to get to me. I know you'll get most of the attention in our lives, and that's fine, but I wouldn't want to be completely ignored all the time. Don't forget my freak sorceress mother," he added helpfully to Lenny, "and my would-be alpha dad."

"Have you left time for another villain rant?" Sean asked anxiously. "We want you to have your say."

"You're all . . . just . . . awful." Lenny was running out of steam. His plan, never very intelligent or thought out to begin with, wasn't going to work. Probably wouldn't have worked if everything had gone perfectly. "Just . . . I hate you. I really do."

"Bad enough to pretend to be my friend, to sympathize," Geoff's dad remonstrated, "but then to kill me and use my body to decorate their steps? I didn't sign on for that, dude. You're just as bad as any of these guys."

"Quit it, Geoff's dad!" Sean roared, startling them all. "Lara saved your smelly ass by boning a guy she barely knew like some loose skank. You owe the new Pack Skank your life!"

"No more classic movies. No more classic TV. No books published before 2015. All of it ends. Right now." Lara pinched the bridge of her nose, where a truly awful headache had sprouted. She'd heard the phrase *didn't know whether to laugh or cry* and never knew how it felt until now. "Right now, Sean. Though he's right. Jack and I saved your life, Geoff's dad."

"What life?" he complained.

Some people, there's just no pleasing them.

"Okay, fuck this." Lenny took a step back, his hands over his head as if Lara was arresting him. "I didn't try to kill you. I didn't try to kill him. I'm not Challenging. You can't kill me."

Lara looked at him thoughtfully. "That's true." She knew other members of the household had been assembling; she could see several through the windows all along that side of the house. Kara had come when called, of course, but realized what was happening and the word had spread, as Lara had known it would. She needed only a few witnesses; the word would get out, as it always did. "*I* can't kill you. But that's all right. I'll just give you to my good friend the vampire queen."

Lenny said nothing, just looked at her with dawning surprise.

"Y'know, Betsy and I have been wondering if a Pack/vamp hybrid would be possible. It's a pretty exciting idea. But it's not like any Packer would *volunteer* for that, right? But it occurs to me I don't need a volunteer." Lara smiled at him. "I've got you. For what it's worth, what you'll do for us will provide valuable research for both our peoples." She turned to Sean. "Peoples? Is that right? Because we're different species? Actually, they're all dead, technically. Are the dead a species?"

"No, you—you can't." Lara barely heard his croaked denial. Lenny had to cough, and then spit, and then try again: "You can't. Do that. You can't."

"You'll find I can. You'll find there's not anyone here who will stop me."

Lenny seemed to realize for the first time that they had an audience, and looked around, his lips moving as he made note of the numbers . . . a dozen, two dozen . . . all watching. All listening.

"You didn't Challenge and you didn't get a chance to kill Geoff's dad. That hardly puts you up with the Knights of the Round Table, but all right. But you *planned harm*, Len. To me, to my family. You insulted my mate's family, you threatened my brother and insulted my mother and her mate. You didn't think you'd walk away from that, did you?" She laughed, delighted. "Did you? Oh my God. You did! Oh, that's hilarious."

He was whitening, stammering, backing away. He shook his head so hard more spittle flew. He tried harder to speak, and stuttered and stumbled and nearly fell. Geoff's dad was saying something, but Lara had no idea what; her full attention was on Len.

"Come on, then," she said. "You don't want to keep my friend the vampire queen waiting. You'll like Minnesota. While you're able to like anything, I guess. After that . . . well, it's likely the winters won't bother you so much. Nothing will bother you so much."

Len turned. He ran. Not blindly; Lara saw at once he had a plan, a path. The new plan went much better than the old: he ran straight to the edge of the cliff, and straight over. Unlike the classic cartoons, he didn't run a few steps on air. He dropped from sight, and even over the sound of the ocean, they could hear him screaming all the way down. Until they couldn't.

CHAPTER
SIXTEEN

In all the years Lara's mother had lived with the Pack, she had never gotten used to post-confrontation anticlimaxes. "The fight or whatever is over, and they just look for a minute, and then everybody goes back to whatever they were doing. *Never* ceases to amaze."

The witnesses—the kitchen staff, a few groundskeepers, some of the interns from the business office—looked for a minute, then went back to work. If she had called any of them to her, they would have come at once, but she didn't, so they left. All but Kara, who knew Lara would want her. A quick whispered discussion, and the older Packer was easily lifting Geoff's dad into her arms. "Get me *outta* here," he was saying, "I wanna go back; chemo's better than this place, anything's better. Jesus!"

Sean walked up to the edge of the cliff, looked down, then

came back, shaking his head. "I don't know which memory to repress first. Also he's deader than shit down there. Are you gonna have some Packers go get him, or let him wash out to sea, or what?"

Hmm. Yes, that was her decision, too. She raised her voice, called over two of the groundskeepers, and had a quick word. Their baseball caps were in their hands the moment she spoke their names, and didn't go back on their heads until they'd heard their instructions and stepped out of her presence.

"I'll go with them," Jack said, and she nodded. Then she looked at her little brother. "What?"

"Nothing."

"Lies, all lies." She smiled. "What is it?"

"Okay. I wasn't gonna say anything—"

Sure.

"—and don't get the wrong idea, I'm glad you didn't have to get ready to rummmmmbbblllle! Expecting you to kill a stranger after you killed all that bacon was too much." He looked back at all the now-empty windows. "But with everybody watching—I don't know. Maybe they think you should have been more, uh, Pack-ey. About handling Lenny. I don't want you to get jammed up from that. I don't want you to have to look over your shoulder forever."

Oh, Sean, you sweetie. I'll have to no matter what happened today. Just like Dad did. "Nope. Never happen."

"Well. I'm not arguing about it or anything. It's just something I was wondering about."

"What's the saying—there's a new sheriff in town? New rules, honey. What do you think would further my rep more? That I killed someone smaller, weaker, and dumber than me in a fight I had every chance of winning? Or that not only did I expose and remove a threat to my Pack, he was so horrified at what I was going to do to him, he killed himself on the spot rather than face it?"

Sean stood there with his mouth open for a few seconds, then snapped it closed so hard she heard the *click* of his teeth coming together. "Okay. Good point. I withdraw my earlier comment. I'm going to my room now to be terrified for the next few hours."

"Okay." She tried not to laugh and, as usual with her bubbly odd beta bro, failed. "Thanks for sticking up for me by telling the world I'm the new Pack Skank."

"Thanks for scaring me shitless pretty much all day." He pulled her close for a quick hug, and she felt her eyes sting with tears that wanted to run down her face and show the world she was a coward. She ruthlessly quashed the urge to cry and stepped back. "Okay, so, I'm looking at waking up screaming up every night for the next few weeks, but by the time the new fall movies come out, I should be back to a less horrible sleep schedule . . ." She could hear him muttering his fall sleep plans as he walked away. ". . . by then only waking up screaming once or twice a week, so I could go to the late shows on Fridays . . ."

Lara looked around; she was alone for the moment. Sean off to his room, Jack to help with the body, Geoff's dad bundled unceremoniously into Kara's car for a trip to the hospital, and Len . . . well.

She sat down quickly, sure her shaking knees weren't going to hold her up another minute.

It was another five minutes before she could stand.

CHAPTER
SEVENTEEN

She ran into Jack's arms the moment he stepped into the bed-room. "Was it very awful?" she asked his chest as he wrapped his arms around her and squeezed. He reeked of soap; he'd washed thoroughly before touching her.

"Not as awful as talking to him," he replied so dryly she chuckled. "Did you know, there's a protocol in place for the disposal of inconvenient bodies on Pack property?" He pulled back and looked at her eyes. "Ah. Of course you knew."

"Doesn't make it any less horrible. And the day of our—you know."

He was still watching her face, his head cocked to the right. "You were wonderful, you know. Ah . . . not just earlier." He winced and rubbed his nipple where she'd pinched him. "Our true leader."

She shook her head so hard she couldn't see for the hair in her eyes. Jack smoothed the strands away. "I wasn't. I wanted my dad the whole time. My mom, too. I kept wishing they were there in case I fucked up. *When* I fucked up," she admitted. "I was pretty sure I would. Bet my mom never worried about stuff like that." She smiled a little. "It's not easy, having a mom for a legend."

She'd been afraid he would think less of her after the confession, but he only looked astonished. "Do you hear yourself?"

"That's such a dumb question. I said it; of course I heard it."

"It's not easy having a mom for a legend?" he asked, incredulous, proving that he, too, heard her. "Lara, you're a legend."

"What? No I'm not. The most interesting thing about me is my parents. Them, it's *them*. I'm just . . . me."

"You were barely whelped when you took on two alphas in their prime. You broke up a fight for dominance and could easily have been fatally stomped."

"That only proves what a dumb kid I was. Not knowing better isn't legendary."

"You know better now," he pointed out. "Would you do the same thing again?" Her silence gave him the answer. "Lara, you drove our enemy to kill himself rather than face your vengeance. Packers don't kill themselves!" (They did, but not nearly as often as humans. It was *almost* unheard of.) "It's unprecedented! Dare I say, legendary?"

"You make it sound so straightforward," she said, uneasy with his admiration. "It's not. My dad thinks I'm not afraid of anything. But I'm always afraid." Even of Jack, although now she knew why. Even as a child, even during her first Change, she was afraid of him because she sensed Jack would change her, and he did. Their mating marked the true end of childhood and entrance to adult responsibilities with far more intensity than turning voting age had.

He kissed her on the mouth. "You're mistaking fear of not fulfilling your responsibilities for cowardice. If you weren't afraid of letting us down, someone else would be Pack leader. Someone else isn't; *you* are. You're supposed to be here. I am, too."

He kissed her again, but she was thinking so hard she barely felt it. Instead she leaned against his comforting bulk and relaxed as he rubbed her back.

Incomer. That word, thrown around like a swear word. And they were wrong, everyone was wrong; Jack wasn't the incomer, or at least not the only one. She was, too. Her hybrid status, a human mother and a Pack father, a Pack *leader* father, an even rarer animal. She'd been raised by parents who didn't fear change, who embraced it. Parents who befriended vampires and mermaids, who helped them through their crises and expected help for their own. Who raised their daughter to seek out change, and never hide from it. A daughter who would take to mate the son of a self-exiled alpha and a sorceress, and think nothing of something so strange.

Incomer. *The cubs will be, too*, she thought, and was glad.

"I'm glad you came back again," she told him, the biggest understatement she had uttered in her life.

"Well, me, too," he replied, pleased. "I can hardly wait to see what happens next. Look what happened your first couple of days! I—" He cut himself off and laughed. "My dad is going to be so upset he missed all this. I can hear the ranting now."

Lara, who'd returned the kiss and was suddenly interested

in doing many more things to Jack's outstanding body besides kissing, stiffened. *Dads? Ranting? Oboy. Yeah, there'll be plenty of that.*

"We should kiss a lot," she said, stretching up on her toes to reach him better. "And more. Starting now."

His hands were sliding down to her hips, cupping her ass, coming around to gently tug on the buttons on her shorts. "Ever the dutiful beta, I obey."

"Oh, shut up. And do that faster. Why aren't we both naked?"

He laughed in her mouth. "Excellent question." And got to work.

CHAPTER
EIGHTEEN

"He what? He just took my daughter on the sideboard—the antique *sideboard—like some—some—and now they think they're mated? 'Hi, Dad, we had sex and now we're a family and I'm likely pregnant, because what birth control?' They— He—They're not—"*

Jeannie Wyndham started to laugh and laugh, which startled her husband almost as much as the first piece of news. "Karma's a bitch," she said at last, wiping a tear from one eye. "She truly is. Michael, you look like an asshat trying to claim the moral high ground on this one. It's done. You've gotta suck it up, just like you expected everyone else to suck it up when you nailed *me*."

"Can we all please stop staying *asshat*?" Michael snapped. "It's—it's not that. That's our way . . . sometimes . . . though going out on a date or two wouldn't have been out of the question . . .

The sideboard. That's the problem. It's an antique! My great-grandmother found it in the basement of the Old Yarmouth Inn and spent years restoring it! Respect for antiques, was that too much to ask?"

"Careful, Mikey," Jeannie teased. "You're the one sounding like an antique."

"But on the *sideboard*? Is that why Sean won't go back in there? The poor kid's been traumatized, the whole staff's probably traumatized, and I'll bet they've ruined the finish. And where's the body of the idiot who thought he could scare my kid into being as stupid as he was? It's gonna be a while before we go out of town again, goddammit."

"The sideboard survived hurricanes. It'll bear up under your daughter's ass imprint."

"Oh, goddammit . . ."